PHANTOMS

HAUNTING TALES
from masters of the genre

Also available from Titan Books

PHANTOMS

HAUNTING TALES

from masters of the genre

edited by **MARIE O'REGAN**

TITAN BOOKS

Phantoms
Print edition ISBN: 9781785657948
Electronic edition ISBN: 9781785657955

Published by Titan Books
A division of Titan Publishing Group Ltd
144 Southwark Street, London SE1 0UP

First edition: October 2018
10 9 8 7 6 5 4 3 2 1

CONTENTS

INTRODUCTION
Marie O'Regan

Anyone who knows me knows my love of ghost stories. From an early age, I read everything I could get my hands on – I have very fond memories of reading Enid Blyton (I especially loved the Adventure series and the Famous Five novels) and Agatha Christie, two of my favourite authors at that time. Then, aged nine, I found a book in the school library called *Thin Air: An Anthology of Ghost Stories* (edited by Alan C. Jenkins, in 1967), and my direction was set. It contained such classics as Dickens' "The Signal-Man", W.W. Jacobs' "The Monkey's Paw" and Saki's "The Open Window", as well as more whimsical stories such as Oscar Wilde's much-loved "The Canterville Ghost" and Hugh Walpole's "The Little Ghost" – thirty stories in total, ranging from gently humorous to downright terrifying. In the end, I took that book out so often that when I left primary school they gave it to me, and it's still one of my most prized possessions.

From then on, my tastes leaned more towards

darker fiction, although it could be said that my love for Agatha Christie had already given me a nudge in that direction. I've read – and continue to read – widely in many genres, but I have a special fondness to this day for a ghost story, well told. A few years ago (2012, to be exact), I edited my first solo anthology: *The Mammoth Book of Ghost Stories by Women*, partly because of this love of ghost stories and partly because at that time I kept hearing that women didn't really write horror of any kind, let alone supernatural. Not true, of course, and I was happy to showcase the talents of both classic and current writers in an anthology I felt displayed a wide range of ghost stories. There was something – hopefully – for every taste.

So why ghost stories? Ghost stories have a quality, for me, that sets them apart from other types of supernatural tale. They tend to be stories that deal with loss, or guilt. There's an emotional resonance that a reader can feel permeating the page; there's no need for a "baddie" if you don't want to include one in your story, as not all ghost stories are to do with evil-doers and their intent or their deeds. They have an atmosphere that's unique to them, a creeping sense of… not fear, necessarily, more of disquiet – a knowledge that something's there, just out of sight, at the far reaches of hearing or vision. At least until the spirit chooses to reveal itself. There's a melancholy, a sadness, that resonates with the reader and creates empathy, leaving a frisson of emotion that often remains long after the reading of the story.

With this volume, I've gone for modern ghost stories, from a very talented range of writers who were kind enough either to write a tale especially for this anthology or to allow me to reprint a favourite of mine from their existing body of work. Within these pages you'll find a range of ghost stories – from John Connolly's incredibly poignant "A Haunting" and Joe Hill's film-loving "20th Century Ghost" to Muriel Gray's tragic "Front Row Rider" and Josh Malerman's tale of guilt, "Frank, Hide", not to mention stories by such authors as the wonderful A. K. Benedict, Helen Grant, Tim Lebbon, Robert Shearman and many more. I've thoroughly enjoyed putting this anthology together, and am very grateful to the authors for trusting me with their words.

I hope you find something you love in this anthology, as I have.

Marie O'Regan
Derbyshire
January 2018

WHEN WE FALL, WE FORGET
Angela Slatter

The mist beyond the low stone wall is thick, now white, now grey, sometimes shading to a black that blends with the night, so it's hard to tell where one begins and the other ends. Never seen anything quite like it; though I've travelled far, this is different from any place I've ever been. Insular people, the small distances between their holdings might as well be a hundred miles for all the interest they take in their neighbours – unless there are secrets in the offing. The little town that clings to the earth sloping down to the harbour is not quite so bad; something to do with being in close proximity, I suppose. The necessity of human contact. And they all go to one church or the other, depending upon their own version of God and Its message. There's a tidy white-washed Protestant place of worship in town, a grey stone Catholic one about ten minutes out of it. The name of this island doesn't matter; it's much like the one where my memories began and ended, those left to me along with my troubles.

I've been sitting on the front stoop for too long. The cold has numbed my backside and legs, made my lower back ache, but I don't get up. Mortal hurts still strike me as novel even after all these years. The sun sank while I sat here, hands wrapped around a cup of tea that cooled far too soon. The fog began in the peat bogs just on the other side of the road that hardly anyone drives down anymore now they're used to me. My cardigan's too thin. If I had any sense I'd have gone in long ago, tended the hearth, had blazes crackling in the sitting room and in my chosen bedroom upstairs; I prefer the fireplaces to the rattling radiators, prefer the true warmth, the ancient warmth. But I am watching the mist, same as every evening, watching it mass above the bogs, creep up and over the road, then press and froth at the low stone wall that encloses my garden. Each night it creaks and clatters the rickety wooden gate, but it never pushes through, not even spilling between the long gaps from paling to paling. As if whatever waits out there keeps it at bay.

Ariel would have liked it here, the way the house is so close to the cliff, overlooking the sea. The rush and roar and crash of the waves on the rocks below, the constant sound of it. I'd have had to watch her, though, so close to the edge; the thing is, we'd not be here if I had not lost her once before.

The house crouches behind me, breathes over my shoulder. The place was already furnished, mostly antiques, not necessarily comfortable, but I make do.

I need so little. It has three storeys: on the ground floor a kitchen, a library, a sitting room; upstairs four bedrooms and a renovated bathroom. Above that the tiny, airless attic with dust on the floorboards and a round window of red, blue and green, small enough for a child to open and push her head through should the mood take. Sometimes I hear what might be footsteps up there, the echoing sighs of forgotten things.

A racket at the gate catches my attention. The mist is shifting, spinning as if it might form into something new, something tall with substance. It brushes against the wooden entrance, shakes it enough to produce a noise that might hide a moan or a groan or even the sweep of a sharp metal object through the air. It struggles, wavers, fails and falls away. It's not time yet; there are more tasks to be done.

I force myself upwards. My knees protest. I arch backwards and feel the little cracks as each vertebra returns to its proper alignment. Sighing, I go inside, closing the door behind me. There are things that need doing, and this body must sleep.

At mid-afternoon, the sun's made half an effort, and though the light is mostly grey there are some shades of gold to it, here and there. The wind alternates between sly nips and outright bites. You can see why the trees, cut down in ancient times, were reluctant to grow again. There are only a few stunted oaks across the island, like the one clinging drunkenly to the side of the granite church. An angry, tenuous tree, ugly and twisted, refusing to go without a fight. My daughter would have squealed with delight to see it, to climb it, to perch triumphantly on branches not that far from the ground.

There's no warmth, though. I settle the knitted cap more firmly on my head so the breeze can't pluck the red locks of hair away, hunch my shoulders, jam my hands back into the pockets of my puffa jacket and continue towards the church and the small rectory beside it which houses the local priest.

As I get closer the stained glass windows seem to glow. I shake my head. *Lighting inside the building.* Nothing to be afraid of. I smile; it's been so long since I've felt fear, the sensation is strange. The glasswork is very fine and I shouldn't be surprised, I suppose. The faithful always want the best for their houses of worship, no matter how remote, will always empty their pockets, go short, starve their own children, if only the structure where they think God resides might be magnificent in some way. As if It's not got better places to be.

The glass angels are exquisite, however, kind and forgiving, strikingly lovely as they deliver tidings of comfort and joy, and lambs to and from slaughter. I'm not sure what I feel as I look at them, whether I hear the singing of metal again, the sound Ramiel told me was the last I ever heard.

Off to my right are ranks of peat bricks and the gutted earth from which they've been dug. They lie like soldiers, waiting. Soon they'll be stacked, herringboned, to dry.

No one's around.

As with every other dwelling here, a low stone wall marks out the boundaries. Inside the graveyard are headstones, the older ones covered in mosses from deep fern green to almost lime, then to a seafoam hue. Many of the names have been weathered away. I focus on the double doors of the church; oak, I think, presumably brought over from the mainland where trees are plentiful, stained by age, smoothed by years of priestly and penitential hands, by the dogged ministrations of the ever-present wind. The lock, if ever it was polished to a shine, is black now. The left door hangs ajar, but the sunlight doesn't creep too far inside.

I take a deep breath and move along the path, through the gap in the wall. Nothing happens; no bolt of lightning, no thunder, the sky does not split. I keep walking, right up to the doors, and there is only a tiny tremor in my fingers when I push them open. As I step over the threshold, that spot between my shoulder blades begins to itch.

It takes a while for my eyes to adjust to the darkness of the tiny porch, and I bump my hip against something hard: a marble font, carved like a gigantic cup with hands wrapped around the rim. The water within shimmers darkly, as if shadows rise to the surface, and I don't dip into it, don't cross myself and hope for the best like

17

others. My reflection in it is an uncertain thing. There are rows of pews in the nave, twenty each to the left and right. On either side of an aisle flagstones also serve as headstones for those who've been judged as good and great. At the far end flicker many points of light: candelabras ranged on both sides of a small altar, and in front of that altar with its white gold-embroidered cloth and carved tabernacle is a man in a black cassock, turned towards me. He's like a stain against the pristine fabric.

A man who gasps as I step from the gloom.

What does he *see*?

He puts out a hand to steady himself, the other comes up as if to ward me off. I smile. The doors behind me swing properly shut, cutting off the watery daylight that's made me a silhouette to him.

"Father McBride?"

I can hear his breathing, it's slowing, calming as he sees me for a human being after all. He nods, trying to collect himself.

What did he see?

"I'm Sarai McEwan."

"Ah. The new girl at the big house on the Old Road." And he smiles as if that might cover the fact he was terribly afraid for however brief a time. That I might be reduced to a series of descriptors. *Girl.* Trying to make me small, unimportant, to make himself feel big again. Once upon a time I'd have given him a lecture about infantilising women, but there are more important matters.

"Not so new," is what I say instead. "Mhairead Spence at the historical society said I might chat with you."

"I'll speak to any who come to me in need," he says, and I sense a homily approaching. I feel the heat of angry blood flooding my face, have to work hard to keep my voice steady. I think how it could all be done with now, that I could take up a candlestick or that fine shiny monstrance and... but no. There's an order to things, steps that need following if I'm to get my wish.

"How kind. But it's not your godliness I'm in need of today, Father." I barely keep the contempt from my tone. "But your archaeological knowledge, that's another thing entirely."

His expression flickers like slides onto a screen, one change after another, subtly different until it settles to a kindly frown. Registering the rejection of one thing and the offering of another, unexpected thing. There's uncertainty, too; his past clings to him as surely as a phantom limb. Doesn't everyone's?

"That was a long time ago, Ms McEwan."

"You're not that old," I say; flattery works even on a priest. I can see it in his face as I draw closer. Especially on a priest. He's in his forties, perhaps closer to fifty than not, but he's handsome: square jaw, features rugged as if carved by his time on this island and eyes the pale shade of blue I associate with a stript soul, with a loss that's leeched part of your very life from you. Eyes like my own. He's tall, bulky, would turn to fat quickly if he weren't careful, going for a run at dawn and dusk, past my house, muscular arms and legs pumping, fighting off whatever cold might try to get into his bones; he's been here so long, the climate shouldn't bother him anymore. The thick, salt and pepper hair is longer and untidier than is seemly for a man of his profession and vintage, but I don't imagine the spinsters and widows who come to listen to his preaching mind so terribly much; nor the married women and some of the men.

"I don't know much about the house where I'm staying, you see, just that an adventurer built it and filled it with his souvenirs." I smile again, take the last few steps and offer my hand. After a moment, he accepts; his skin is warm, rough with calluses from years of digging that no amount of time will smooth away. His pupils dilate at the touch. I don't look my age, and my lips are full, my eyes full-lashed; all the tales I've heard say that Gunn McBride always did have an eye for a beautiful woman. No reason why that would have changed just because he found God. I release his hand at last, feel the sudden cold.

"Thomas Earnchester, one of those Englishmen with too much money and a fascination with things that didn't concern him. He died without heirs and left the estate to the Free Church. Everything's been gradually sold off until only the house remains, and they let that out as a holiday rental."

"There you go, Mrs Spence was right," I say. "You're very well informed."

He shrugs. "I've been here the better part of twenty years. A body picks up bits and pieces of rumours and tales."

"There's a mummy," I tell him, and he tilts his head, arctic gaze narrowing. "In a glass case."

"I've never heard of it," he says as if he should have. I ask casually, "Have you visited there before?"

He shakes his head.

Good.

"It was up in the attic. I was exploring. That's how I found it. Her. It. It's not terribly big so I moved her to the sitting room." I pull the knitted cap from my head and curls tumble out, catching the light from the candles; his eyes follow the fall. "A peat mummy, I think, judging by the tea colour of the skin, but I'm no expert."

He nods. "The constitution of the bogs does that. Depending on the acid concentration in the water, it will either eat the bones away and leave the skin and hair, or strip away the flesh and skin and leave the bones. They tend towards the former here."

"Will you come and look? Please? Mhairead said you'd been an archaeologist once, that you'd know best. Only I feel it should be better looked after, not just gathering dust like some old fake mermaid sewn together by carnival shysters. If it's valuable, it should go to a museum, but I don't want to trouble anyone unless…"

He smiles and I know what he's thinking: *Don't want to trouble anyone but me.* I smile back, thinking: *What else are you doing with your time?*

"Besides, I'd be happy for the company if only for a little while," I say, fully aware of the power of a woman's attention, even on a priest. Especially on a priest.

"Tomorrow afternoon, then," he says, and I release a breath. "I've evening Mass and community visits to make tonight. I don't imagine your girl's in any great hurry."

"Tomorrow afternoon will be perfect," I say, though my pulse is loud in my temples. My girl's waited a long time; what's one more day? My heart aches at the delay. "I look forward to it."

I hesitate a little longer, stare at the stained glass windows once more, at the beatific faces that might or might not be familiar. Feel the itch between my shoulder blades again. Feel a similar itch at the back of my memory where the forgotten things wait.

"Anything else I can do for you, Ms McEwan?" he asks and his voice is soft, so soft it might contain an invitation.

I give another smile, a brilliant thing. "Just admiring your angels, Father, they're lovely."

He looks at them as if for the first time. "They're doing their duty. It makes them beautiful."

I laugh. "Oh, Father, the fallen are lovely too, and don't you forget it. Didn't Lucifer keep his good looks? Otherwise how might he tempt righteous souls?"

I walk towards home faster than I left it. Almost there, I have to pause at the side of the road until the shaking rage passes. I don't throw up, though I feel I might. I straighten, take in the height, the breadth, the many stones that went into the house's make-up. I look up at the attic window and think I see a shape pressed against the glass, but I know nothing's there, not really. Just a sliver, a memory, a shade. Not a whole thing, not yet.

The night drags on. When I finally sleep, I dream of wings and old things that were given up, sacrificed. I dream of the things I yearned for, the things I gained and then lost. I wake in the dark hours to the certainty that someone is in the room, but when I open my eyes no one is there. Tiptoeing to the window, I peer out through the sliver between the thick curtains.

Beyond the low stone wall, the fog roils, agitates, rebels, but does not enter the garden.

"Did you speak to him, love?" Mhairead Spence asked when I ran into her in the village store. I stocked up on coffee and biscuits, which is basically what I exist on, and she on items far more appropriate, like fresh fruit and vegetables, flour and tea.

"Thank you, Mrs Spence."

She nodded, a housewifely gesture, pleased that matters had gone as she'd expected. "He's a good man for all he's a Catholic. I've always thought him a little haunted."

"Ah, Mrs Spence, we drag our ghosts behind us whether we want to or not."

"You've an old head on you." *She's got no idea.* "Have a lovely evening, Sarai."

"And you, Mrs Spence," I said and watched her bustle her groceries up to the counter.

Now I press my fingers against the pane, feel it cold despite the double-glazing. The fire in the hearth has gone out and the chill is palpable. Down below one of my ghosts waits, stoic, with the patience of a statue. Eventually, I go back to bed and find a dreamless slumber awaits.

"She's a lovely thing," Father Gunn McBride says, crouching in front of the case, two fingers resting against the glass as if to steady his balance. His eyes are avid, almost warm with interest.

The little tea-brown girl lies on a bed of dirt, her head and shoulders twisted one way, the rest of her body the other, as if she was shifted and warped in the earth's damp embrace. The long plaits are bright ochre red; once they were golden, but the bog has changed them too. The acid of the water has eaten away most of her clothing, so it's not likely he'll recognise that as an anachronism. And there's that strange sheen to the skin; that and the colour of her, the distortion of her features from the pressure of liquid and peat, make her unrecognisable except to one who loved her.

"Exquisite in death, isn't she? I think you've got a prize here, Ms McEwan."

"Sarai, please."

"Then I'm Gunn," he says and smiles. "Of course, she'll need to be x-rayed, all the usual tests conducted to make sure she's what she appears. I can put you in contact with some people at one of the universities on the mainland. I'm sure they'll be keen to help. I imagine the letting agent will want to be notified, though."

"I'll tell her," I say. "Can I interest you in a drink? Sherry?"

"What do you take me for? A reverend?" He laughs as he says it.

"Whiskey, then?"

"No alcohol for me, thank you." Yet there's longing in his eyes, a whisper of it in his tone. Gunn McBride used to love his booze just as he loved his beautiful women. Probably more, and that's where he came apart.

"I wonder where she's from?" His voice is quite soft, musing. He sounds oddly kind and tender, as if he feels some responsibility for her, which he should. "I wonder what happened to her? A sacrifice, do you think? I can't see a garrotte around her neck, or any obvious stab wounds. Perhaps poison or a blow to the back of the head?"

I wonder that he can discuss the death of a girl so casually. I turn away so he can't see my face. "I'll make tea, then."

When we're settled in the sitting room, the fire crackling merrily, the glass case between us, I say, "May I ask a question, Father?"

"You just did," he says and chuckles as if it's terribly funny. I want to tell him it's not, but I just smile. "Of course you may, Sarai. And it's Gunn, don't forget," as if his name is an intimacy he can force upon me.

"What did you see? When I walked into the church yesterday?" I sip at my own beverage, a dash of whiskey to fortify it.

His gaze slides away, latches onto the flames in the hearth, is held there for a few beats too long, then he lamely produces, "A trick of the light was all," and says no more.

We sit in silence for a while, drinking, looking anywhere but at each other, until he breaks at last. "And what about you, Sarai? What do you do? What brings you to us?"

"I travel," I answer, and smile. "I read, I research, sometimes I write. I witness and I watch, and if I can I set things to rights."

"Independently wealthy and aimless, then?" He misunderstands, of course, though he can't know it. "Nice thing to be."

"It costs me sure enough, Gunn," I use his name and see him blink. "And I only appear aimless to those who don't pay enough attention."

His gaze moves once again, to something behind me, or that he thinks is there. The stare traces an outline I can only imagine. "And you, Gunn, what made you change? From archaeologist to shepherd?"

It takes an effort for him to refocus, and his grin is uncomfortable.

"Mid-life crisis, shall we say? I found I had insufficient faith to support the life I was living. I needed something else, something that didn't come at the bottom of a bottle or beneath a short skirt." He shakes his head as if hit by the confessional urge. "Life was easy for me, Sarai. Things came easily to me: jobs, successes, women, and I let them go just as easily because I didn't value them. I assumed that something new would replace whatever slid away. For a long time I was right; and then… then came a hole so deep I couldn't fill it no matter what I poured down my throat or snorted up my nose or stuck my cock in." His gaze flits to see if that shocks me. I wonder how often he's given this speech, if it's a standard he pulls out when trying to convince someone of his sincerity. I might have believed him, too, if not for that little glance. If I didn't know what he'll never actually confess.

"And you found what you needed in a black robe, performative cannibalism and the fairy story of a dead god come back to life?" I raise my cup as if in toast, see his flare of annoyance – not panic, too arrogant for that – to realise I've not fallen for his act.

"Will you look at the hour, Ms McEwan? Time for me to go." He goes to put his cup on the coffee table and misses. The delicate vessel falls to the carpet, doesn't smash, but the remnants of dark bitter liquid soak into the weave. He's apologetic, embarrassed. "I'm sorry, how clumsy of me! I must have misjudged…"

"Nothing to apologise for, Father McBride. No harm done. Just leave it." I crouch in front of him, right the cup and put it on the table, then take his hands and rise, pulling him with me. We stand so close I can feel his breath on my face. He stares at me. I let one hand drop, turn and lead him behind me. His feet seem to drag when we pass the stairs that go up, but I don't pause. I guide him to the front door, open it and let his hand go. His fingers dance across my palm and he wavers on the stoop as if I might change my mind.

"For all you've found God, you don't always want him around, do you?" I breathe into his face, all whiskey and sugar sweetness, and I can see it excites him. I think about the core of him, that he sometimes fights, but eventually gives in to. There's too much of him that favours the darkness. And I want to put my hands around his thick throat and squeeze.

But I don't.

I push him away, out into the night. He staggers a little down the steps, watches me close the door ever so slowly. I don't know how long he'll stay out there. But he'll be back, I do know that much.

Once upon a time, Gunn McBride hid after he did what he did. He hid the result of his careless act and avoided the consequences. He hid from himself, from his conscience, pretended to find salvation in a new life. But it's all a façade, all a dream, all make-believe. It's just for *show*.

Two days and he doesn't return.

Two days and I think I've lost him.

Two days and I fear he's fled. I'll have to trace him,

track him, stalk him. Hunt him. As if I haven't done that enough all these years.

Was I overconfident? Have I lost my chance? What if he sensed something? What if, when given the choice, he elected not to descend? Not to seal his own fate? What if he's been genuine in his repentance? For long moments, I'm convinced I don't have the energy to pursue him anymore. That it will be easier, simpler to just let him go. To forgive, if not to forget.

Then I remind myself what I would be giving up. What I already gave up, *before*. I remind myself that was enough, if not too much, that I will not surrender this. I will not abandon her. I will not fail her again.

And in that darkness sitting vigil over the glass coffin, in that deepest pit of anguish, when what passes for my soul kindles and reaches, when I recall the determination that's kept me going, the doorbell rings.

There are shadows under his eyes. He's forgone the cassock, is in his running gear, perspiration pouring off him despite the chill air. I wonder if he's been drinking; I can smell the stale sweat with a hint of barley. Fallen off the wagon into the whiskey vat.

I'm pulling the door open as he's pushing it, then he's on me and soon in me, and I don't care. This act is needed to show his fall is entire, that he's not true to the life he claims. That he's faithless.

And for me there's relief in the physical contact, in the animal nature of the act, in knowing I've not lost. Who'd begrudge me that small comfort? I run my nails down his back, digging furrows that draw grunts from him but don't slow him down. Then I'm on top of him and his eyes widen, go to a point behind my shoulders, and I hiss, "What do you see?"

This time he answers, gasping, "Wings. Wings!" and reaches up to touch them, to outline their feathery tips, but I know he won't be able to make contact, that they're not really there. Just ghostly things clinging to my back like cobwebs, impossible to shift, to leave behind. "How can you have these? Have I gone mad?"

"No more than the rest of us, Father." I laugh, moving against him until he's caught once again in what we're doing and forgets to ask questions for a while.

When we're done and lying on the hall rug, he runs his fingers across the skin of my back as if he might feel what he can no longer see, and asks, "What are you? One of *them*?"

"Once, or so I've been told. No longer."

"Do you not know?"

"When we fall, we forget. Our wings are taken, sliced away with a great scythe, and our memories of our time aloft are removed, too."

"Then how..."

"Writings." I sigh. "And those who remain Above, who are not Fallen, they come to us. When we despair, they give us tasks, offer hope that perhaps we might one day find grace again if we are obedient."

"But if you can't remember then how do you know they're not demons tempting you? That you're not...?"

"Mad? I've asked myself that time and again, especially when the one who came to me first appeared. I can't remember, but I feel these." I point to the wings that are both there and not there. "They make us promises, that we can earn back what we lost. Most of us want our wings back, when we discover the things we fell for weren't worth the sacrifice."

"And you? What did you lose?" he asks tenderly, and I can almost believe he's genuine. But I think of how casually he spoke of my girl's death, thinking her an ancient sacrifice, how he never confessed to his deed, not even to another priest in the sanctity of confessional.

"Her. I'm told I chose to fall so I could have her. I'm told I questioned our nature, demanded to know why we did so little beyond fetching and carrying; why we created so little, why nothing we did was *generative*." I shake my head. "Some days I wonder if I *do* remember: if there are cracks in the world, between what was and what is, if my memories are bleeding through." I raise a hand as if I might catch at something, at a truth, then sigh again. "Yet, really, I remember nothing but her, and that's because she came after I fell. I chose to be human so I could have her. All I ever wanted was a child; it must have been what I wanted because that desire was the only thing I could recall the day I awoke, wingless. I found a man who was kind. I conceived, nothing miraculous in that. I had her, my little one, my tiny joy. I had her for eight years." I shrug as if it were all so simple, as if the time passed as easily as I've made the tale sound.

He says nothing, just watches my face. No sign from him that he recognises any of this story, no sign of compassion or even fleeting discomfort to hear of the death of a girl-child.

"Surely I knew from *before* that nothing lasts, that you mortals are so ephemeral – surely that piece of knowledge would have stuck – but I had her and thought she'd be there forever." I smile, but there's no warmth in it. "It's hard for angels to understand precisely how fragile life is. That humans are God's goldfish, pretty, circling, soon to be dead and flushed."

"What happened?" he asks, still stroking me. His touch raises goosebumps, or perhaps it's just this part of the telling.

"A man killed her, a bright young man, an archaeologist on a dig. A drunk on an island not so terribly different to this one. He didn't know me, didn't know my child; it was purely coincidental. Hit her as she rode her bicycle home from school. Hit her and hurt her and instead of calling for help and taking the consequences, he feared for his reputation, his career." He's gone terribly still, his fingers frozen in the small of my back. "He was too drunk to slow down, too drunk to avoid hitting my Ariel, but sober enough to think to hide her body in the peat bog not far from the road. Sober enough to know she'd turn to a sack of leathery skin with her bones eaten away by the acid of the mire, that given enough time she'd look like an ancient mummy, a sacrifice from long ago."

I sit up and lean against the wall, nesting amongst our discarded clothes. It's cold here, but I don't care: the chill reminds me I'm alive. That I *feel*. His face hangs as if all the muscles have been cut.

"How can you know?" he manages. "I told no one. Not ever."

"You didn't need to. You can't hide from the angels. God perhaps – It's very busy, gets distracted – but the angels... Well, their job is to watch, and they're terribly good at that." I lean forward, push a stray strand of hair out of his pale blue eyes. "*His* name is Ramiel, the one who came to me, and we were siblings, or so he says. He has dominion over those who rise from the dead. God lets us go if we ask, but It doesn't like to, not really – doesn't like losing souls any more than your Church does. So, when the chance comes to bring one back to the fold..."

"I didn't mean it."

"It took me so long to find her. Too long. There was nothing that could be done. The skeleton was gone. She's just a piece of old leather now, my little girl. Or, more correctly, she was broken into a trinity: the body, the ghost that waits upstairs and the soul that lives in the mists outside, waiting." I wipe away my tears. "Some just want to take their place amongst the heavenly host once more. But I couldn't have cared less about that, about the wings. Ramiel didn't come to me until I despaired, didn't offer anything until I was in a place where I'd do anything to get my daughter back."

I lean forward. "And I have done so much to earn my reward, Father McBride. I have hunted so many evil-doers, so many sinners whose very existence is anathema to the Godhead. I have been the instrument of punishment for so many years since you killed my Ariel, but finally I am told I have earned my reward."

"I didn't mean it," he says again, plaintive as a boy who feels he's wrongly punished, struggling upwards to pull his shorts back on, his shirt over his sweating torso. But he doesn't run, doesn't break for the door, as if needing the end of the story keeps him rooted. "I didn't mean it, Sarai. I'm sorry. I was a different man, then, fearful of my freedom, my reputation."

"And yet you never came forward. You hid in the priesthood as if you were somehow absolved, as if prayers and lip service might free you of all your sins. You never spoke of what you'd done, not even in the confessional booth." I look at him, pitiless, and say, "It doesn't matter. Whether you meant it or not, you did it. And you tried to hide it. Her. You *did* hide her. My little one." And I can see in his eyes how I look. I wonder if I appeared like that when I had wings, when, Ramiel had told me, I made judgments and handed down wisdom and punishment.

"What will happen to me? What do you want?"

"Ah, you've made your own choices, taken your own steps, which is why I've not killed you myself." I rise. "It's time for you to leave. Away with you, then." I open the door, feeling the wind lick at my bare skin; I point out to the terribly thick fog dancing just beyond the gate. "That's the way you need to go."

And he nods, befuddled and drunk on all that's happened, all he's learned, all that's been taken from him even as it's been given, drunk on the idea that he's escaped consequences one more time. He walks with an assurance that surprises and angers me. He doesn't notice even as he goes out the garden gate the creature in the mist, the one with wings such as I once had. Ramiel doesn't follow him, doesn't need to, just waits, as do I.

Waits for Gunn McBride's feet to take the trail that's irrevocably changed, that no longer goes towards his church and the tiny rectory beside it where he'd be warm and safe and comfortable. We linger expectantly, Ramiel and I, in the terrible cold until we hear the trickle of falling rocks, then a cry from Father McBride's lips, a single sharp sound that breaks over my ears like shattering glass, and sets everything in motion.

I look towards the fog that takes a shape that is *not* Ramiel who has dominion over those who rise, but another, smaller form that shudders and shivers as if it too has wings or is being birthed. I feel a sympathetic tremor on my bare shoulder blades. A stream of mist breaks through the gate palings and shoots its way up the path, past me with the coldest breath of air, and into the sitting room where the display case lies. From the attic comes a cry.

I scramble to follow. A shape, pale and elongated, flows down the stairs, reaches the case just as the mist does;

they mingle and, as I watch, find their way into the casket through cracks and crevices invisible to the naked eye.

The glass is icy beneath my fingertips as I flick the hidden latch and lift the lid. The vapour pours into the holes in my daughter's body, up nostrils, into parted lips and seashell-curved ears. She slips inside herself once again, into her skin, into that empty shell I've carted from place to place for so long. She reaches for me, mouths *Mama*, as though she's no voice left to her, as though it's yet to return.

Ariel is warm and soft, her skin growing paler by the second, her limbs firmer as the bones are reinstated, as her head and face lay claim once more to a pleasing, recognisable shape. I can smell the vinegary whiff of the acid that preserved her and hid her so no one but those who watch would know what Gunn McBride had done. So I wouldn't know where she'd gone until Ramiel at last decided it was my time, and told me where to look. Told me what I had to do to get her back, to earn her resurrection from the angel of those who rise; and I never questioned him, simply obeyed.

And here she is at last, breathing once again, and I feel as if each breath goes some way to filling all the absences in my life. My child, all I wanted, all I needed. Whatever memories were taken when the great scythe removed my wings have no value beside this restoration. I know one thing with utter certainty: my daughter was a worthy reason to fall.

TOM IS IN THE ATTIC
Robert Shearman

Young Tom is playing in the attic again. You call him Young Tom, of course, to distinguish him from the other Toms, though you doubt it's his real name. Young Tom hasn't appeared for a while, and you had wondered whether you'd scared him off. But, no, there he is, if you stand at the bottom of the staircase, right at the very point where it begins to bend around into a spiral, and you listen closely, you can hear all the sound from above funnel down – and you do that now, and there he is, it's Young Tom, it's unmistakable.

And you go up to see him. You take the flashlight, and turn it on full beam. He's silent suddenly, but that's because you're there – you can never be sure whether the reason he hides in the shadows is because he's frightened or whether it's just another one of his games. But if you're patient, and you can be patient, he'll come out of hiding soon enough; he'll play in front of you quite amiably. The games he knows! Sometimes it's hopscotch. Sometimes he'll spin around in a circle, laughing, until he falls down. Sometimes he plays musical chairs, even though there's no music, and there's no chairs – and yet you know that's what he's playing, you just *know*.

You can watch Young Tom play for hours. It's more fun than television. In the summer, when the attic was baking in the heat, you would sometimes watch him stripped down to your undies, and take up an ice cream.

Today it takes him a while to come out of hiding. "Come on, I can see you," you say, although you clearly can't, and although Young Tom has never acknowledged you in any way, he never talks to you or looks at you, you're sometimes not really sure he even knows you're there. You train the flashlight on all the usual nooks and crannies, the little gaps between the cardboard boxes and the water tank, and at last he emerges. He's got a new game today. "Varoom," he says. "Varoom!" He's on his hands and knees, and he's playing with a toy car, he's pushing it along the ground, he's making it speed through imaginary traffic lights and jump off imaginary cliffs.

You've never seen him play with a real object before; he'll just make do with his pretending. And you flash your light on it, and you see it isn't a toy car at all. It's a hairbrush. He's running the hairbrush along the floor, and making out the bristles are wheels.

It's your hairbrush, the one from your bedroom. You don't know whether to be angry or amused. "Hey, hey!" you say. "Did you steal that?" Because the bedroom is out of bounds, Tom has never been in the bedroom before, not *Young* Tom. He's crossed a boundary. It's not really out of bounds, though, because you've never needed to set up boundaries before, you've never seen Young Tom outside the attic. "Hey," you say again, though there's really no point, it's not as if he's listening; "Varoom!" he says, and crashes your hairbrush into the side of a cardboard box. You consider taking the hairbrush from him, but think that would be a little mean. He's enjoying himself, and it's not as if you're going to want to use the hairbrush again, not now it's been scraped along the attic floor with all the dust and dirt and cobwebs.

You have an idea, and having an idea is exciting in itself. "Stay here," you say to Young Tom, and the child will stay there or he won't, but the chances are he'll still be around when you get back, once he starts playing he's usually at it for hours. You get dressed. You put on your hat and your coat. You haven't been outside for a while, the people come and deliver all of the shopping you need, but this requires the personal touch, a little expedition all of your own. You catch the bus into town. You look for a toy shop. They're rather hard to find, don't they make toy shops any more, not for all the children in the world, and at last you settle for a children's department within a big supermarket. The sales assistant listens politely to you, and she's little more than a child herself. You tell her you want a gift for a young boy. "How old is he?" you're asked, and you don't know, it's hard to tell, sometimes he seems about two, other times he's as old as nine or ten. The assistant shows you lots of toys, but all of them require batteries or computer cables or digital media players – "Don't you have anything more old-fashioned?" you ask. At last you come up trumps in a charity shop off the high street. You find a toy car, a Rolls-Royce no less, not quite as big as your hand, and there's a little smiling man sitting in the driving seat, and the paintwork on the chassis is a bit chipped. "Genuine antique, that," you're told, and they charge you a tenner, and a tenner's outrageous, but you don't care, you pay the tenner anyway, the toy is perfect.

You're so thrilled as you climb the stairs, as you take the flashlight and wave it about. "I'm home!" you say. Young Tom hasn't gone into hiding. But he's standing on his feet now, stock still, and the hairbrush has gone. "I have a present for you," you say, and this is new, you've never bought him a present before, you've named him and you've spent time with him and watched him play in your knickers, but it's not as if he's your responsibility, he's not your child. "Here," you say and you hold the toy out to him, and he looks at you, he actually looks at you, and he smiles, and your heart starts racing, maybe now you can be friends! He holds out his hand, and you think he's reaching for the toy, but he isn't.

You turn the flashlight on to his hand. You see he's got a little tooth there, small and white and perfect. And you turn the light up to Young Tom's face, and he's smiling, and he seems proud, and the smile is with the mouth open, and you can see, yes, the little gap in the front where the tooth comes from.

You think he's just showing it to you. But now he picks the tooth up between finger and thumb, gingerly, as if it's some sort of specimen, as if it's really nothing to do with him any more, and he offers it. Before you can think, instinctively, you open your hand out to receive it. You don't want it – why would you want some kid's tooth? – and he drops it on to your palm, drops it carefully, so his fingers do not touch yours. You're welcome to the tooth but that's all he'll give you, thank you very much – and you clench your fist around the tooth, you don't know why, you ball up your fist to keep the tooth safe. And he turns away. Goes back on to his hands and knees. Begins playing once more in the dust and the dark, this time cupping a pretend car in his hand, no hairbrush there now.

You put the Rolls-Royce down beside him. He doesn't look up. "Varoom," he says, he's happy with the toy he can create out of thin air. And you feel as if you've been dismissed, and you leave him to it.

You go back to the attic that afternoon. And it's not to see Young Tom, because you stand at the bottom of the staircase and listen hard and there's not a trace of him. You go back because you want to see whether he took the present with him. And you know what to expect, but as the light makes out the Rolls-Royce, standing there on the floor, neat, precise, untouched, there's still a pang of disappointment. You wonder whether to leave it there, or to take it down with you, try to offer it to the boy again later. And then you hear a cough in the shadows, just a little cough, well-mannered, quite polite, really – and you know you're not alone.

Old Tom is the only one who speaks to you. He seems to enjoy your company. Young Tom's age appears to fluctuate, sometimes even as you're looking at him, but Old Tom stays the same. He's a hundred years old if he's a day. He's thin and white and the skin around his face is pulled in tight so you can see the skull beneath poking through. But he's not unkind, you think, and there can be a twinkle to his eyes, though you suspect that may be the flashlight reflecting off them.

"Hello, Rachel Taylor," he says. Because he asked for your name when you first met, and you didn't see any reason not to tell him, not then. And he remembers it, he remembers it every time.

"Hello, Old Tom," you reply, and he never attempts to correct you, even though it's a name you invented. Sometimes you think Old Tom is Young Tom, but a century later. Sometimes you think they're two separate people altogether, and indeed Old Tom seems to know little of Young Tom and whenever you ask about his infant namesake the old man looks confused.

Old Tom is in reminiscent mood again. "Come here, Rachel Taylor," he says. Oh, how he likes to use your name. "Come and look out of the window with me."

There is no window. But you do your best to look where he is looking anyway. "When I was young, this was all fields. Fields as far as the eye could see. And that's where I worked, tilling the fields, from dawn to dusk, me and my pappy." He starts to tell you the story of his life, and smokes a pipe as he does so – you don't like it when people smoke, but it doesn't matter, the pipe doesn't make a smell, it doesn't make any smoke either, and sometimes as he puffs away on it you see there isn't even a pipe at all, he's sucking on his thumb, it's all just pretend. Old Tom often tells you the story of his life. Sometimes it's this one, when he worked hard in the fields, in the sun and the rain and the snow, all to build a better life for his family. Sometimes he's a mariner on the high seas, fighting naval battles against the French, or discovering new lands in the Indies. Sometimes he is a priest, sometimes a pirate. Sometimes he owns a shop.

You haven't got time for this today. "Did you see the little boy?" you ask. "He left behind his toy car, look."

But you know it's pointless because he never answers your questions. You answer his. He's polite, and sometimes seems genuinely interested, and over the months he has learned everything about you – your name, your childhood, your past loves and near-loves and never-really-loves, why you're living in a house like this. He tells you things too, but never anything you want to know. What's your name, where do you come from, why are you here. Are you dead.

You asked that only once, "Are you dead?" you said. And at that he looked almost offended, and he gripped you by the hand, and he said, "Do I *feel* like a dead man?" And you said he didn't, but the truth was he might have done, a bit; there was something cold and unnerving about that grip, but only if you thought hard, only if you really concentrated on it – it was almost as if the sensation was trying to slip away from you, as if the sensation wanted nothing to do with you, as if, if you took your attention off it it'd seize the chance to escape you altogether and slip from your grasp like mist. So you didn't ask him again.

"When I was young, all this was fields," says Old Tom.

"I know that," you say. "But the toy."

"This was all fields. As far as the eye could see."

"Yes, yes," you say. "If you can pass the toy on, though, that'd be great."

And he looks at you, and there's a twinkle to his eye – and it *is* a twinkle, isn't it! And he looks so kind. And you know that if he sees the kid, of course he'll give him the toy, like a regular Santa Claus. He opens his mouth to speak. "All this was fields," he starts. And then he coughs. A good spluttering cough too, and you're not alarmed, you've heard it often before, it's all that pipe smoking he may or may not really be doing.

But the spluttering goes on, he puts his hand over his mouth, he doubles over. And this is something new. "Are you all right?" you say. And you're going to clap him on the back, but resist the urge to touch him in time.

And he straightens up now, and he smiles. He opens his hand out, the hand he coughed into. He invites you to look. You recoil at that.

Sitting there on his gnarled palm are two teeth. Yellow with tar and brown with decay.

"For the tooth fairy," he says, and smiles wider, and you can see his gums, and where he's coughed those teeth right out of his mouth.

You don't want to take the teeth, but there's no choice – he's taken your hand now, tightly. And once again it feels cold and insubstantial, and, yes, *unearthly*, and there's something suddenly nauseous and too too sweet in your mouth.

The teeth feel real enough, mind. They weigh heavy.

"For the tooth fairy, Rachel Taylor." Oh, how he loves your name. Because you don't know his name, like this is some little power he has over you. Old Tom puts his pipe in his mouth, and it is a pipe this time, you'd swear it is. He turns back to his fields, looks out on them with a pride that is almost territorial.

Old Tom is the only one who speaks to you, but that doesn't mean you like him very much.

You suppose the other Tom should be called Middle-Aged Tom, or Inbetween Tom, but you just think of him as Tom. No, in truth, you don't think of him by name at all. You just wait for him there in the dark, hoping he'll come. And often he doesn't, and sometimes he does.

The lights have to be off, he won't come if there's even a chink of light, not light from the room next door, nor light from behind the curtains. And so you don't entirely know what Tom looks like. But you can always hear him coming. Because this Tom won't talk to you either, he's more like the little boy in that respect, but still he talks, how he talks, he never pauses for breath, it all comes out in one long mutter. You lie there in the bed, hoping he'll be with you soon, and telling yourself not to be disappointed if he won't be – though, of course, you can't stop the disappointment, no matter how hard you try. And then, if you're lucky, you'll hear it, there'll be the muttering – getting louder as he approaches, but never so loud you can make out what it is he's saying really, it's like a background rumble, it's rather soothing. And you shift over to the edge of the bed to make room, but there's really no need; he's not going to worry about the space you're taking up, you can't even be sure he knows you're there.

Though you think he knows. Surely he knows. Sometimes, when you're especially sweet to him.

There's something nice about another body being next to yours again. And it's better than before, because this time it'll just lie there, like a dead weight; each night he stays he sleeps on his back, and he never moves, he never complicates things, he never tries to *accommodate* you. That was always what put you off in the past, all that accommodation, the way the men would respond to you, it made bedtime feel like such a responsibility.

Not for Tom – he'll mutter on and on regardless of you, he'll sleep when he's ready, he'll snore, he'll cough, fart. There's something nice about another body. Something reassuring. "Good night," you'll say, and sometimes, "Good night, my love," and he'll just keep on chatting away to himself. Oh the restful rhythm of it, it makes your head light and drowsy.

And you touch him. You touch him if you can. You touch the right part. He's like the old man, the body feels insubstantial and cold, you feel that if you pressed hard enough you'd put your hand right through him, and you wouldn't want that! But there's always a piece of him that's firm and warm. And human. And manly. It's not hard to find that warm bit, in a cold bed it radiates heat like a beacon. A little lighthouse in the cold flat ocean of his body, and sometimes it's his chest, and you cuddle up to it, and wonder whether what's tickling you are chest hairs, does he have hair on his chest? – you put your head down upon that chest and that maybe-hair which might really be your hair, how can you tell, and you fancy you can hear his heartbeat. Which might really be your heartbeat, how can you tell. – And sometimes it's the neck. Sometimes it's the forehead. One time it was the lips. Most often, it's just the elbow.

Tonight it's just the elbow again, but there's nothing *just* about the elbow, it's not one of your favourite parts of his anatomy, but it's still him, it's still warm. Nice. A bit hard and bony, there's not much give to an elbow, but you lean into it anyway, and you feel it's as if he's holding you to him, holding you close, keeping you safe from the ghosts of the night.

But that time with the lips! – and you cradled on top of him, on top of his face, you pressed your lips against his own. And the funny thing was, as you kissed him, he never stopped his muttering. You were up so close that you could even hear it, or most of it. It didn't make much sense. *Good morning. Good morning. Good morning. Toast, please. And did you. Did you. Oh. Good morning.* And more like that. *Good morning. Yes. Yes. Thank you. Good morning. A single to Piccadilly Circus, please. Thank you. Good morning. Excuse me.* Running on, no matter how much you tried to smother it with your kisses, he wasn't having it, the words had to come out, he was forcing them past your mouth, each little syllable squeezed out through the tiniest gaps between lip and lip and out into the world, *Good morning. Hello? Yes, could you just. Yes. Good morning, thank you. Good morning. Good morning.* It seemed to you that it was every conversation he had ever had, all run together without the pauses, no room left for another person's response. Half-phrased questions, greetings, apologies, thank yous, occasional requests for cups of tea. Once in a while you heard an *I love you.* There it was, *Good morning. Good. Thank you. I love you. Excuse me. I love, yes. Good morning.* "I love you too," you said, and kissed him again, long and hard, and his mouth squirmed with further conversation underneath your lips and teeth and tongue, although you knew the *I love you* wasn't for you.

Some nights the warm part of his body is below the waistline. But you never go there. You've never liked to go there, not with any man, not even with the living ones. No good ever came of it. Yours is a very platonic love. As you nuzzle at his elbow. As you kiss and suck every bit of the body heat you can get from it.

Tonight feels wrong, and different, and it did from the moment he first arrived; the muttering was no louder, but there was more edge to it, does that make sense? *Good morning*, he says, but now it feels more deliberate, even sarcastic, as he pronounces the words so clearly. He won't settle, you can't calm him, no matter what attentions you pay his elbow – is he asleep anyway, is he having a nightmare? For that dead weight body is beginning to thrash, he's really not supposed to do that – and as he thrashes he's getting warmer, not just the elbow now, but the whole body, it's like being in bed with a real man. You don't want that, that's not the game, that's out of bounds. And suddenly you can see that he's reaching out to you, as dark as it is you can make out his hands coming towards your neck, and you cry out, though he'd never hurt you, surely, not Tom, not your very own Inbetween Man? But he's not reaching for your neck. He's not reaching for you at all. It's the pillow, your pillow, his hands are underneath it now, bulging it right behind your head so you have to sit up

– he's *searching* for something, and it's desperate, the muttering begins to turn into a whisper, so scared – and really, this is more the sort of behaviour you'd expect from Young Tom, a baby, not a grown man, what can he be after?

What could be under a pillow? You remember Old Tom, giving you his teeth for the Tooth Fairy.

So – "Is it these? Do you need these?" And you've taken them off the dressing table. You can't see them, but can feel which one is young and healthy, the two that are soft and diseased.

He snatches them from you then. His hand so warm it's burning. His whole body burning hot.

And he thrusts the teeth under the pillow. And he holds down the pillow over them tight. And he wraps his arms around the pillow, so nothing can get in or out.

He's quiet at last. The muttering gentle.

There's no room in the bed for you now. You sit upright in the armchair, watching the contours of your lover rise and fall as he sleeps.

At some point you doze off. Because by the morning you have a crick in your neck, and the bed is empty.

You think to check under the pillow. The teeth have gone. Instead, there is a large silver coin. You pick up the coin. There are no markings on it, not on either side; it can't be a real coin. But it feels flat and heavy and rich.

* * *

You go for breakfast, and at the bottom of the stairs you hear Young Tom is playing in the attic. And you never go to him before breakfast, you want your breakfast first, there's a right time for fun and games. But he's not playing quietly. There's stomping and shouting and goodness knows what. And you rush right up there.

You turn the flashlight on. "Come out!" you call. But Young Tom is already out, he isn't hiding this time. He's playing with the little Rolls-Royce. He's dropping it upon the floor, he's kicking it. He's smashing it hard against the walls.

"Stop that!" you say.

And there's a look on his face that isn't angry or spiteful. It's utterly intent. And it isn't childish either, that's what makes you shiver suddenly. It's adult intent.

He drops to his hands and knees, starts beating the ground hard with the car.

"I said stop!"

He looks up at you. In bewildered surprise, as if he's only just seen you. Maybe he has. And all that intent is gone, and his face falls into that of an embarrassed child.

"If you don't play with your toy nicely," you say, "I'll take it back." But you won't take it back, look at his sweet little face, he's sorry now.

He sets the car upon the floor, dented as it now is, with great care and utter precision.

"I have something for you," you think to say. And you open up your hand, and show him the coin. You weren't even aware you were still holding it. You turn the flashlight upon it, and it seems to burn in the glare.

Young Tom looks interested, but cautious.

"It's yours," you say. "From the Tooth Fairy."

And Young Tom takes it. He looks at it quizzically. Sets it upon the floor next to the car. He turns the coin on to its side, starts rolling it around in the grime. "Varoom," he says, quietly. He looks up at you. He likes this game. He smiles.

No, he beams. He beams the broadest grin, his mouth open in childish happiness. And you realise there isn't a tooth in his head. It's all gum. And his face can't take it, there's nothing to support its shape properly now, it's collapsing in on itself.

And he holds out little fists, and he's raising them towards you. And you don't want to take what he's got in there, but your hands are opening in response, your palms are stretched out wide.

You take his teeth. Every last tooth he has.

"For the Tooth Fairy?" you ask, and it isn't really a question. And because it isn't really a question, Young Tom doesn't really answer it. He's playing with his coin now. With his big shiny coin, shiny even though the flashlight isn't on it.

You put the little boy's teeth under the pillow, every single one of them. The pillow teeters awkwardly on the mound. You press it down firmly.

You lie in bed that night, and wait for Tom. But he doesn't join you. Perhaps he's busy.

In the morning you wake up and check under the pillow. Sure enough, the teeth have gone. You'd have thought for all the teeth you gave her the Tooth Fairy would have left you a treasure trove. But there's just one coin, silver, no bigger than the last.

You hear Young Tom playing in the attic, and he hasn't done so for a while. You race up there as fast as you can. But it's not Young Tom at all. Old Tom is playing hopscotch. He bounces up and down on one foot, laughing, and wheezing through the laughter.

"Greetings to 'ee, Rachel Taylor," he says. He's in pirate mode today. He speaks in an accent of richest Mummerset, he squints his eye a lot. He talks about pieces of eight and treasure chests, and pretends he has a parrot on his shoulder. The first time you saw him play the pirate you thought it was quite funny. But it really, really isn't. He says to you, "When I was young, this was all oceans, as far as the eye can see."

"Where's the little boy?" you ask, and he ignores that. "Where's the other man?" you ask. "Why won't he sleep with me any more?" And at that he actually laughs. He lights his pipe, and puffs out smoke. No, he lights his thumb. He puffs out smoke.

"Where be my treasure?" he says.

"I don't know of any treasure," you say.

"I've scoured the oceans for treasure," he says. "You dog. You landlubber. You scurvy knave."

"You're not getting a thing," you insist, "until I get Tom back. My Tom."

He chuckles at that, but not unkindly. He reaches out, and strokes your chin. You flinch, but his fingers now are warm. It's not like before, his fingers are warm and his touch is tender.

He strokes away at your chin, and his eyes twinkle, and you know now it's nothing to do with the flashlight. His second hand joins the first, they're both at your chin now, they're not stroking, they're rubbing, hard – and you try to pull away, but why would you want to, it's hard, yes, but it's nice, isn't it? It feels nice, and you've so missed being touched. And Tom, he never touched you, not really, he never even knew you were there, admit it now, he's never cared whether you live or die. Old Tom puffs on his pipe, and he has to use a pipe because his thumbs are busy, his thumbs are pushing deeper into your skin, into your jaw, and his eyes twinkle all the more, they sparkle now, and the eyes then are lost behind the clouds of tobacco smoke, and then his entire face is lost.

He takes his hands away. He holds out a tooth to you.

You hadn't even felt it pop out of place. You touch your face, you're shocked to find the gap. It's not one of the front teeth, it won't be that visible, but even so – how rude. Your tongue can't but help explore the missing space in your mouth.

"I'll be wanting my treasure," says Old Tom softly. And then, of course, in your hand, you're holding the silver coin. He takes it, pockets it, doesn't even look at it.

He gives you back your tooth. "Shall I give it to the Tooth Fairy?" you hear yourself ask.

"Oh, Rachel," he says, and smiles – and you see there's nothing in that mouth now, no teeth, but not just no teeth, there's no gums, there's no tongue, there's blackness, that's all there is, void. "Oh, you're our Tooth Fairy now."

And he pops his pipe back into the blackness; the void bites down the stem and sucks hard.

You look down at your tooth. It's yellowing by the second.

"Everything I touch turns to shit," says the old pirate, and then he's in the shadows, and then he's gone.

The tooth is dust now. You wipe it from your hand.

As you walk, your foot kicks at a discarded toy. You bend down to the Rolls-Royce, start to play with it.

Your tongue has settled down in the exciting new gap your missing tooth has created, it loves to loll about in there. It goes to sleep.

He comes for you that night, and you were sure he would. In preparation you had a bath and washed your hair. You put on that perfume you never wear. You make your skin smooth and soft, just for him, and lie there, spread out like a banquet, and wait.

He comes, and you were sure he would, but you still feel so relieved when you hear his muttering in the dark. You haven't heard it for so long now. You hadn't slept well for the loss of it.

A body gets in at the right side of the bed. A body gets in at the left side. The muttering stays apart, it feels a long way away.

To your left the body feels very small. To the right, you can smell the faint whiff of pipe smoke.

And you think, no. No, this really has crossed a boundary now.

The light comes on, and you don't know how, because Young Tom is to one side and Old Tom is to the other, and besides, they're so busy, they've both taken one of your arms and they're holding on to you tight. And you don't want the lights on because it'll scare your Tom away, you couldn't bear that.

You don't want to see him. Just in case he's not beautiful.

Oh, but he is. And he does have chest hair, you thought he must. And his eyes are dark and strong, and it doesn't matter that they keep rolling in his head, darting this way and that, like he's asleep with his eyes open, like this is all some dream for him. And he has teeth, such white teeth. He has all the teeth in the world.

You hope you smell nice for him. You know you do.

And he's over you now. Straddling your body with his, as the other Toms hold you down. And you can hear his muttering.

Good night, good night, good night, sleep well, love you, good night, sleep well, have a good sleep, night night, night, good night, g'night, love you, love you. And it's every bit of his pillow talk, every single word he's ever said as he's settled down to sleep, all in order, and they're for you, he's giving them to you.

He takes the pillow, and he presses it on to your face. And for a moment you think he's going to suffocate you, but he wouldn't hurt you, you love him and he loves you, didn't he just say? And the little boy and the old man keep you from struggling, but you aren't going to struggle, don't be silly.

You can feel the teeth melt away. There's no pain. You spit some out. Others just slide down your throat, already liquid, or near liquid, and the taste of spearmint, it's all so fresh.

Your tongue loves it, it's like a child on Christmas morning, such excitement, so many new crevices to explore – and then, no crevices to explore, the crevices are gone now, there's just a wide open field in which he can play! When you were young, this was all fields, as far as the eye could see, as far as the tongue could roll.

It's over now. The pillow just slides off your face. No one's holding it down any more.

They all have their silver coins now. Each of the Toms are holding them out, offering them – but to whom? Because you can't see anyone. But they can see something, and they can't see you, or can't be bothered to see you, there's no interest in you any more, that's what hurts.

They don't even vanish. They were never there.

They were never there, and you're all alone.

You go to the bathroom mirror, and open your mouth, and you think your red gums look so clean and pretty now the teeth don't get in the way.

You don't leave the house again. You're not sure whether you even can. But it doesn't matter. You simply don't feel the urge.

The people keep bringing you food. It's hard to eat with no teeth, but that's okay. It's not as if you're especially hungry. You haven't eaten in days. Months? Ever? No, you must have eaten once upon a time, that's just crazy talk. Anyway, one day they stop leaving you food.

Your gums fall out, and you don't mind, you were getting bored of them anyway.

Sometimes you hear a little child playing in the attic. You like to go up there and watch. It's not Young Tom. Tom has gone. It's you. It's you. It's you. Look at that face, don't you know that face, it's you! Oh, the games she plays. She plays hopscotch. She spins herself around until she falls over. She plays musical chairs, and you know it's musical chairs, because you hear the music in your head, and you can turn it off the moment you feel like it.

She doesn't talk to you, you're not sure she knows you're there. Maybe it's easier that way. And in the summer months, when the attic just bakes, you go up and watch her in your undies.

You can make her scratch her head if you want. You scratch yours, she scratches hers. Usually.

It doesn't always work, but still. She's playing, and you're playing with her.

She is so pretty. You were so pretty.

She is so pretty, she has such bright white sparkling teeth. How you'd love to have those teeth. How you'd love to knock them out of her head, with a hammer maybe, ever so gently, one by one, one little tap, and out they'd pop! How you'd love to liquefy them, and drink them down, and taste that rush of spearmint fresh.

Just to taste it again. Just once more. Once more in your life, and you wouldn't ask for anything else.

Sometimes there's an old woman in the attic, and she looks a bit like your mother, but she's kinder than your mother, and she didn't give you away. This old woman is the only one who speaks to you. "Hello, Rachel Taylor," she says, and she loves to use your name, like it's a matter of personal pride. She looks about a hundred, and she smokes a pipe, and that's ridiculous, because you've never smoked a pipe, and you're pretty sure your mother never smoked a pipe either.

She tells you stories of her childhood, and they

should be your childhood too, but she gets them all wrong. She tells of when she was a farmer, or a priest, or a pirate. You don't recognise any of it. Frankly, the daft old crone is talking bollocks. She puffs at her pipe, and sometimes she touches your hand, and she feels so warm and alive, and you don't like that very much. You don't see why she should be so warm when you feel chilled to the core. And she talks to you her bollocks, and you don't talk back.

You can't talk back, not since your tongue went the way of your gums. But she talks enough for both of you. You prefer it when it's the little girl who's in the attic.

And when neither the little girl nor the old crone are in the attic, you go up there to play by yourself. You play with a little Rolls-Royce car. Varoom. But it's not an out loud varoom. It's the sort of varoom you make silently in your head.

And at night. Most nights. But not every night. The good nights, she'll come to you.

She comes in muttering, and she says such rubbish, and her concerns are all so very trivial, and her problems really so small. And you want to say *ssh*, you want to tell her it'll be all right, relax now, easy, easy. You love her.

She doesn't even know you're there, there's nothing you can do.

And she only comes in the dark, but you can feel how beautiful she is. The very shape of her is perfect, the imprint she leaves upon the bed after she's left in the morning is as correctly proportioned as an imprint can be. You wish she knew she was beautiful. And if no one has ever wanted her beauty, well, that was their loss – and if no one has ever made her feel beautiful, their shame.

Nothing you can do, but you nuzzle into the elbow. It's bony and hard and there's such little feeling to an elbow, she won't know that you're kissing it. But you do your best.

And she should get out of this house. Whilst she has the chance. Because this can't be all there is. There's a better life waiting for her, she should just reach out and take it, what's stopping her? You're stopping her. You couldn't bear it if she were to go.

You love her so much.

You want to see her, but she only comes in the dark.

You want to see her, but you daren't turn the light on, you might alarm her. And you mustn't do that. Not with all her teeth, all the teeth in the world. If she's scared, she'll bite.

20TH CENTURY GHOST
Joe Hill

*T*he best time to see her is when the place is almost full.

There is the well-known story of the man who wanders in for a late show and finds the vast six-hundred-seat theater almost deserted. Halfway through the movie, he glances around and discovers her sitting next to him, in a chair that only moments before had been empty. Her witness stares at her. She turns her head and stares back. She has a nosebleed. Her eyes are wide, stricken. My head hurts, *she whispers.* I have to step out for a moment. Will you tell me what I miss? *It is in this instant that the person looking at her realizes she is as insubstantial as the shifting blue ray of light cast by the projector. It is possible to see the next seat over through her body. As she rises from her chair, she fades away.*

Then there is the story about the group of friends who go into the Rosebud together on a Thursday night. One of the bunch sits down next to a woman by herself, *a woman in blue. When the movie doesn't start right away, the person who sat down beside her decides to make conversation.* What's playing tomorrow? *he asks her.* The theater is dark tomorrow, *she whispers.* This is the last show. *Shortly after the movie begins she vanishes. On the drive home, the man who spoke to her is killed in a car accident.*

These, and many of the other best-known legends of the Rosebud, are false... the ghost stories of people who have seen too many horror movies and who think they know exactly how a ghost story should be.

Alec Sheldon, who was one of the first to see Imogene Gilchrist, owns the Rosebud, and at seventy-three still operates the projector most nights. He can always tell, after talking to someone for just a few moments, whether or not they really saw her, but what he knows he keeps to himself, and he never publicly discredits anyone's story... that would be bad for business.

He knows, though, that anyone who says they could see right through her didn't see her at all. Some of the put-on artists talk about blood pouring from her nose, her ears, her eyes; they say she gave them a pleading look, and asked for them to find somebody, to bring help. But she doesn't bleed that way, and when she wants to talk, it isn't to tell someone to bring a doctor. A lot of the pretenders begin their stories by saying, You'll never believe what I just saw. *They're right. He won't, although he will listen to all that they have to say, with a patient, even encouraging, smile.*

The ones who have seen her don't come looking for Alec to tell him about it. More often than not he finds them, comes across them wandering the lobby on unsteady legs; they've had a bad shock, they don't feel well. They need to sit down a while. They don't ever say, You won't believe what I just saw. *The experience is still too immediate. The idea that they might not be believed doesn't occur to them until later. Often they are in a state that might be described as subdued, even submissive. When he thinks about the effect she has on those who encounter her, he thinks of Steven Greenberg coming out of* The Birds *one cool Sunday afternoon in 1963. Steven was just twelve then, and it would be another twelve years before he went and got so famous; he was at that time not a golden boy, but just a boy.*

Alec was in the alley behind the Rosebud, having a smoke, when he heard the fire door into the theater clang open behind him. He turned to see a lanky kid leaning in the doorway – just leaning there, not going in or out. The boy squinted into the harsh white sunshine, with the confused, wondering look of a small child who has just been shaken out of a deep sleep.

Alec could see past him into a darkness filled with the shrill sounds of thousands of squeaking sparrows. Beneath that, he could hear a few in the audience stirring restlessly, beginning to complain.

Hey, kid, in or out? *Alec said.* You're lettin' the light in.

The kid – Alec didn't know his name then – turned

his head and stared back into the theater for a long, searching moment. Then he stepped out and the door settled shut behind him, closing gently on its pneumatic hinge. And still he didn't go anywhere, didn't say anything. The Rosebud *had been showing* The Birds *for two weeks, and although Alec had seen others walk out before it was over, none of the early exits had been twelve-year-old boys. It was the sort of film most boys of that age waited all year to see, but who knew? Maybe the kid had a weak stomach.*

I left my Coke in the theater, *the kid said, his voice distant, almost toneless.* I still had a lot of it left.

You want to go back in and look for it?

And the kid lifted his eyes and gave Alec a bright look of alarm, and then Alec knew. No.

Alec finished his cigarette, pitched it.

I sat with the dead lady, *the kid blurted.*

Alec nodded.

She talked to me.

What did she say?

He looked at the kid again, and found him staring back with eyes that were now wide and round with disbelief.

I need someone to talk to, she said. When I get excited about a movie I need to talk.

Alec knows when she talks to someone she always wants to talk about the movies. She usually addresses herself to men, although sometimes she will sit and talk with a woman – Lois Weisel most notably. Alec has been working on a theory of what it is that causes her to show herself. He has been keeping notes in a yellow legal pad. He has a list of who she appeared to and in what movie and when (Leland King, Harold and Maude, '72; Joel Harlowe, Eraserhead, '77; Hal Lash, Blood Simple, '85; and all the others). He has, over the years, developed clear ideas about what conditions are most likely to produce her, although the specifics of his theory are constantly being revised.

As a young man, thoughts of her were always on his mind, or simmering just beneath the surface; she was his first and most strongly felt obsession. Then for a while he was better – when the theater was a success, and he was an important businessman in the community, chamber of commerce, town-planning board. In those days he could go weeks without thinking about her; and then someone would see her, or pretend to have seen her, and stir the whole thing up again.

But following his divorce – she kept the house, he moved into the one-bedroom under the theater – and not long after the 8-screen cineplex opened just outside of town, he began to obsess again, less about her than about the theater itself (is there any difference, though? Not really, he supposes, thoughts of one always circling around to thoughts of the other). He never imagined he would be so old and owe so much money. He has a hard time sleeping, his head is so full of ideas – wild, desperate ideas – about how to keep the theater from failing. He keeps himself awake thinking about income, staff, salable assets. And when he can't think about money anymore, *he tries to picture where he will go if the theater closes. He envisions an old folks' home, mattresses that reek of Ben-Gay, hunched geezers with their dentures out, sitting in a musty common room watching daytime sitcoms; he sees a place where he will passively fade away, like wallpaper that gets too much sunlight and slowly loses its color.*

This is bad. What is more terrible is when he tries to imagine what will happen to her if the Rosebud closes. He sees the theater stripped of its seats, an echoing empty space, drifts of dust in the corners, petrified wads of gum stuck fast to the cement. Local teens have broken in to drink and screw; he sees scattered liquor bottles, ignorant graffiti on the walls, a single, grotesque, used condom on the floor in front of the stage. He sees the lonely and violated place where she will fade away. Or won't fade… the worst thought of all.

Alec saw her – spoke to her – for the first time when he was fifteen, six days after he learned his older brother had been killed in the South Pacific. President Truman had sent a letter expressing his condolences. It was a form letter, but the signature on the bottom – that was really his. Alec hadn't cried yet. He knew, years later, that he spent that week in a state of shock, that he had lost the person he loved most in the world and it had badly traumatized him. But in 1945 no one used the word "trauma" to talk about emotions, and the only kind of shock anyone discussed was "shell—."

He told his mother he was going to school in the mornings. He wasn't going to school. He was shuffling around downtown looking for trouble. He shoplifted candy-bars from the American Luncheonette and ate them out at the empty shoe factory – the place closed down, all the men off in France, or the Pacific. With sugar zipping in his blood, he launched rocks through the windows, trying out his fastball.

He wandered through the alley behind the Rosebud and looked at the door into the theater and saw that it wasn't firmly shut. The side facing the alley was a smooth metal surface, no door handle, but he was able to pry it open with his fingernails. He came in on the 3:30 P.M. show, the place crowded, mostly kids under the age of ten and their mothers. The fire door was halfway up the theater, recessed into the wall, set in shadow. No one saw him come in. He slouched up the aisle and found a seat in the back.

"I heard Jimmy Stewart went to the Pacific," his brother had told him while he was home on leave, before he shipped out. They were throwing the ball around out back. "Mr. Smith is probably carpet-bombing the red fuck out of Tokyo right this instant. How's that for a crazy thought?" Alec's brother, Ray, was a self-described film freak. He and Alec went to every single movie that opened during his month-long leave: *Bataan*, *The Fighting Seabees*, *Going My Way*.

Alec waited through an episode of a serial concerning the latest adventures of a singing cowboy with long eyelashes and a mouth so dark his lips were black. It failed to interest him. He picked his nose and wondered how to get a Coke with no money. The feature started.

At first Alec couldn't figure out what the hell kind of movie it was, although right off he had the sinking feeling it was going to be a musical. First the members of an orchestra filed onto a stage against a bland blue backdrop. Then a starched shirt came out and started telling the audience all about the brand-new kind of entertainment they were about to see. When he started blithering about Walt Disney and his artists, Alec began to slide downwards in his seat, his head sinking between his shoulders. The orchestra surged into big dramatic blasts of strings and horns. In another moment his worst fears were realized. It wasn't just a musical; it was also a *cartoon*. Of course it was a cartoon, he should have known – the place crammed with little kids and their mothers – a 3:30 show in the middle of the week that led off with an episode of *The Lipstick Kid*, singing sissy of the high plains.

After a while he lifted his head and peeked at the screen through his fingers, watched some abstract animation: silver raindrops falling against a background of roiling smoke, rays of molten light shimmering across an ashen sky. Eventually he straightened up to watch in a more comfortable position. He was not quite sure what he was feeling. He was bored, but interested too, almost a little mesmerized. It would have been hard not to watch. The visuals came at him in a steady hypnotic assault: ribs of red light, whirling stars, kingdoms of cloud glowing in the crimson light of a setting sun.

The little kids were shifting around in their seats. He heard a little girl whisper loudly, "Mom, when is there going to be *Mickey*?" For the kids it was like being in school. But by the time the movie hit the next segment, the orchestra shifting from Bach to Tchaikovsky, he was sitting all the way up, even leaning forward slightly, his forearms resting on his knees. He watched fairies flitting through a dark forest, touching flowers and spiderwebs with enchanted wands and spreading sheets of glittering, incandescent dew. He felt a kind of baffled wonder watching them fly around, a curious feeling of yearning. He had the sudden idea he could sit there and watch forever.

"I could sit in this theater forever," whispered someone beside him. It was a girl's voice. "Just sit here and watch and never leave."

He didn't know there was someone sitting beside him and jumped to hear a voice so close. He thought – no, he knew – that when he sat down, the seats on either side of him were empty. He turned his head.

She was only a few years older than him, couldn't have been more than twenty, and his first thought was that she was very close to being a fox; his heart beat a little faster to have such a girl speaking to him. He was already thinking, *Don't blow it*. She wasn't looking at him. She was staring up at the movie, and smiling in a way that seemed to express both admiration and a child's dazed wonder. He wanted desperately to say something smooth, but his voice was trapped in his throat.

She leaned towards him without glancing away from the screen, her left hand just touching the side of his arm on the armrest.

"I'm sorry to bother you," she whispered. "When I get excited about a movie I want to talk. I can't help it."

In the next moment he became aware of two things, more or less simultaneously. The first was that her hand against his arm was cold. He could feel the deadly chill of it through his sweater, a cold so palpable it startled him a little. The second thing he noticed was a single teardrop of blood on her upper lip, under her left nostril.

"You have a nosebleed," he said, in a voice that was too loud. He immediately wished he hadn't said it. You only had one opportunity to impress a fox like this. He should have found something for her to wipe her nose with, and handed it to her, murmured something real Sinatra: *You're bleeding, here.* He pushed his hands into his pockets, feeling for something she could wipe her nose with. He didn't have anything.

But she didn't seem to have heard him, didn't seem the slightest bit aware he had spoken. She absent-mindedly brushed the back of one hand under her nose, and left a dark smear of blood over her upper lip... and Alec froze with his hands in his pockets, staring at her. It was the first he knew there was something wrong about the girl sitting next to him, something slightly *off* about the scene playing out between them. He instinctively drew himself up and slightly away from her without even knowing he was doing it.

She laughed at something in the movie, her voice soft, breathless. Then she leaned towards him and whispered, "This is all wrong for kids. Harry Parcells loves this theater, but he plays all the wrong movies – Harry Parcells who runs the place?"

There was a fresh runner of blood leaking from her left nostril and blood on her lips, but by then Alec's attention had turned to something else. They were sitting directly under the projector beam, and there were moths and other insects whirring through the blue column of light above. A white moth had landed on her face. It was crawling up her cheek. She didn't notice, and Alec didn't mention it to her. There wasn't enough air in his chest to speak.

She whispered, "He thinks just because it's a cartoon they'll like it. It's funny he could be so crazy for movies and know so little about them. He won't run the place much longer."

She glanced at him and smiled. She had blood staining her teeth. Alec couldn't get up. A second moth, ivory white, landed just inside the delicate cup of her ear.

"Your brother Ray would have loved this," she said.

"Get away," Alec whispered hoarsely.

"You belong here, Alec," she said. "You belong here with me."

He moved at last, shoved himself up out of his seat. The first moth was crawling into her hair. He thought he heard himself moan, just faintly. He started to move away from her. She was staring at him. He backed a few feet down the aisle and bumped into some kid's legs, and the kid yelped. He glanced away from her for an instant, down at a fattish boy in a striped T-shirt who was glaring back at him: *Watch where you're going, meathead.*

Alec looked at her again and now she was slumped very low in her seat. Her head rested on her left shoulder. Her legs hung lewdly open. There were thick strings of blood, dried and crusted, running from her nostrils, bracketing her thin-lipped mouth. Her eyes were rolled back in her head. In her lap was an overturned carton of popcorn.

Alec thought he was going to scream. He didn't scream. She was perfectly motionless. He looked from her to the kid he had almost tripped over. The fat kid glanced casually in the direction of the dead girl, showed no reaction. He turned his gaze back to Alec, his eyes questioning, one corner of his mouth turned up in a derisive sneer.

"Sir," said a woman, the fat kid's mother. "Can you move, *please*? We're trying to watch the movie."

Alec threw another look towards the dead girl, only now the chair where she had been was empty, the seat folded up. He started to retreat, bumping into knees, almost falling over once, grabbing someone for support. Then suddenly the room erupted into cheers, applause. His heart throbbed. He cried out, looked wildly around. It was Mickey, up there on the screen in droopy red robes – Mickey had arrived at last.

He backed up the aisle, swatted through the padded leather doors into the lobby. He flinched at the late-afternoon brightness, narrowed his eyes to squints. He felt dangerously sick. Then someone was holding his shoulder, turning him, walking him across the room, over to the staircase up to balcony-level. Alec sat down on the bottom step, sat down hard.

"Take a minute," someone said. "Don't get up. Catch your breath. Do you think you're going to throw up?" Alec shook his head.

"Because if you think you're going to throw up, hold on till I can get you a bag. It isn't so easy to get stains out of this carpet. Also when people smell vomit they don't want popcorn."

Whoever it was lingered beside him for another moment, then without a word turned and shuffled away. He returned maybe a minute later.

"Here. On the house. Drink it slow. The fizz will help with your stomach."

Alec took a wax cup sweating beads of cold water, found the straw with his mouth, sipped icy cola bubbly with carbonation. He looked up. The man standing over him was tall and slope-shouldered, with a sagging roll around the middle. His hair was cropped to a dark bristle and his eyes, behind his absurdly thick glasses, were small and pale and uneasy.

Alec said, "There's a dead girl in there." He didn't recognize his own voice.

The color drained out of the big man's face and he cast an unhappy glance back at the doors into the theater. "She's never been in a matinee before. I thought only night shows, I thought – for God's sake, it's a kids' movie. What's she trying to do to me?"

Alec opened his mouth, didn't even know what he was going to say, something about the dead girl, but what came out instead was: "It's not really a kids' film."

The big man shot him a look of mild annoyance. "Sure it is. It's Walt Disney."

Alec stared at him for a long moment, then said, "You must be Harry Parcells."

"Yeah. How'd you know?"

"Lucky guesser," Alec said. "Thanks for the Coke."

Alec followed Harry Parcells behind the concessions counter, through a door and out onto a landing at the bottom of some stairs. Harry opened a door to the right and let them into a small, cluttered office. The floor was crowded with steel film cans. Fading film posters covered the walls, overlapping in places: *Boys Town*, *David Copperfield*, *Gone With the Wind*.

"Sorry she scared you," Harry said, collapsing into the office chair behind his desk. "You sure you're all right? You look kind of peaked."

"Who is she?"

"Something blew out in her brain," he said, and pointed a finger at his left temple, as if pretending to hold a gun to his head. "Six years ago. During *The Wizard of Oz*. The very first show. It was the most terrible thing. She used to come in all the time. She was my steadiest customer. We used to talk, kid around with each other—" His voice wandered off, confused and distraught. He squeezed his plump hands together on the desktop in front of him, said finally, "Now she's trying to bankrupt me."

"You've seen her." It wasn't a question.

Harry nodded. "A few months after she passed away. She told me I don't belong here. I don't know why she wants to scare me off when we used to get along so great. Did she tell you to go away?"

"Why is she here?" Alec said. His voice was still hoarse, and it was a strange kind of question to ask. For a while, Harry just peered at him through his thick glasses with what seemed to be total incomprehension.

Then he shook his head and said, "She's unhappy. She died before the end of *The Wizard* and she's still miserable about it. I understand. That was a good movie. I'd feel robbed too."

"Hello?" someone shouted from the lobby. "Anyone there?"

"Just a minute," Harry called out. He gave Alec a pained look. "My concession-stand girl told me she was quitting yesterday. No notice or anything."

"Was it the ghost?"

"Heck no. One of her paste-on nails fell into someone's food so I told her not to wear them anymore.

No one wants to get a fingernail in a mouthful of popcorn. She told me a lot of boys she knows come in here and if she can't wear her nails she wasn't going to work for me no more so now I got to do everything myself." He said this as he was coming around the desk. He had something in one hand, a newspaper clipping. "This will tell you about her." And then he gave Alec a look – it wasn't a glare exactly, but there was at least a measure of dull warning in it – and he added: "Don't run off on me. We still have to talk."

He went out, Alec staring after him, wondering what that last funny look was about. He glanced down at the clipping. It was an obituary – her obituary. The paper was creased, the edges worn, the ink faded; it looked as if it had been handled often. Her name was Imogene Gilchrist, she had died at nineteen, she worked at Water Street Stationery. She was survived by her parents, Colm and Mary. Friends and family spoke of her pretty laugh, her infectious sense of humor. They talked about how she loved the movies. She saw all the movies, saw them on opening day, first show. She could recite the entire cast from almost any picture you cared to name, it was like a party trick – she even knew the names of actors who had had just one line. She was president of the drama club in high school, acted in all the plays, built sets, arranged lighting. "I always thought she'd be a movie star," said her drama professor. "She had those looks and that laugh. All she needed was someone to point a camera at her and she would have been famous."

When Alec finished reading he looked around. The office was still empty. He looked back down at the obituary, rubbing the corner of the clipping between thumb and forefinger. He felt sick at the unfairness of it, and for a moment there was a pressure at the back of his eyeballs, a tingling, and he had the ridiculous idea he might start crying. He felt ill to live in a world where a nineteen-year-old girl full of laughter and life could be struck down like that, for no reason. The intensity of what he was feeling didn't really make sense, considering he had never known her when she was alive; didn't make sense until he thought about Ray, thought about Harry Truman's letter to his mom, the words *died with bravery, defending freedom, America is proud of him*. He thought about how Ray had taken him to *The Fighting Seabees*, right here in this theater, and they sat together with their feet up on the seats in front of them, their shoulders touching. "Look at John Wayne," Ray said. "They oughta have one bomber to carry him, and another one to carry his balls." The stinging in his eyes was so intense he couldn't stand it, and it hurt to breathe. He rubbed at his wet nose, and focused intently on crying as soundlessly as possible.

He wiped his face with the tail of his shirt, put the obituary on Harry Parcells' desk, looked around. He glanced at the posters, and the stacks of steel cans. There was a curl of film in the corner of the room, just eight or so frames – he wondered where it had come from – and he picked it up for a closer look. He saw a

79

girl closing her eyes and lifting her face, in a series of little increments, to kiss the man holding her in a tight embrace; giving herself to him. Alec wanted to be kissed that way sometime. It gave him a curious thrill to be holding an actual piece of a movie. On impulse he stuck it into his pocket.

He wandered out of the office and back onto the landing at the bottom of the stairwell. He peered into the lobby. He expected to see Harry behind the concession stand, serving a customer, but there was no one there. Alec hesitated, wondering where he might have gone. While he was thinking it over, he became aware of a gentle whirring sound coming from the top of the stairs. He looked up them, and it clicked – the projector. Harry was changing reels.

Alec climbed the steps and entered the projection room, a dark compartment with a low ceiling. A pair of square windows looked into the theater below. The projector itself was pointed through one of them, a big machine made of brushed stainless steel, with the word VITAPHONE stamped on the case. Harry stood on the far side of it, leaning forward, peering out the same window through which the projector was casting its beam. He heard Alec at the door, shot him a brief look. Alec expected to be ordered away, but Harry said nothing, only nodded and returned to his silent watch over the theater.

Alec made his way to the VITAPHONE, picking a path carefully through the dark. There was a window to the left of the projector that looked down into the theater. Alec stared at it for a long moment, not sure if he dared, and then put his face close to the glass and peered into the darkened room beneath.

The theater was lit a deep midnight blue by the image on the screen: the conductor again, the orchestra in silhouette. The announcer was introducing the next piece. Alec lowered his gaze and scanned the rows of seats. It wasn't much trouble to find where he had been sitting, an empty cluster of seats close to the back, on the right. He half-expected to see her there, slid down in her chair, face tilted up towards the ceiling and blood all down it – her eyes turned perhaps to stare up at *him*. The thought of seeing her filled him with both dread and a strange nervous exhilaration, and when he realized she wasn't there, he was a little surprised by his own disappointment.

Music began: at first the wavering skirl of violins, rising and falling in swoops, and then a series of menacing bursts from the brass section, sounds of an almost military nature. Alec's gaze rose once more to the screen – rose and held there. He felt a chill race through him. His forearms prickled with gooseflesh. On the screen the dead were rising from their graves, an army of white and watery specters pouring out of the ground and into the night above. A square-shouldered demon, squatting on a mountaintop, beckoned them. They came to him, their ripped white shrouds fluttering around their gaunt bodies, their faces anguished, sorrowing. Alec caught his breath and held it, watched with a feeling rising in him of mingled shock and wonder.

The demon split a crack in the mountain, opened Hell. Fires leaped, the Damned jumped and danced, and Alec knew what he was seeing was about the war. It was about his brother dead for no reason in the South Pacific, *America is proud of him*, it was about bodies damaged beyond repair, bodies sloshing this way and that while they rolled in the surf at the edge of a beach somewhere in the Far East, getting soggy, bloating. It was about Imogene Gilchrist, who loved the movies and died with her legs spread open and her brain swelled full of blood and she was nineteen, her parents were Colm and Mary. It was about young people, young healthy bodies, punched full of holes and the life pouring out in arterial gouts, not a single dream realized, not a single ambition achieved. It was about young people who loved and were loved in return, going away, and not coming back, and the pathetic little remembrances that marked their departure, *my prayers are with you today, Harry Truman*, and *I always thought she'd be a movie star.*

A church bell rang somewhere, a long way off. Alec looked up. It was part of the film. The dead were fading away. The churlish and square-shouldered demon covered himself with his vast black wings, hiding his face from the coming of dawn. A line of robed men moved across the land below, carrying softly glowing torches. The music moved in gentle pulses. The sky was a cold, shimmering blue, light rising in it, the glow of sunrise spreading through the branches of birch trees and northern pine. Alec watched with a feeling in him like religious awe until it was over.

"I liked *Dumbo* better," Harry said.

He flipped a switch on the wall, and a bare lightbulb came on, filling the projection room with harsh white light. The last of the film squiggled through the VITAPHONE and came out at the other end, where it was being collected on one of the reels. The trailing end whirled around and around and went *slap, slap, slap.* Harry turned the projector off, looked at Alec over the top of the machine.

"You look better. You got your color back."

"What did you want to talk about?" Alec remembered the vague look of warning Harry gave him when he told him not to go anywhere, and the thought occurred to him now that maybe Harry knew he had slipped in without buying a ticket, that maybe they were about to have a problem.

But Harry said, "I'm prepared to offer you a refund or two free passes to the show of your choice. Best I can do."

Alec stared. It was a long time before he could reply. "For what?"

"For what? To shut up about it. You know what it would do to this place if it got out about her? I got reasons to think people don't want to pay money to sit in the dark with a chatty dead girl."

Alec shook his head. It surprised him that Harry thought it would keep people away if it got out that the

Rosebud was haunted. Alec had an idea it would have the opposite effect. People were happy to pay for the opportunity to experience a little terror in the dark – if they weren't, there wouldn't be any business in horror pictures. And then he remembered what Imogene Gilchrist had said to him about Harry Parcells: *He won't run the place much longer.*

"So what do you want?" Harry asked. "You want passes?" Alec shook his head.

"Refund, then."

"No."

Harry froze with his hand on his wallet, flashed Alec a surprised, hostile look. "What do you want, then?"

"How about a job? You need someone to sell popcorn. I promise not to wear my paste-on nails to work."

Harry stared at him for a long moment without any reply, then slowly removed his hand from his back pocket. "Can you work weekends?" he asked.

In October, Alec hears that Steven Greenberg is back in New Hampshire, shooting exteriors for his new movie on the grounds of Phillips Exeter Academy – something with Tom Hanks and Haley Joel Osment, a misunderstood teacher inspiring troubled kid-geniuses. Alec doesn't need to know any more than that to know it smells like Steven might be on his way to winning another Oscar. Alec, though, preferred the earlier work, Steven's fantasies and suspense thrillers.

He considers driving down to have a look, wonders if he could talk his way onto the set – Oh yes, I knew Steven when he was a boy – wonders if he might even be allowed to speak with Steven himself. But he soon dismisses the idea. There must be hundreds of people in this part of New England who could claim to have known Steven back in the day, and it isn't as if they were ever close. They only really had that one conversation, the day Steven saw her. Nothing before; nothing much after.

So it is a surprise when one Friday afternoon close to the end of the month Alec takes a call from Steven's personal assistant, a cheerful, efficient-sounding woman named Marcia. She wants Alec to know that Steven was hoping to see him, and if he can drop in – is Sunday morning all right? – there will be a set pass waiting for him at Main Building, on the grounds of the Academy. They'll expect to see him around 10:00 A.M., she says in her bright chirp of a voice, before ringing off. It is not until well after the conversation has ended that Alec realizes he has received not an invitation, but a summons.

A goateed P.A. meets Alec at Main and walks him out to where they're filming. Alec stands with thirty or so others, and watches from a distance, while Hanks and Osment stroll together across a green quad littered with fallen leaves, Hanks nodding pensively while Osment talks and gestures. In front of them is a dolly, with two men and their camera equipment sitting on it, and two men pulling it. Steven and a small group of others stand off to the side, Steven observing the shot on a video monitor. Alec has never been on a movie set before, and he watches the work of professional make-believe with great pleasure.

After he has what he wants, and has talked with Hanks for a few minutes about the shot, Steven starts over towards the crowd where Alec is standing. There is a shy, searching look on his face. Then he sees Alec and opens his mouth in a gap-toothed grin, lifts one hand in a wave, looks for a moment very much the lanky boy again. He asks Alec if he wants to walk to craft services with him, for a chili dog and a soda.

On the walk Steven seems anxious, jingling the change in his pockets and shooting sideways looks at Alec. Alec knows he wants to talk about Imogene, but can't figure how to broach the subject. When at last he begins to talk, it's about his memories of the Rosebud. He talks about how he loved the place, talks about all the great pictures he saw for the first time there. Alec smiles and nods, but is secretly a little astounded at the depths of Steven's self-deception. Steven never went back after The Birds. He didn't see any of the movies he says he saw there.

At last, Steven stammers, What's going to happen to the place after you retire? Not that you should retire! I just mean – do you think you'll run the place much longer?

Not much longer, Alec replies – it's the truth – but says no more. He is concerned not to degrade himself asking for a handout – although the thought is in him that this is in fact why he came. That ever since

*receiving Steven's invitation to visit the set he had been
fantasizing that they would talk about the Rosebud,
and that Steven, who is so wealthy, and who loves
movies so much, might be persuaded to throw Alec a
life preserver.*

The old movie houses are national treasures, *Steven
says.* I own a couple, believe it or not. I run them as
revival joints. I'd love to do something like that with the
Rosebud someday. That's a dream of mine, you know.

*Here is his chance, the opportunity Alec was not
willing to admit he was hoping for. But instead of
telling him that the Rosebud is in desperate straits, sure
to close, Alec changes the subject... ultimately lacks the
stomach to do what must be done.*

What's your next project? *Alec asks.*

After this? I was considering a remake, *Steven says,
and gives him another of those shifty sideways looks
from the corners of his eyes.* You'd never guess what.
Then, suddenly, he reaches out, touches Alec's arm.
Being back in New Hampshire has really stirred some
things up for me. I had a dream about our old friend,
would you believe it?

Our old – *Alec starts, then realizes who he means.*

I had a dream the place was closed. There was a
chain on the front doors, and boards in the windows.
I dreamed I heard a girl crying inside, *Steven says, and
grins nervously.* Isn't that the funniest thing?

*Alec drives home with a cool sweat on his face, ill at
ease. He doesn't know why he didn't say anything, why*

he couldn't *say anything; Greenberg was practically begging to give him some money. Alec thinks bitterly that he has become a very foolish and useless old man.*

At the theater there are nine messages on Alec's machine. The first is from Lois Weisel, whom Alec has not heard from in years. Her voice is brittle. She says, Hi, Alec, Lois Weisel at B.U. *As if he could have forgotten her. Lois saw Imogene in* Midnight Cowboy. *Now she teaches documentary filmmaking to graduate students. Alec knows these two things are not unconnected, just as it is no accident Steven Greenberg became what he became.* Will you give me a call? I wanted to talk to you about – I just – will you call me? *Then she laughs, a strange, frightened kind of laugh, and says,* This is crazy. *She exhales heavily.* I just wanted to find out if something was happening to the Rosebud. Something bad. So – call me.

The next message is from Dana Llewellyn, who saw her in The Wild Bunch. *The message after that is from Shane Leonard, who saw Imogene in* American Graffiti. *Darren Campbell, who saw her in* Reservoir Dogs. *Some of them talk about the dream, a dream identical to the one Steven Greenberg described, boarded-over windows, chain on the doors, girl crying. Some only say they want to talk. By the time the answering machine tape has played its way to the end, Alec is sitting on the floor of his office, his hands balled into fists – an old man weeping helplessly.*

Perhaps twenty people have seen Imogene in the last twenty-five years, and nearly half of them have left messages for Alec to call. The other half will get in touch with him over the next few days, to ask about the Rosebud, to talk about their dream. Alec will speak with almost everyone living who has ever seen her, all of those Imogene felt compelled to speak to: a drama professor, the manager of a video rental store, a retired financier who in his youth wrote angry, comical film reviews for The Lansdowne Record, *and others. A whole congregation of people who flocked to the Rosebud instead of church on Sundays, those whose prayers were written by Paddy Chayefsky and whose hymnals were composed by John Williams and whose intensity of faith is a call Imogene is helpless to resist. Alec himself.*

After the sale, the Rosebud is closed for two months to refurbish. New seats, state-of-the-art sound. A dozen artisans put up scaffolding and work with little paintbrushes to restore the crumbling plaster molding on the ceiling. Steven adds personnel to run the day-to-day operations. Although it's his place now, Alec has agreed to stay on to manage things for a little while.

Lois Weisel drives up three times a week to film a documentary about the renovation, using her grad students in various capacities, as electricians, sound people, grunts. Steven wants a gala reopening to celebrate the Rosebud's past. When Alec hears what he wants to show first – a double feature of The Wizard of

Oz *and* The Birds – *his forearms prickle with gooseflesh;
but he makes no argument.*

*On reopening night, the place is crowded like it hasn't
been since* Titanic. *The local news is there to film people
walking inside in their best suits. Of course, Steven is
there, which is why all the excitement... although Alec
thinks he would have a sell-out even without Steven,
that people would have come just to see the results of
the renovation. Alec and Steven pose for photographs,
the two of them standing under the marquee in their
tuxedoes, shaking hands. Steven's tuxedo is Armani,
bought for the occasion. Alec got married in his.*

*Steven leans into him, pressing a shoulder against his
chest.* What are you going to do with yourself?

*Before Steven's money, Alec would have sat behind
the counter handing out tickets, and then gone up
himself to start the projector. But Steven hired someone
to sell tickets and run the projector. Alec says,* Guess I'm
going to sit and watch the movie.

Save me a seat, *Steven says.* I might not get in until
The Birds, though. I have some more press to do out
here.

*Lois Weisel has a camera set up at the front of the
theater, turned to point at the audience, and loaded
with high-speed film for shooting in the dark. She films
the crowd at different times, recording their reactions
to* The Wizard of Oz. *This was to be the conclusion
of her documentary – a packed house enjoying a
twentieth-century classic in this lovingly restored old*

movie palace – but her movie wasn't going to end like she thought it would.

In the first shots on Lois's reel it is possible to see Alec sitting in the back left of the theater, his face turned up towards the screen, his glasses flashing blue in the darkness. The seat to the left of him, on the aisle, is empty, the only empty seat in the house. Sometimes he can be seen eating popcorn. Other times he is just sitting there watching, his mouth open slightly, an almost worshipful look on his face.

Then in one shot he has turned sideways to face the seat to his left. He has been joined by a woman in blue. He is leaning over her. They are unmistakably kissing. No one around them pays them any mind. The Wizard of Oz is ending. We know this because we can hear Judy Garland, reciting the same five words over and over in a soft, yearning voice, saying – well, you know what she is saying. They are only the loveliest five words ever said in all of film.

In the shot immediately following this one, the house lights are up, and there is a crowd of people gathered around Alec's body, slumped heavily in his seat. Steven Greenberg is in the aisle, yelping hysterically for someone to bring a doctor. A child is crying. The rest of the crowd generates a low rustling buzz of excited conversation. But never mind this shot. The footage that came just before it is much more interesting.

It is only a few seconds long, this shot of Alec and his unidentified companion – a few hundred frames of *film – but it is the shot that will make Lois Weisel's reputation, not to mention a large sum of money. It will appear on television shows about unexplained phenomena, it will be watched and rewatched at gatherings of those fascinated with the supernatural. It will be studied, written about, debunked, confirmed, and celebrated. Let's see it again.*

He leans over her. She turns her face up to his, and closes her eyes and she is very young and she is giving herself to him completely. Alec has removed his glasses. He is touching her lightly at the waist. This is the way people dream of being kissed, a movie star kiss. Watching them, one almost wishes the moment would never end. And over all this, Dorothy's small, brave voice fills the darkened theater. She is saying something about home. She is saying something everyone knows.

A MAN WALKING HIS DOG
Tim Lebbon

I was still shaking when I returned home, so I made myself a cup of tea and sat on the decking in my back garden, wishing I'd added a shot of something stronger but feeling too traumatised to go back in and find the whiskey. My regular seat on the timber bench welcomed me, knowing my shape and affording me some level of comfort. But I was still shivering, and not only from the deep winter chill. It's not every day you see a dead body.

It was cold but dry, January just heading into February. There'd been a heavy snowfall just after New Year, but since then the weather had been crisp and freezing, frost-speckled landscapes the perfect canvas for my regular morning walks with Jazz. I loved the sound of frozen leaves crinkling underfoot and the sight of Jazz rooting through the undergrowth, sniffing out scents I would never know. She lived in a whole different world from me – one of exotic senses and tastes, different colours, and drives I can only pretend to understand – but that's why our friendship had always meant so much. She relied on me, I relied on her. I wouldn't have it any other way.

I held the mug tight in both hands, comforted by the warmth and staring through the steam. My back garden had the sparse, bleached appearance of winter, colours muted and growth paused between seasons. It felt like the whole world was holding its breath today.

I breathed out, and the steam spiralled and dispersed in the cool, clear air.

"A body has been found."

She has been expecting it. She'd convinced herself it was the only likely outcome, given the circumstances. But it is still a shock when the words come out of the policewoman's mouth. Taking form and meaning, given the weight of reality compressing air he had once breathed, the words' finality is like a punch to the chest. Her heart stutters and she blinks, eyelids fluttering as the echo of the statement weaves its way through the house and rebounds inside her skull.

"I'm very sorry, Mrs Jones. This is not a formal identification, but the clothing matches your description."

She can't look at the policewoman. She's been very kind, has sat with her for many hours over the past few days, but she is an invader in Jenny's home. Yesterday, Jenny went into the kitchen and found that John's cup had been washed and wiped and placed on the wrong hook, and the wrong way around. He wouldn't have liked that. They had their routine, their organisation, and John would have tutted and rolled his eyes. The policewoman didn't belong here. John did, sharing Jenny's space as he had done for the past four decades.

Jenny takes in a deep, shuddering breath and goes to stand, one hand flat on the table top, the other pressed against her bad hip. She senses the policewoman moving close and concentrates harder, not wanting her help, not needing it.

"Maybe you should stay sitting down," the woman says, and Jenny hears the pity in her voice. The caring, the humanity. It's been there all along.

"Yes," she says, easing herself back into the chair. "Maybe I should."

"I'm very sorry, Mrs Jones."

"Yes," Jenny says, and as she sits again she looks across the table at John's seat. He's there, newspaper folded on the table before him, toast and marmalade half-eaten on the plate, cup of tea half-empty, and he's frowning at the crossword as he has every morning for as long as she can remember. Soon he'll sigh and sit back, sliding the paper across to her again so that she can have another look. *Seven down's a bugger*, he'll say, and she'll hear him crunching the rest of his toast as she looks at the offending clue, half-hoping she'll get it instantly, half-hoping she won't. They both love their morning ritual. It is the foundation upon which the rest of their day is built, whatever that day is destined to bring.

John is not there. This day has no foundation. The previous few days have been the same, but now she knows that solid base will never be built again. She is floating free in her own home, her own chair. It makes her feel sick.

"We like to do the crossword," she says, and she senses the policewoman's discomfort. She hears movement behind her, a shuffling of feet, and Jenny silently berates herself for saying something so foolish. The woman will think she's just a confused old lady. She's not confused at all.

She's angry.

"He's left me," she says, looking up at the policewoman for the first time since hearing those dreaded words.

"I'm sure he didn't mean to," the woman says. She has a very caring face.

"I told him he was being stupid," Jenny says. She's already told the police about his failing health. They wrote down what she said with a blank expression.

"He sounded like a very proud man," the woman says, and the past tense makes Jenny blink. John will never be in the past for her.

"Where?" she asks.

The policewoman scoots a chair over and sits down next to her, taking Jenny's hand in her own. It's a sudden, surprising gesture, the first time the woman has made physical contact, and it makes everything more real. *The foundation of my new future*, Jenny thinks. *A stranger holding my hand*.

"Up by the canal," the policewoman says. "I don't know where, exactly."

"Five days," Jenny says. "He's been lying there on his own for five days."

No answer. Only a squeezed hand.

"Who found him?"

"A man walking his dog."

Jenny laughs. She surprises herself so much that she pauses, then laughs again. The policewoman frowns, uncertain.

"Isn't that always the way," Jenny says. "Poor man. Poor, poor man. Just out for a walk with his dog and he finds…" *He finds my dead husband.*

"I suppose it is something you hear a lot."

"I'd like to meet him," Jenny says. "The man. His dog. I'd like to meet them to say sorry."

"I'm not sure if…"

"Not straight away. After all this is…" Sorted. Put away. After everyone but me has moved on.

"I'm sure it can be arranged," the woman says. Her radio makes a funny noise and she lets go of Jenny's hand, standing and moving to the doorway into the dining room to speak. She must be grateful for the distraction.

Jenny looks across the table at her husband's empty chair. *Seven down's a bugger*, he says.

"I'll get it for you," she whispers.

The policewoman glances at her and frowns. Just another confused old lady whose husband wandered away to die.

* * *

Jazz went off on her own again. I didn't mind, because she was a good dog and I knew she wouldn't get lost or run away. Jazz always came back.

But now, something was different. She was barking. She didn't bark very often, and it sounded agitated and afraid. I followed, slipping down the steep slope from the canal towpath and into the woods. A stream flowed down there. I'd heard it countless times, but I'd never been tempted from the path to go exploring. There was a barbed wire fence, fallen trees, holes from old forestry work, and I had no wish to injure myself and lie there in pain waiting for someone to come and help. I glanced back up towards the canal. It was interesting seeing it from this perspective. From down here, you could make out some of the heavy stone retaining walls that had been built over a century before, when the canal was being constructed. Such a familiar place, and now I was seeing it afresh.

"Good girl, Jazz," I said. She had shown me something new once more. She was always good company, and she enriched my life.

I heard another bark. I paused, head tilted, and the barking came again. I fought my way down the slope, climbing over fallen trees, avoiding the snares of tangled undergrowth.

The barking continued, guiding me, and by the time I saw her I knew that something was wrong. A darkness had fallen over the day. The sun was still out, but the fir tree canopy shielded me from the cool sky, and frost clung to the shadowy forest floor.

As soon as I saw the shape ten feet from Jazz I knew what it was. I froze, heart hammering, and for the longest few seconds of my life I waited for movement. *He's a drunk, a vagrant, a bird watcher, an explorer.* But all of those were wrong, and my first reaction was right. This was a dead man. From the state of his body, the colour of his skin, I believed he had been dead for some time.

I reached down to stroke and calm Jazz.

Which was when the man's head turned with a crunching sound and he said, "She's a good dog."

I snapped awake, gasping for breath. It was the third time I had dreamt about the dead man, the dreams waking me each morning since finding him. They unsettled me, because a dead man shouldn't talk. They were mostly the same – me and Jazz walking, her disappearing down into the woods, me looking for her. Then the barking, her calling me onwards with an obvious alarm. Drawing me closer to the body. The only real changes were the memories of how the weather had been that day. In one dream there was snow, a couple of inches coating the landscape and settling on the canal's frozen surface. In another, it was raining a constant, soaking drizzle. In this final dream, it was cold and sharp, and my exhalation of shock upon finding the body hung in the air before me. I didn't like waking to these dreams. It was as if the poor man's death drew me onwards, day by day, towards my own inevitable future.

Perhaps the events of today would help me move on.

I glanced at my bedside clock and sat up. Standing and opening the curtains, I was struck by the strange beauty of this normal, new day. It was cool and frosty once again. For the third morning in a row, I dwelled upon how the dead man would see no more mornings.

His wife would be here soon. A police officer would be accompanying her. After an initial deep sense of anxiety at the prospect, I had at last accepted to meet her. She was the one who mattered in this. The police had filled me in a little about her background, and the more I heard, the more I understood why this day must be so important to her. I might have been having strange dreams, but her waking hours had become a nightmare. If I hadn't found her husband's body, it might have been many days before his fate was discovered. Even weeks. Perhaps he might never have been found at all, hidden from the towpath as he was by a large holly bush and a couple of fallen trees. I was the person who had changed her life.

Jazz and I had changed everything.

I dressed and ate breakfast, then went about cleaning the house. I kept it in good condition anyway, but having a stranger visit gave me the impetus to vacuum and dust once more. Dog hair gets everywhere. But as I cleaned, I realised that I would not be letting the widow inside. Not after what had happened. Not after the dog had snuffled at her husband's corpse.

There was no way that she could meet Jazz.

* * *

"Why didn't you tell me this before?" Jenny asks. She's sitting in the back of the police car, and the policewoman is turned around in the passenger seat, eyes wide.

"I only found out myself this morning," she says. "And, really..." She shrugs. *Does it matter?*

Jenny frowns and looks at the hedgerows and fields flitting by. *Did* it matter? She wasn't sure how it could, yet it did. If this were a TV series or a book, not real life, it would hint at a malevolent pattern, a twisted thread leading to more murder and mourning. In truth, it's nothing but a sad coincidence. It is always a woman out for a jog or a man walking his dog, isn't it? They are the people out early in the morning. They are the ones who find what the night leaves behind.

"How long ago?" Jenny asks without looking at the policewoman.

"Fourteen years."

"Not the same dog, then."

"Huh?"

It doesn't matter. They swing from the main road onto a lane leading along the hillside, and across a couple of fields she can see the line of trees that marks the route of the canal, and the hump of an old stone bridge. They're still three or four miles from where John was found, but the towpath that leads there is now very close by. From here, all routes lead to his lonely, sad death.

A tear rolls down her cheek. She leaves it to drip from her jaw. She has wiped away too many tears.

"I hope he won't want to talk about it," Jenny says. "The other body he found all those years ago, I mean."

The policewoman doesn't reply. Jenny suspects that he's already had to talk about it enough with the police. She feels sorry for the man and hopes he's not nervous.

They finish the journey in silence, parking across the road from a neat little cottage. It's small but well kept, render-painted a pale yellow, its garden large and ordered. There's a Ford in the driveway, and a curl of smoke rising from the chimney. Jenny realises that she doesn't know a single thing about this man, other than what he found three days ago. She hasn't asked his name, whether he's married or alone, how old he is, what he does. She's suddenly embarrassed by that. He's been through a trauma too.

She wonders what he thinks about her wishing to meet him.

"Are you ready, Jenny?" the policewoman asks.

She nods. "Yes."

The policewoman leaves the car and opens Jenny's door for her, and as she does so the cottage's front door opens and a man emerges. He's tall and perhaps a decade older than her John, well dressed against the cold, and as he closes the door behind him and smiles, Jenny wonders, *So, where's the dog?* He crosses the country lane and stands close to the back of the police car.

"I thought we might go for a walk," he says.

* * *

He took the woman – the widow – and the policewoman along a track by his house and into a small woodland. They walked away from the canal, not towards it. The silence was awkward and heavy, punctuated only by the sound of their footsteps on the frozen ground, the crinkle of leaves beneath their shoes, the birdsong from the bare trees and bushes. He walked side by side with the woman, and if he glanced to the left and away from her he might have been alone.

He often came to these woods with Jazz. He knew the area well, and he led them to a place in the centre where several fallen trees provided somewhere to lean or sit.

"I'm so very sorry," he said at last.

"Yes," the woman said. She pressed her lips tight and a tear flowed down her cheek. It dripped to the forest floor, and he thought, *I wonder if it will freeze there?*

"I thought walking might be better, you know, fresh air and…"

"And you didn't want me to meet your dog."

He blinked, not sure what to say.

"I understand," the woman said. "That's very thoughtful of you." She looked around. "It's very lovely here."

"Yes, it is," he said. "You should see it in springtime. We walk here often, Jazz and I, most days in fact. Here and the… the canal."

"Good companionship, I imagine. Maybe I should get a dog."

"I couldn't do without her," he said.

"John and I used to walk," she said. "He liked getting up into the hills, but lately my hip's been getting worse and we've ended up finding flatter places to walk. Along the river, sometimes, you know? We always end up at a coffee shop somewhere. You feel like you've earned your cake after walking for several miles. John likes Victoria sponge, the bigger the better. He usually has two coffees." She paused, looking over his shoulder. "*Had* two coffees. *Liked* Victoria sponge." She was having trouble balancing the present and past, and he was not surprised. It was early days.

"Do you have a wife?" the woman asked. The question surprised him, and he took a few seconds to gather himself, moments in which memories danced and sang, and emotions made him their plaything.

"Not for a long time," he said at last. The woman smiled in sympathy. He smiled back. And like that the ice was melted, the awkwardness between them broken, and they were just two lonely people in their autumn years taking a stroll in winter sunlight.

Later, he went for his usual afternoon walk with Jazz. He left the cottage and headed up the gentle slope to the canal, crossing the small bridge and descending three steps onto the towpath. It would be getting dark within half an hour, but that was still long enough to stretch his legs and let Jazz have a good sniff around to do her business. And after today, he needed a walk.

For the first couple of minutes, he was on his own. He whistled softly and uttered her name under his breath. "Jazz. Jazz." He felt a faint tugging on the lead he was carrying. "Good girl," he said. He looked down and saw a shimmer around the end of the lead. "You always come when I call you."

It took his old dog a few more minutes to fully appear. And then he let her go and she was gone, darting along the canal to pick up the ghostly scents of other dogs, sniffing at forgotten dead things in the undergrowth, being with him as he had always been with her, and always would.

CAMEO
Laura Purcell

Stephen had never thought to see the old place again. *Hoped* not to, in all honesty. Five years later and it was just the same. That dreary stone terrace and the urns that decorated it, stretching towards the fringe of an oak forest. It was late September now. Acorns everywhere underfoot, dropping from the trees and narrowly avoiding Gwen's head as she and Stephen made their way, trembling, towards the steps that led to the front door.

Where was the sunshine they'd driven through this morning? Gone. Stonevale Hall sustained its own atmosphere. He wouldn't be surprised to see a cloud hovering perpetually over the roof. Take the oaks, for example. In other parts of the country they blushed, a charming array of bronze and russet. Here they were dirt brown. As if they had skipped over the autumnal phase in a rush to die and be rid of the place.

He raised the polished knocker and let it fall against a shining, black door. Footsteps sounded in another part of the house. Gwen's fingers gripped his coat sleeve.

Poor old girl. The shame of knocking for admittance to her former home must be crushing. But if he was supposed to feel guilty for taking her away from this life, he didn't. Already the return was making her look pinched and anxious, the grey stone walls throwing a pallor over her skin. What with the black dress, she hardly resembled his wife at all. No; setting her free from this house had been the best thing he'd ever done.

The door opened slightly to reveal the hawk of a butler, Jones. A beak nose and hooded eyes lurked beneath two bristling brows. "May I help you?"

A deliberate snub. As if he did not know Gwen, had not seen her grow from a child. On another occasion, Stephen would bloody the fellow's nose, but that would hardly raise Gwen's spirits now.

"What, Jones, grown forgetful in your dotage, have you? Or is it your eyesight that's gone?" Unintimidated, Stephen pushed at the door, forced it open wider. "It's Mr and Mrs Fletcher here for the reading of the will, just like everyone else."

The old man's mouth quirked. "So it is. I did not recognise Miss Gwendoline."

"Mrs Fletcher."

"Yes… Marriage has *altered* her." Jones pressed on the word like a bruise. His eyes ranged over Gwen's unfashionable dress, the black shoes that had seen better days, and the hair she could not afford to keep styled.

She blushed, but the anger seemed to ginger her up a bit. "Just let us in, Jones. It's going to rain."

It was darker inside. The windows only admitted a depressing, grainy sort of light. There was no glint on the heavy gold frames around the paintings, no shine from the glass in the grandfather clock. Everything was matt and dull.

"This way, if you please."

Stephen followed reluctantly through the mahogany-panelled hallways, wrinkling his nose at the hunting trophies that snarled from the walls. Gwen huffed, slowing her pace to keep behind the butler.

How had this starched place ever been a home to her? The woman he knew was warm and sweet. Not simply an attentive mother, but a fun one too. Such qualities did not take root inside Stonevale Hall. They were smothered beneath the perfume of dried flowers and waxed wood. God, it made him feel like all the life was being slowly choked out of him. The sooner they got this blasted will over and done with, the better.

Jones came to a halt and opened the door to the drawing room. At this proximity, Stephen could see flakes of dandruff on the shoulders of his coat. The old man was crumbling like some decayed relic of a bygone age.

"Mr and Mrs Fletcher," Jones announced with cool disdain. Voices murmured; a spot of red burned in each of Gwen's cheeks.

Seizing her hand, Stephen marched in and pulled her after him. He hadn't fought in a war to be cowed by snobbish parasites, thank you very much. And there they were, the old crowd, vapid as ever. Men with oiled hair, the young women flat-chested in their unflattering gowns. Gwen's sisters now sported locks cropped to their jaws. It made them look strangely androgynous.

"Good day," Stephen said, with a touch more force than he intended.

No response. He hadn't expected one.

Two Wedgwood chairs were left vacant next to the General, one of those moustachioed buffoons who had sent so many good men to their death. Gritting his teeth, Stephen sat down beside him. Gwen perched on the edge of her seat, hands bunched in her lap.

Anger flared in his chest, but he stifled it. Christ, what *wouldn't* be stifled in that drawing room? It was worse than the hallways: papered the red of a corked wine, an unnecessary fire smoking beneath the grey marble mantelpiece. Above it, the old Tartar herself glared down over them in oil paints, more vivid and alive than she had ever appeared in the flesh.

Lady Strange's painted expression was precisely the one she had bestowed upon Stephen the last time they had met. He remembered the cloud of powder that fell from that nest of carefully coiffured white hair, and the thin top lip, set in its habitual sneer. "You might have possessed the impudence to marry her, but she will never be yours. Never. She is *my* daughter, and I will take her back."

He waggled his eyebrows at the portrait. *Bad luck, your ladyship.*

A suited, spectacled man who must be the lawyer stood with a sheaf of papers tucked under his arm. He cleared his throat. "I believe that everyone concerned is now present. If I might begin."

A creak as the black-clad family shifted in their seats, leant forward with gleaming eyes. Carrion birds.

Stephen lolled back and let the lawyer's voice drone over him. There would be nothing for Gwen. Lady Strange had stipulated that her youngest daughter attend the reading of the will, but he wouldn't put it past her to do that out of spite. To make Gwen bear the shame of her disinheritance in public. He was only sorry they'd been foolish enough to come at the dead woman's bidding.

But there you had it. Gwen loved her mother. *Why* was a question he was never able to answer, but he wasn't a brute. If she wanted to visit Stonevale Hall one last time, he wasn't the one to begrudge her. She'd given up everything for him.

The bequests fell out in the order he expected. Stonevale Hall to Winifred, the eldest. Daphne got a chunk of money, and the General received an amount so similar it must have been the portion originally allotted to Gwen. Well, the old butcher was Lady Strange's brother; he deserved it. But it chafed one to think of what might have been. Little Camilla would be off to a much better school with that sort of cash. But perhaps it was healthier for the child to make her own way in the world and not be trapped in the clutches of these people, as her mother had been.

Pensions for servants. Gifts to cousins, worth more than Stephen earned in a year. The list went on, the relations becoming more obscure. He uncrossed his legs, crossed them the other way. Gwen sank lower in her seat with every name read.

But then suddenly, "To Gwendoline Abigail Fletcher, my antique cameo brooch."

Heads swivelled in their direction. Gwen raised her chin, eyes sparkling with tears. She had something. The wording of the will did not even acknowledge her as Lady Strange's child – yet still, she had *something*. She had not quite been forgotten.

It clearly meant the world to her.

Gwen waited until they were inside the parked car before she ventured to untie the ribbon on the black velvet box. They huddled together in expectation, almost like a couple on Christmas Day. Rather less jolly, though. Gwen's fingers trembled.

"I never saw my mother wear a cameo brooch," she observed. "I didn't realise she owned one."

"Well, women have so many gimcracks," he reasoned. "It must have been something from the old days, before you were born."

"But my sisters and I knew every item in Mamma's jewellery box, Stephen."

They hadn't been able to discuss their inheritance with the superior sisters. Winifred and Daphne had stood in a cluster with their own, wealthy husbands who had gone to public school and not the local grammar, like Stephen. They even had the audacity to sneer at his motorcar, saying real gentlemen would never need such a contraption. Bloody idiots. Antiques, just like the thing in Gwen's box.

He sensed her reluctance to pull up the lid, a superstitious dread, as if she held a coffin in the palm of her hand and not a simple item of jewellery.

"Maybe you will remember the brooch when you see it?"

"Maybe." She did not look convinced. Squaring her shoulders, she took a deep breath and prised open the clasp.

The lid creaked on its hinges. Inside, the box was lined with dark satin. A jet oval scalloped with gold filigree nestled amongst it. A cameo, as the will had said. The profile depicted was that of a young lady, hair piled on her head, one loose curl springing free at the nape of her neck.

She looked ghostly amidst all that black, ephemeral. A little wisp of a nose, a pointed chin. Not true to life. The brooch must date from a time before the method was refined. Stephen did not like the way the artist had indicated her eye by shadowing the socket. There was no pupil, only a dead, white eyeball gazing blankly to the side.

"Oh." Gwen ran her fingertips over the jet. "It's... quite beautiful."

Stephen nudged her. "How much do you think it will fetch?"

His jest did the trick, broke the spell. Gwen laughed, batting him playfully on the arm. "Beast."

How good it was to hear her laugh again. The last week or so had been an awful trial for her, what with the grief, which tended to strike even when one hated one's parents, and the odious family in contact again. He raised a hand to her cheek.

"You know, I think you were tremendously brave in there, darling. I've never been prouder of you."

Her lower lip trembled. She cast her eyes down, back at the brooch. "I'm glad there was something. At the end. She didn't go hating me."

"No. Of course not." He turned from her, put his hands on the wheel. Talking to Gwen about her mother was a bit like conversing with Camilla. One had to be careful, to guard her from certain truths.

"It was a gesture of forgiveness," she insisted.

"Yes, dear."

A piece of broken jewellery, at the end of the will. Even a fool could decipher Lady Strange's true message.

By the time they returned to Sussex the gloom was gone, the day honey-glazed once more as the sun sank behind the hills. Their home might not be Stonevale Hall, but it was a damn sight more welcoming with the small lake twinkling at them and the warm, red hue of the bricks.

Before the car had stopped, the front door flew open. Camilla rushed out with poor distracted Nanny hot on her heels.

At four years old, having never met her maternal grandparents, Camilla was not in a position to grieve for Lady Strange. But she could understand that Mummy was sad and dressed in black now. Perhaps it was that knowledge which caused her to pull up a few feet from the car, watching them shyly under her fringe. Unsure of her welcome.

"Darling!" Parking, Stephen threw the car door open and advanced on her with arms outstretched. There could be no doubt now. She leapt into his embrace and squealed.

What a bonny thing she was, with Gwen's light hair and fair skin: a living doll, he often thought. But she was a good deal stronger and heavier than a doll these days. It cost an effort to haul her up into his arms, her mourning dress rucking around her knees and revealing black woollen stockings. "Did you miss us?"

"Yes. You were gone a long time," she chided.

"It's a fair drive to Stonevale Hall."

"You could have taken me with you, Daddy."

"No… It was all lawyers and legal papers. You would be bored senseless."

Only then did he hear Gwen's passenger door thud shut. Balancing Camilla on his hip, he turned to see his wife dawdling towards them. She held the closed jewellery box with both hands.

"Mummy, what's that?"'

Gwen gazed up as if from a dream. A wan smile played on her mouth. "Hello, Camilla."

"What have you got?" the child demanded, reaching. Gwen took a step back, clutched the box protectively to her chest.

"Don't pester Mummy today, darling. She's had a stressful time of it. Why don't you run along and play with Nanny? It will be dinner time soon."

Camilla pouted as he stood her back on her feet.

"Actually, I'll just take tea tonight," Gwen said. The poor thing was done in, pale-faced with black smudges beneath her eyes.

"But you must keep your strength up," he protested. "Eat something. You've had a hell of a day."

"I've no appetite. Early to bed, I think."

"What's in the box, Mummy?"

Ruffling Camilla's hair, Gwen did not answer but traipsed wearily away from them, towards the house.

Stephen raised a slice of toast to his mouth, eyes focused on the opposite end of the dining table. It had been four days since their trip of penance to Stonevale Hall and still Gwen picked at her food, uninterested. She looked like a maiden under an enchantment. A face of wax and the blue eyes sparkling, dangerously bright.

Perhaps it was the black dress heightening her pallor, and that inevitable cameo clasped at her chest. He didn't like to see it, suspended there. Day by day, the lady in the brooch appeared more lifelike than Gwen.

It was beastly of him, but he resented her grief. Good people had fallen into unmarked graves across Europe without even a tear shed for them, yet here was Gwen, pining like a dog for the loss of a cantankerous old woman.

"I don't want you to go away again," Camilla whined, swinging her legs over the edge of her chair.

Gwen didn't answer, as she usually would. How distracted she was. Worse than when she'd first heard of Lady Strange's death. Rather than settling her mind, the bequest seemed to have raked everything up again, rekindled the guilt. No doubt that was just what the old crone had wanted.

"We have to go, darling," Stephen said at last. "Your grandmother is to be buried tomorrow."

"Why can't I come and watch?"

"You're too young. It would upset you."

"No, it wouldn't. I didn't even know Grandma."

Gwen blinked, a radio signal fading back in. "Suppose she did come, Stephen? It wouldn't hurt her to meet my family. She has never had the chance before."

He bit into the toast, hard. Was she mad? The image of sweet Camilla inside that tomb of a house, sneered upon by the reptilian relatives! It was like seeing her in a winding sheet; it made him feel sick, and angry beyond reason.

"They don't view us as family, Gwendoline, as well you know."

Her fingers fiddled with the brooch. They looked pale, bloodless. "But they might, if we—"

"I want to go!" Camilla shouted.

A sudden gasp. Gwen had twitched the brooch too hard. The clasp gave way and it clattered upon the table, falling to the floor.

She might have dropped a grenade for all the commotion it caused.

Camilla was off her chair, groping under the table. "I'll get it, Mummy."

Ordinarily, Gwen would upbraid her for unladylike behaviour, but now she was frantic, grasping the edge of the table. "Oh hell, don't let it be broken. Don't say I've broken the last gift she ever gave me."

As if the damn thing wasn't old and falling apart from the beginning! That was the only reason Lady Strange had let Gwen have it in the first place.

Camilla's blonde head emerged from beneath the tablecloth, triumphant. "Don't worry, Mummy. I've got it!"

Gwen did not wait for her to advance. Greedily, she snatched the unfastened brooch from the child's hands.

"Ouch!" Camilla whimpered.

"What is it, darling?"

Camilla held up her index finger, her face scrunched and threatening tears. Even from across the table he could see the trickle of blood running to the palm of her tiny hand. "Mummy scratched me! She scratched me with the pin."

Gwen did not apologise, did not even notice. She was fixing the brooch back onto her dress with quaking fingers, feverish in her activity.

"Poor old thing!" Tossing his napkin aside, Stephen went over to Camilla and kissed her. "When you were being so brave and helpful to Mummy as well! Go and see Nanny. She can wash your cut and put a bandage on it. Tell her I said you could have a sugar lump, too."

With baleful eyes upon her mother, Camilla sloped off. Gwen was oblivious, settling the folds of her collar around her brooch, as heartless as her uncle the General surveying his fallen soldiers.

"It isn't broken," she exhaled. "The brooch is safe."

"Well that's all right then, isn't it?" he snapped. "Never mind that the damned rusty pin will probably give her the tetanus."

She blinked up at him, blue eyes very pale in the morning light.

"Who, Stephen?"

That was the night that he saw it.

Maybe he wouldn't have if the cold hadn't awoken him. A cold so deep it pierced the bones. The weather had sharpened over the past weeks, honing the edges of its fangs, but nothing like this. His limbs trembled beneath the sheets. A muscle ticked in his jaw, and he knew that in a moment his teeth would start to chatter.

What time was it? He opened his eyes, flung out a hand for his pocket watch. And then he realised.

It was not quite dark. Wisps of something – fog? – floated against a black backdrop. Just like gun smoke, gliding through the air, forlorn after the battle has ended. He exhaled, watched his breath steam and join the billowing clouds. How was this possible?

All the windows were closed; he'd locked them himself. There was no way mist from outside could flow down the chimneys and seep through cracks in the window frames. Was there?

With difficulty, he climbed out of bed. The vapour had a texture to it, damp.

It only took a moment to grab his dressing gown and fling it about his shoulders. That was better, but hardly warm – the flannel seemed moist. Gwen's silky little creation hung from a hook. He should drape it over her, prevent her from taking a chill. Heaven only knew how she had managed to stay asleep.

As he turned around, dressing gown in hand, a sense of oppression seized him, a feeling he could not explain. His wife's side of the bed was shrouded in vapour. He couldn't see her, only hear her cavernous breathing. Surely that wasn't right?

He edged forward a few steps. Shapes with wispy edges appeared, but they were ill-defined, lacking substance. There – was that a movement? Impossible to tell. More of that cold mist spilled in from under the curtains, obliterating his view.

"Gwen?" he whispered.

Another step forward. Another. By turns, the mist seemed to take form, resolve itself into a face.

No. A figure.

Vague, but certainly there. A woman made of clouds. She wore a gown with a high, tight waist. Her hair was piled on her head. Her skin seemed to smoke, its fumes blending with the mist.

Stephen dropped the dressing gown. It must be a dream. Nothing but a bad dream, like he'd suffered after the war.

Indeed, it was with a nightmare slowness that the woman of mist bent over the bed. Her eyes, two blank pearls, peered down at the sleeping form of Gwen. She opened her mouth, revealing a great void. Gwen's lips parted.

It was the most horrific thing he had ever seen. What was that substance, feathery and luminescent, that flowed from one to the other? Gwen's back arched, and he realised: the lady was drinking. Sucking the life from her.

"No! Gwendoline!"

He lurched blindly into the mist. Something hard whacked against his shin. The bedframe, it must be. Pain burnt up to his knee, and before he could help it, the leg crumpled. He went down. Hard.

Dust from the carpet filled his mouth. Somehow, he had expected the mud of the trenches. Light flashed; instinctively he raised his hands to cover his head.

"Stephen? What are you doing? Are you all right?"

Her voice fetched him back to the present. Of course, it was a lamp, not a shell that had made the flash. What a simpleton he was – and yet, the feeling had been the same. The visceral fear of battle, the real awareness of danger. Gingerly, he lifted his head.

The mist had gone. The woman had gone. Gwen was awake, leaning over the end of the bed to stare at him.

Alive. Unharmed. Or was she?

She didn't look well. She looked like the ephemeral woman who had stood by her side, feeding.

The woman in the brooch.

"Did you have another bad dream?"

He cleared his throat. "Yes, love. A bad dream. That's all it was."

It wasn't a dream. He could sense it as he sped down the roads towards Stonevale church, the unease that made him irritable, forced him to take the corners too wide. He'd never driven wildly like this, but you wouldn't know it from the fossil of a wife that sat beside him. No flinches, no reaction as she lolled against the seat. Just a white face with all the essence bled out.

"Daddy, you're going too fast."

Camilla had won her way, as she always did. She looked sorry for it now, in his rear-view mirror, clinging to the door for dear life. Somehow, her pleas did not encourage him to slow down. He wanted to go even faster. Get his family away, somewhere safe.

They all wore black, naturally. It was only fitting, yet it increased his sense of doom. Funeral clothes emphasised his wife's wasted condition, the distinct *lack* of Gwen. And of course, she'd pinned that brooch in pride of place on her dark overcoat. It winked in the light. Mocking him.

Was it his imagination, or did the woman in the cameo appear fuller? The strokes bolder, her profile less colourless? As if she truly had drained something from Gwen, that night.

"Daddy, I'm scared. Stop it."

Camilla was right. Any of his friends would tell him to get a hold of himself, say that Gwen was naturally distraught and ill following the death of her mother. But Stephen *knew* that brooch was evil. As wicked as the woman who had willed it to Gwen in the first place. He couldn't explain it, nor should he have to. He'd been in the trenches, he'd seen men shot, men drowned in mud. He knew something dark and wrong when he saw it.

Wind rushed past his ears, numbing them. Over the county border and right on cue, a pearly fog began to haze the road and the low-lying fields. He thought of the mist in the bedroom, and that cloud of hair powder wafting from Lady Strange.

I will take her back.

Not if Stephen had anything to do with it.

As the great spire of the church pierced the horizon, he cursed. Speed hadn't carried them to safety, rather the opposite. They were here early, and now he'd have to spend even longer with the hateful family. He glanced in the mirror at Camilla's bright innocence. It didn't seem possible that she had a blood connection to these people, this place.

They parked and climbed out. A bell tolled, muffled by the fog. It was rolling in thicker now, moving restlessly amongst the graves.

"Camilla, give me your hand. It's hard to see the ground. You'll trip."

She obeyed, but a pout remained on her lips.

He hadn't the energy to apologise for speeding and frightening her. Neither could he summon the will to console Gwen. He seized her arm and dragged her after him. She made no resistance.

It was lucky he'd been there before and remembered the way. A stranger could become lost in this mist. Stonevale church had never carried the same stifling atmosphere as the hall, but it was dreary in its own right, damp and chill. Exactly the place blasted Lady Strange belonged.

Of course she'd chosen the best plot, on the east side, as close to the church as possible. The family bunched around it, the way he'd seen crows gather to feast on a body. Their faces were expressionless – as if they were corpses themselves. Gwen fitted right in.

There were no coloured flowers, nothing bright or pretty, simply cold, stately lilies. Their honeyed scent bloomed, its power diluted by the fog.

The floral tributes set the tone for the service:

emotionless. No tears were shed. Even the vicar's prayer lacked fervency. Not that Lady Strange deserved their sorrow, but still it felt uncomfortable, embarrassing, even, that *this* should be Camilla's first view of death: a process without grief.

The girl was as good as gold, looking on with silent wonder as the coffin descended into the earth. All the same, he wished her a thousand miles away.

Gwen stood apart as one hypnotised. Mist teased at her edges, seemed to breathe with her. Like a sleepwalker, she edged nearer to the pit. Closer to Mamma.

And then he saw her again.

Not the entire woman, but her arms. Tendrils stealing up from out of the grave. Misty hands with long, thin fingers. Caressing Gwen's shoes, her ankles. Reaching.

"Enough!" he cried.

Everyone stared. It was bad form, but to hell with it. He'd got Gwen free of that woman once; he'd be damned if she took her again. Releasing Camilla's hand, he rushed forward, grabbed his wife by the shoulders and dragged her away.

"Stephen! What on earth are you doing?"

Maybe the mourners were tittering. He didn't hear them over the blood thundering in his ears like mortar fire.

"I'm saving you."

Across the grass, past the cedars, into the graveyard. Gwen whimpered, propelled helplessly on.

There was no clear path, only mist, mist, everywhere he turned. Uneven ground made him stumble, but he couldn't slow his pace. He had to get Gwen away from those hands, her mother's hands, which yearned to drag her into the grave…

"Stop it! You're traipsing all over the tombstones. Have you no respect?"

As if that mattered. With every step the mist was building, closing in. He couldn't keep her safe. Unless…

He pulled up suddenly, taking Gwen by surprise. She fell against him and in that instant he ripped the cameo from her coat and flung it to the frosted earth.

"Stephen, no!"

He stamped his heel down. *Crack*. The brooch yielded satisfyingly beneath his shoe. He ground it into the dirt, again and again, without mercy. "She won't take you from me!"

Gwen began to sob.

Panting, he looked down at his handiwork. The white woman lay shattered. Pale again, without that weird, lifelike quality. A jagged crack ran across her brow, stretching down the cheek.

"Have you lost your mind? How could you? On the day of her funeral! You *brute*!"

Weeping, Gwen pummelled him with her hands. He let her do it. She'd never forgive him for this, but he'd done the right thing. Her anger, the colour flooding back into her cheeks proved it. The spell was broken. Lady Strange would not get her daughter back.

A scream ripped through the graveyard, high-pitched, clear as cut glass.

Their heads jerked up. Gwen's pounding fists fell still.
"Camilla," she gasped. "Where's Camilla?"
Dear God.
Together, they plunged back the way they had come.
A sea of fog, and they were swimming against the tide
with shaking limbs. Camilla must have followed them
into the mist, trotting at speed, unable to see... Why had
he let go of her hand? How could he have been so stupid?

This was worse than the fear he'd felt for Gwen,
even worse than the war. A blinding terror that seized
control of every fibre. They should never have brought
Camilla with them. Hadn't he said that? He should
have forbidden it, made her stay at home, but all he'd
been able to think about was that damned brooch...

Gwen branched off towards the sound of bells, and
all at once, the fog drew back like a curtain.

"No!" She plunged to her knees.

Lady Strange had taken someone else.

It was a tree root that had tripped her. One tiny,
orphaned shoe remained wedged beneath its arch. And
there she was, his darling daughter, sprawled on her
side. Offering a face in profile.

Blonde hair piled up around her head. One delicate
cheek lay smashed against a flat tombstone. A crack
splintered across her forehead. Identical. The same
pattern, blood dripping down to the chin.

Shattered.

Just like the lady in the brooch.

LULA-BELLE

Catriona Ward

Lula's last words to Irene were, "You stupid old woman." That was on Friday when she could still speak. "Always looking at me with those cow eyes. No wonder I'm ill."

"I hope you get better soon, Lula," said Irene and took her sister's hand.

"Don't touch me. I'll catch stupid from you."

Soon after that Lula went into a coma.

On Sunday, Irene signed the forms that allowed the tired young man in blue scrubs to switch off her sister's ventilator. The machine ceased its wheezing. Irene slept in a chair by her bed while it happened. She didn't want Lula to be alone.

Lula died on Tuesday. For a few moments afterwards her body still seemed tenanted. Then something was gone.

Irene went back to the home that they had shared for forty years. The bus stop was a mile away. Irene had no umbrella. She tied her plastic scarf tight, bowed her head to the cold darts of rain and began her cautious shuffle.

Irene imagined her arthritis as a black slug that lived in the crevices of her joints. It glutted itself on cold, wet; it swelled, filled the spaces of her, slowed her to a deathly pace.

The carcass of a shopping trolley listed on the bald verge. Torn plastic fluttered in strips, ghost fingers. Towers rose black in the night, freckled with bright pinpricks. Fairy lights cast colourful haloes on drawn curtains. It was almost Christmas. Irene tried not to flinch as she went, at the deep shadows that might conceal hostile eyes, watching her slow progress. Hands, chains, sticks, blades... Such things happened. Irene scolded herself. She could not run. Fear served no purpose. *Cowardy pudding custard*, Lula had sometimes called her. *Fat cowardy milky pudding!*

Irene greeted their familiar yellow door with relief. Her knees were molten. She made tea with turmeric and ginger for the arthritis, took aspirin. Next to the aspirin was the unopened bottle of whiskey, given years before by a neighbour. "Alcohol is a weakness," Lula used to say. "Those who drink it have no iron at their core." After a moment's thought, Irene opened the bottle. The scent sliced sharp at her nostrils. She took the whiskey tea upstairs, step by careful step.

Lula's room smelled of despair and eucalyptus. She was bedridden before the cancer raised its black pennant for the final assault. Irene had given Lula a little brass bell to ring when she needed something. Lula rang it day and night. "You are too fat to come up the stairs, too slow when I ring." Irene grew to dread the pretty tinkle.

Lula's childhood nickname had been Lula-belle. Irene hadn't thought of it in years; how amusing! She shook out a rubbish bag with a joyful crack. "The bin for you, Lula-*bell*," she whispered, dropping it in. She laughed to herself. In went Lula's clothes, the bright, patterned leggings she liked. The collection of teddy bears staring with beetle eyes. Irene hated teddy bears. In went the yellowed sheets, thin after many boiling washes, mounds of greying tissues, gossip magazines, pages soft with use. Irene took a long drink of turmeric whiskey tea. It really did help with pain. No wonder people said it was medicinal.

When she had finished, the room was strange. The bedstead bare, the skeleton of an ancient beast picked clean. With the mattress gone the seeping stain on the floor was prominent, dark. Sometimes when Irene was out shopping or at the post office Lula could not wait for the bathroom. She went where she lay. Afterwards, Lula crawled out of the wet sheets, under the bed, and curled up in her urine-soaked nightdress to sleep on the boards. Irene thought that if Lula could get herself that far, she could have made it to the bathroom.

Lula's room was Irene's now. She could have a lodger. She imagined a nice young man, perhaps a student of some interesting subject like archaeology. She would cook for him and he would tell her about excavations. Imagine having company that was not Lula! It would mean money. She could go on holiday. She thought of sunshine and parrots and white-capped waves, glassy deeps, coral waving in unseen currents.

Her knees didn't hurt at all as she dragged the black bags down the stairs, out of the back door to the bin. She poured herself more whiskey. She hummed as she drank it in bed, squinting at *Nicholas Nickleby*. She always read Dickens at Christmas time. Little urchins, dust piles, missing heirs, fog that stalked the world like a monster... Sleep came gently without interrupting her thought.

"Coming," Irene murmured. "Hush, hush, I am coming now." She surfaced sadly, pulled from a dream where warm arms held her and she was deeply kissed by lips that tasted of meringue. Irene loved meringue.

She sat up. The room was as dark as it ever got. The streetlight on the far side of the close burned through the thin curtains like a vengeful moon. The whiskey had become something foul. It lined her eyes and mouth and nose; pulsing, astringent. Irene rubbed her head.

It came again, the sound that had woken her. She stilled, hand on her aching brow. It could not be. Cold fingers walked up and down her spine. Once more from the empty room next door it sounded: the imperious tinkle of a little bell.

Irene's lips parted. Her heart was a warm plum in her mouth. The bell rang. "Coming," Irene breathed before she could stop herself. Years of habit.

She stood before Lula's door. Inside, it went on. *Tinkle, tinkle.* She promised herself that she would not scream.

"Lula?" Irene whispered. "Sister?" The knob was slippery in her palm. The door yielded with a creak, swung wide.

Bare of curtains, Lula's room was flooded with ashy yellow streetlight. All seemed as usual. The bedframe, white and spectral in the corner. Beneath it, the dark stain. The scuffed walls, the slight catch of eucalyptus lingering in the air. Irene stood, fists clenched white. She waited. Her knees ached, trembled. Nothing. No sound but the wet *shush, shush* of her heart. At last Irene gave a little whoofing sigh. Shame flooded her. She should not have drunk that whiskey. She was not used to it. Exhaustion, the grief of the day. She was confused. It was natural. A waking dream.

She turned to go back to bed. A shrill tinkle rang out behind. She turned, flesh thrilling. Beneath the bed, the stain was moving. It shifted in patterns of dark on dark. Two eyes, the plane of a cheek, the curve of a chin... It was a face made of shadow, and Irene knew whose it was.

Lula's voice was that of creaking timber, wildfire. She said her sister's name the old way. In Lula's dark eye sockets were tiny pupils of flame.

Irene's slippered feet moved without her will, towards the smoky outline of her sister's face. It was a natural thing, both right and true, to go to Lula and be a part of her... Lula's mouth opened slowly, impossibly wide to receive Irene, a snake dislocating its jaw. From the yawning depths of her throat there came a brassy tinkling. A long black tongue flickered about her lips. The world began to tear in half.

Something shrill and terrible rang out, ululating, drowning the bell. Irene had broken her promise to herself, for she was screaming. She ran from the disembodied head of her sister, which formed and scattered on the bedroom floor, calling with her bell voice for Irene to come, come down into the dark.

Irene sucked a boiled sweet. That helped. Her head ached all the time now since the ringing had begun three weeks earlier. It went on day and night. She drank a little more whiskey. That helped too. She was stiff from sitting on the floor, back against the door. Her swollen knees burned. She imagined the slug within, fat and preening. The bell rang on. Each peal a dent in her skull. She slept lightly in the odd intervals when the bell stopped. She went to the shops every few days but she was jumpy, irrational. She thought she saw a man and woman following her. Faces slid as if melting. Everywhere she went, she heard the bell ringing.

"*Okhti al-koubra*, I don't understand!" Irene said tearfully to the thing behind the door. Arabic and English had begun to slide into one another. "You don't like me! Or this house or anything in this life! Why don't you go?" Inside the room, the bell rang on, whether in answer or indifference, she could not say. Irene knew better than to open the door. It was not safe. The sucking mouth, the hungry dark, the sound of the world, tearing… Instead, she beat the wood with her fist. "Why are you here?" she shrieked. "*Atrukini lewahidi*. Leave me alone!" The little bell rang on and on.

Irene blew her nose on her skirt. She wondered how long she would last without going mad. Perhaps it had already happened.

She sat upright. She must have slept. Night had come. The dark, silken. The streetlamp was out. Silence. No bell. What woke her?

Irene heard it then. The crunch and tinkle of glass. A panel in the yellow front door giving to a fist. She could picture it. The gloved hand reaching carefully through. Sure enough, in a moment it came: the sound of the key turning slowly in the lock.

The door swung open. A quiet male voice said, "All right?" Another answered, unintelligible.

Knowledge of danger flooded Irene like dye. She tried to stand. Her joints blazed. She mouthed silent curses. Tears streamed down her cheeks. Downstairs, footsteps. Irene pulled herself across the hallway floor into her bedroom. She slid over to the window. Her fingers shuddered and slipped, useless on the latch. But then she had it and the window swung open, letting in the good night. The yard looked very concrete, far away. How long was the drop? Eighteen feet perhaps. Irene grasped the windowsill and strained to haul herself upright. As she did, gloved hands took her shoulders. They pulled her gently away from the window. Irene fell to the floor with a painful thump.

Two shapes bent over her, giant against the dark. They wore ski masks. Irene considered screaming. She looked at the hunting knife, shining in a fist. She did not scream.

"What do you want?" Her voice was not her own, but that of a frightened old woman.

"Tie her up," the large man said.

When the second figure came close Irene saw that it was a woman. She lifted Irene onto the bed with little trouble. She taped her wrists to the bedposts. Irene started at each crack of the tape. "Please don't hurt me," she said.

The woman hit her on the temple and everything trailed fiery stars. "This isn't for pleasure," the woman said. "We need to make an example or we'll have more and more of your sort coming over here."

Irene was flooded with relief. *There has been a misunderstanding*, she said to the woman. *I was born here*. That was what she meant to say. What came out was a wet moan.

"This isn't personal," the woman said again.

The man stood over Irene. "You don't have to watch this part," he said to the woman. She nodded and turned away.

He lit a candle stub and put it on top of Irene's copy of *A Christmas Carol*. He stuffed handfuls of gauze into her mouth. He pulled down the neck of her blouse and rested the point of his knife below her collarbone. The knife was sharp, and when he began to cut her flesh parted like butter. Irene was glad of the gag because the pain was bad, and she was ashamed to cry out in front of them.

At last, it was finished. "Show her," said the woman. She had watched, after all.

The man brought Irene the little hand mirror that she kept on the chest of drawers. It had pink roses on the back and around the rim. He held it up so she could see. Irene blinked away tears. She stared. He had carved the symbol into her breast. It was an old sign. Irene knew what it meant. Everyone knew. The intersecting arms, the cross.

Softly, from the neighbouring room, a little bell began to ring. The man paused with Irene's rose pattern mirror in his gloved fist.

"She's alone," the woman said. "We watched all week."

The man put down the mirror and gathered Irene's throat gently in his hand. "Who's here?" he said. He took the gag off so she could answer.

"My sister," said Irene, mouth strange and numb. "Please, don't hurt her, she is ill… She has no money, nothing valuable – leave her alone!" Irene made her eyes flicker quickly, like the actors on *EastEnders* did when their character was lying. "She has nothing," she said again. The bell tinkled, insistent.

The man put the gag back into her mouth. "You watch her," he said to the woman. "I'll go."

"We don't know who's in there." She took his arm. "Together, remember?"

He touched her face gently through the balaclava. They went.

Irene heard Lula's door open. The tinkling rose. The door closed. The world tore. Irene felt it in her body. A hole opened in the fabric of things: a terrible passage. Wrongness enveloped her. Black covered the world. She gasped, cried out and fainted to the sound of the ringing bell.

Irene woke in silence, in the guttering candlelight. The only sound was of wax dripping onto *A Christmas Carol*. The book would be quite ruined.

She knew that she was alone in the house. Irene began to work her wrists patiently against the tape.

Irene stands in the doorway of her dead sister's bedroom. The black stain under the bed is gone. There is no sign of the man or the woman. Irene is the only living thing here. Outside, the wind moves in the close.

"*Shukraan, habibti*," she says. "Thank you, Lula-belle."

Irene remembers a day when she and Lula were just little girls, holding hands by the banks of a stream which ran brown in the morning sun, each curve and wavelet limned with light, when their father put one hand on each of their heads, and they knew that they were loved. Irene knows the bell will not ring again, except perhaps once, years from now. Until then, she must learn to live alone.

FRONT ROW RIDER
Muriel Gray

She's not a morning person. Never has been. But lately, mornings have become harder than usual. Blinking in the putty-hued square of light from her window she accepts that she has become a cliché, and she can't bear clichés any more than she can bear the assault of the work-day alarm clock. Yet here she is, lying in a corner of her double bed, bought in a moment of optimism never fulfilled, clutching a damp, compressed pillow. What can be more clichéd than the sleeplessness of the haunted?

There is little originality, she thinks, in the troubled creature that nightly thrashes the duvet to the edge of the bed, and hers hangs tantalisingly this morning, as it has on others, waiting to slither from the edge like a linen coin push as she shifts and squirms. Her waking is not gentle, following another night of sweats and nightmares, of falling and screaming and bright lights and hard surfaces, the knowledge presenting itself in the daylight that she won't be able to bear much more of it.

She coughs, out of habit rather than necessity, tugging back the escapee duvet, trying to find solace in its softness, its familiar insulation. Feeling nothing, she huddles and crouches, making a ball of her body like an armadillo expecting trouble.

No part of her even wonders anymore. She simply accepts it will happen. Time ticking, days counting, something inevitable approaching. On a good day, she asks herself if it might be the same for everyone. Death approaching. The sands running down. Then her heart tells her it's not the same. She won't die an ordinary death in a hospital bed; fixed-smile, grown children at her side, framed by wilting petrol station-bought chrysanthemums. She writhes at the vision she has just conjured. Is that ordinary? Is that desirable? She coughs again, turns, and questions for a moment why she forged an image so dismal.

No matter. She feels certain she will never die a picturesque death. Her future is a blur and not a Norman Rockwell tableau. She has no children, no lover, no life that can be filed under satisfactory. She blinks at the ceiling. Recently painted, it offers little Rorschach relief, mocking her with its absence of distraction in peeling patches or dampening blooms. A bland, plain, desert of magnolia, leaving her alone with reality.

She closes her eyes, sighs deeply and gives herself over to the day's simmering fear. She frames the thought by saying the words. Says them in her head and faces the day.

Is he here?

If he isn't here already, then when will he be here? It's the same thought. Every day. On waking. Sometimes the dread cools as the day wears on and she dares to hope. Maybe he isn't here at all. Maybe he's busy somewhere else. Where would that be? Is her haunting unique, personalised, bespoke? Why should it be? What's so special about her? Maybe it's a chain store haunting. Why shouldn't it be happening at the same time to an Amazonian monkey hunter, a Korean care worker, or an Icelandic property developer? Are they afraid to look people in the eye? Fearful of reflections and shadows? Terrified they will see the face in the crowd, that person who shouldn't be there, who has no right to be there, but who is always, unfailingly, reliably there? What vanity says a ghost is for you alone?

But such musings bring little comfort. The hope of a day without him is always dashed. He will come. Early, late. Day or night. Sooner or later. He will come. She realises her breath is coming fast, her heart beating too hard. She closes her eyes and composes herself. She can do this. It's a new day, and she reminds herself that in this indifferent, enigmatic, ineffable universe, she is lucky to be here.

Without knowing how, she is already at the breakfast table. She stirs her tasteless, colourless cereal mechanically, without joy.

She is at work, staring into the deep of a computer screen, her colleagues moving around her like choreographed dancers.

She is in a café, the fat proprietor watching the evening news on the wall-mounted TV, arms crossed over his ample belly. Summer bluebottles drone and bump against the glass. Her coffee and half-eaten plate of food sit cold in front of her.

The temperature drops. She bows her head in despair. Here it comes. As always, she feels him approaching before she sees him. Many times she's tried not to look. Tried closing her eyes, or reading a book. But like floating gutter leaves sucked down a drain, her gaze is helplessly pulled towards the point of his appearance. So now, against her will, she looks up, a fearful glance from half-closed lids, her breath blowing vapour into cold air that has no right to exist in this summer heat. The café owner shudders and rubs his arm against the sudden icy chill. She waits, heart thumping, but doesn't have to wait long. This time it's fast. He walks swiftly past the grimy café window, left to right, adjusting a jumper knotted round his neck, a bundle of newspapers held beneath his bare arm. That's all. It's over. The room regains its steamy warmth. That brief, tiny glimpse, she knows, was all there would be for the day. Just once. Just enough to drain her, tire her, chill her. Defeated, she heads home.

Each night, before she tumbles into scorched sleep, she tries to relive it, to work out what she did wrong, and each night she knows the answer. She turns over on the pillow, draws her knees to her chest. Face it, she thinks. Face the thing that she dreads, the error she made, the turning in life she took that led to this limbo of low-level terror that hums in the background of her life like an electric fence penning her in.

She shouldn't have bought the photo.

She can watch that day in fast forward now. Picking it apart used to take longer. These nights it lays itself out chronologically like a storyboard. This night, it feels different. The story feels alive. She gets out of bed and walks to the darkened sitting room. Pressing back into the hard, worn sofa, a single table light burning low in the bedroom she left behind, she lets her chin fall to her chest and the playback commences.

Jill talking. You're only forty once. Travelling. A package to Orlando, Florida. All four of them. Just the girls. A theme park birthday. Disney, Universal, SeaWorld; the greatest roller coaster rides on earth.

Forty and fat. Forty and a smoker. Forty and making drinking alone a habit. Forty and never having taken a risk, or climbed a mountain or run a marathon. Forty and never having been properly in love. At least never loved back. Never ridden upside down in a chair on rails at forty miles an hour. Shorthand: forty, never really lived.

The girls gabbling. Shouting advice. Make it change. Make it happen. Turn-your-life-around time. Do those things. Stop watching time tick by. Start living, why don't you, gal?

* * *

Details of the holiday, now just fragments of memory in a blender. Laughing, drinking, neon lights and the faux antique wooden booths of cheap, themed restaurants. The girls cackling, ruby red lips open in constant shrieking mirth in their tireless quest to catch the attention of incurious Americans while she cowers in embarrassment. Look at us. Look at the time we're having. Highways crawling with slowly moving oversized cars. Outsized people, outsized food. *You must feel like a supermodel here*, laughs Jill. She laughs too, but wants to cry. Jesus Loves You, sky-written in vapour from a tiny plane, the disintegrating words floating against an azure Floridian sky. She photographs it. Wishes it were true.

All leading towards the moment. The decision.

Her heart couldn't beat any faster in the queue. The Hulk. The fastest, hardest ride in the park.

Libby makes them stand in line for the front row. Keeps barking statistics. *World's tallest cobra roll: 110 feet. Launch lift that shoots you from zero to forty miles per hour in under two seconds.* Stop it, she thinks. Stop it, stop it, stop it. Front row seats have a bigger queue. *Worth the wait*, says Jill. Forty-five, maybe fifty minutes. Every one a hundred hammering heartbeats of panic. She sweats. She trembles. And then, the bitches. The rotten, lousy bitches see a gap for three people, two rows back, and dive for it. Squealing with delight. Waving to her as they strand her in that front row line. Shouting and guffawing.

Roaring that they'll see her at the bottom. She's alone. Made to wait for the next ride. It takes a thousand years to come by, arriving, clunking into place like a mechanised abattoir. A couple of sullen Americans behind push her roughly forward onto the row, the seat at the far side already filled by a young man, staring ahead, calm, like he's waiting in a doctor's surgery. Must have boarded from the fast pass queue on the other side.

It's him.

Alone and waiting.

Ahead, a mountain of rails. A metal serpent waiting to receive its sacrifice.

She hugs her knees tighter. It's time to play the next frame again in her head. Again. Again. She plays it until she knows it by heart, because she knows this matters. Somehow it does.

She's shaking. Nearly crying. She's tried speaking to the American couple, her voice too high, too hysterical to sound casual. But Americans don't make small talk. They tell you to have a nice day if you pay them to, but to those without a name badge on their shirt you might as well be invisible. The big man grunts when she giggles the truth that she's scared. The girl stares ahead, chewing gum like it's a chore.

The coaster car jerks up and then down, bouncing as the automatic harnesses lower, pinning her to the back of the seat. She starts to cry. Silently. More alone than she could ever remember.

She can see his face now, still clear, remembering every detail as he turns slowly to look at her, savouring the memory of his irresistibly sympathetic gaze that follows the fat tear coursing down her cheek until it lands on the restraining bar of the seat. She can see that wide, friendly face, a shadow of stubble around the jaw, round hazel eyes, and a head of thick brown hair cut tight to tame the curls. Of course she looks at this face every day in the photo by her bed, but the memory, the real sweet memory is more vivid than the picture. He was English. She thinks she knows that now. She swallows, climbs back into the moment.

He's smiling. Comforting, gentle. He reaches out his hand, places it on the bloodless, tightly clenched claw that's hers, and speaks, a laugh just beneath the voice, but a kind one. Not Jill or Libby's broken glass laugh, full of taunts; his hints of mischief and joy.

"You're going to be fine. Just fine."

Then nothing. A void of suffering. Screaming. Pressure. Held back, upside down, body pinned in a vice. Forces working on her, stealing her breath, twisting her gut. But somewhere in the maelstrom of pain, his hand has found hers again, a warm, kind hand, squeezing and reassuring.

And then it's over. She's walking, slowly, like in a dream, weaving unsteadily, sick and sore, to the air-conditioned little booth where a bored Hispanic woman is presiding over photographs of the ride. So dazed she feels she's the only customer, though the ride was full, and the woman leans on her elbow and points with long acrylic talons up at the screens showing digital snaps of every row just disembarked.

There she is. Mouth open in a silent scream, eyes clamped shut, hair flying back, hands gripping the harness. The couple pictured on her left are stony-faced.

And then there's him. He's not looking ahead. He's in profile looking directly at her. What she can see of his face is full of concern. His hand is cupping hers.

There's no hesitation. She buys it. She buys it and now she lives with it. Day and night. On her bedside table from then until now. His face the most familiar in her universe.

A man who isn't there.

The first time she saw him after returning home was like a miracle. It was the best time. Close to joy. Stole her breath away. Oxford Street. A Saturday. His face, unmistakable in the crowd. He looked haggard. World-weary, but it was him alright. Her heart in her mouth, she ran, and waved, and ran again, but he'd gone. And oh, the thrill of that moment of recognition. The excitement of that chance sighting. An opportunity to thank him. Who knows? Maybe more than that. A coffee? A reminisce? A laugh? Would he remember her? Did he buy the photo too? Is she somewhere in his life? Maybe not on his bedside table, but – dare she hope – perhaps, on his office desk, or propped up on some shelf full of books? All over the world people cherish their roller coaster photos taken with strangers they will never see again. Faces glimpsed once, then preserved forever. Why not hers? There she would be. The stranger he rode the front row with. She had never wanted anything so much in her life as to catch up with him and put her hand on his arm. But he was gone. His curls lost in the bobbing sea of heads that flowed along the street. She stood for a long time, alone again. Then she went home.

The second time. In the cinema. Too good to be true. Another chance. It must be fate. He left before she could reach him. Then the third. He was on a boat on the Thames. She was on a bridge. When was it? The twentieth time? The fiftieth? The hundredth? When did she wake up and realise that not only can he not see her or hear her when she shouts, screams sometimes, but that maybe, actually, genuinely, he isn't really there at all? Too frightened to call up the theme park, to try and find witnesses to that day, to maybe track down the digital trail of the photo. Too scared in case what she fears turns out to be true. What is he? A spirit? A demon? Worse. A figment of her imagination? She has been beaten. There is no part of her left now that wants to see an alternative photo of her front row ride. A photo in which she is sitting next to an empty seat. So she lives with it. Deals with it.

But tonight she feels different. Tension has been building in her like the close summer air outside. This must come to a conclusion. The burden on her heart is too heavy and tomorrow it will end. She will make it end. She is going to face him, whatever the consequences. She walks back to her bed and curls into her roller coaster sleep.

Come morning, she waits outside a shop, staring into its dusty window displaying foreign newspapers and bottles of sweet drinks, still and passive, knowing he is coming. No need to look. She keeps her back to the street, and shudders against the cold as she feels him pass by.

A deep breath. This time he won't get away. It's now or never. She walks quickly, weaving in and out of the rush hour crowd folding over his wake. He can't outrun her today. Today her feet have wings. He turns and enters King's Cross Station. She breaks into a half-run. He's through the turnstile. She has no ticket. She jumps the barrier. Back behind her, maybe someone shouts. Maybe not. She's not sure. She carries on. He's on the escalator. She pushes forward, lightly tripping down the metal stairs, commuters twitching away in dreamy irritation as she brushes by. He turns into the tunnel for the Circle Line. A train is just leaving. The set of his body registers exasperation. He's missed it.

It's the moment. It's now. There's nowhere to run. In just a few moments this will be over. She closes her eyes and sighs. Deep, satisfied. Her eyes open and she calms herself as she walks slowly and deliberately towards him, her breath cooling in the hot, stifling underground air. Everything around her has slowed. The movement of the crowd has been quieted as though caught in treacle. The platform is an eddy in this sluggish human stream, the passengers at rest, self-absorbed, patient, waiting. His back is to her as he faces the rails, his body tightly flanked on his left by an expressionless man with a rucksack, and on his right by a bespectacled woman, laden with parcels yet attempting to read a book. A train is screeching from the tunnel, its lights beginning to bathe the rails. The crowd shifts and pushes behind her in anticipation and she glides forward.

She takes a deep breath, turning it to icy vapour on the exhale, as her heart beats calmly and steadily now. The train stops and the doors open. He shuffles forward, penned between the man and the woman. She moves towards him. Her hand comes slowly, slowly, gently, up from her side. She lays it on his shoulder and the touch is like an electric shock. He halts, his head turns and he looks her straight in the eye.

He's trying to piece together what's happening, but his breath has been punched from his body and he's gasping like a beached fish. Everything has slowed. The noise of the train, the people pushing past him, even the hot, brisk wind of the underground has turned to sluggish, still cold air around his head. The noises of the station sound like a clockwork music box that's wound down.

He's not ill anymore. He knows he's not ill. Dr Sutton has told him he's not ill. Today is a big day. The interview is at ten. He's left himself enough time to get there and he's calm, prepared. There's no reason for a panic attack. Especially not today. In fact, there's no reason for an attack at all. He's worked hard, he's focussed and he's not anxious. He tries to breathe. Breathe like Dr Sutton showed him. But he can't. He feels faint.

It's not her. It's impossible. He knows it's impossible, and yet the icy chill of terror is spreading through him like black ink poured into a beaker of water. He wants to look away from those eyes, to tear this freezing hand from his shoulder. But he's solid with fear, immobilised and breathless.

His brain works feverishly to rationalise. It's his fault. This is entirely his fault. He should never have accepted, let alone kept the photo they sent. It's the familiarity of her face that's making him recreate her so perfectly now in this madness. It has to be. He might have forgotten how she looked if he'd just binned it. It was nearly two years ago. But they meant well, the family. It was loving, not ghoulish, hunting down and retrieving the photo from the theme park after what had happened. They wanted to honour her last great thrill. To remember her. Remember her not as the fat, lonely, quiet girl they raised, but as a risk-taker. Someone who lived large. A front row rider.

And they wanted to thank him for all he did. What did he do? How did that go again? What order did Dr Sutton say he should remember it in? Her screaming. His laughing. Her screaming again, and again, too much, too shrill, too long, too gurgled for an outburst of joyful abandonment. Then her jerking, and gasping and slumping. His screaming for help as the ride stopped, and no-one coming to help. Screaming more and more as the harness didn't lift, then when it finally loosened grunting and heaving to get the bulk of her big, sweat-slicked body out of the chair onto the hard concrete. Still screaming for a doctor, with everyone standing, watching as though it were an act. Then putting his mouth to hers, and blowing, and pumping her chest with his palms, and crying and still shouting for help.

And then slumping himself, realising she was gone and he hadn't helped, hadn't saved her. This poor, frightened, lonely stranger. His was the last face she saw. The last hand she held. And now he was here, recreating it all in his crazy brain, just as he was about to start afresh. Sabotaging himself. That's what Dr Sutton calls it.

His anxiety has won. He blinks as he watches his guilty creation lower her hand and he listens, numb with horror, as she speaks. She is stern. Almost angry.

"If you follow me onto this train, it won't be fine. It won't be fine at all."

He stays perfectly still. She holds his horrified gaze for a beat then walks past him, steps onto the train, and sits herself gracefully and serenely next to the man with the rucksack. The doors close. The train begins to move away, and as he watches her through the glass she smiles, an expression of release playing in her darkened eyes. She turns her head away from him, lifts a hand and lays it gently over that of the woman with the parcels. She disappears with the train into the darkness of the tunnel.

His chill is gone now. He's sweating. His fevered imagination has made him miss the train that today, at 8.50 a.m., could have taken him to a new job and a new chance and a new life. He has no stomach to wait for another.

He weaves slowly and shakily off the platform and heads for the stairs.

He should feel defeated. He should feel insane, a failure, a casualty. But right now as he jostles through the crowds pushing in the opposite direction, he feels strangely elated, light of heart, released and invigorated. Baffled, he takes a breath and gives himself over to the emotion. In the months and years to come, he will recall that this instant, these precious few moments of confused elation were to savour and not to fear.

In four and a half minutes' time the man with the rucksack in the train will detonate his bomb.

A HAUNTING
John Connolly

The world had grown passing strange. Even the hotel felt different, as though all of the furniture had been shifted slightly in his absence: the reception desk moved a foot or two forward from its previous position, making the lobby appear smaller; the lights adjusted so that they were always either too dim or too bright. It was wrong. It was not as it had once been. All had changed.

Yet how could it be otherwise when she was no longer with him? He had never stayed here alone before. She had always been by his side, standing at his left hand as he checked them both in, watching in silent approval as he signed the register, her fingers instinctively tightening on his arm as he wrote the words "Mr & Mrs", just as it had done on that first night when they had arrived for their honeymoon. She had repeated that small, impossibly intimate gesture on every annual return thereafter, telling him, in her silent way, that she would not take for granted this coupling, the yoking together of their two diverse personalities under a single name.

She was his as he was hers, and she had never regretted that fact, and would never grow weary of it.

But now there was no "Mrs", only "Mr". He looked up at the young woman behind the desk. He had not seen her before, and assumed that she was new. There were always new people here, but, in the past, enough of the old had remained to give a sense of comforting familiarity when they had stayed here. Now, as his electronic key was prepared and his credit card swiped, he took time to take in the faces of the staff and saw none that he recognized. Even the concierge was no longer the same. Everything had been altered, it seemed, by her departure from this life. Her death had tilted the globe on its axis, displacing furniture, light fixtures, even people. They had died with her, and all had been quietly replaced without a single objection.

But he had not replaced her with another, and never would.

He bent down to pick up his bag, and the pain shot through him again, the impact so sharp and brutal that he lost his breath and had to lean on the reception desk. The young woman asked if he was all right, and, after a time, he lied and told her that he was. A bellhop came and offered to bring his bag to his room for him, leaving him with a vague sense of shame that he could not accomplish even this simple task alone: to carry a small leather valise from reception to elevator, from elevator to room. He knew that nobody was looking, that nobody cared, that this was the bellhop's purpose, but it was the fact that the element of choice had been taken from him which troubled him so. He could not have carried the bag, not at that moment, even had he wanted to. His body ached generally, and every movement spoke of weakness and decay. He sometimes imagined his insides as a honeycomb, riddled with spaces where cells had collapsed and decayed, a fragile construction that would disintegrate under pressure. He was coming to the end of his life, and his body was in terminal decline.

He caressed the key card in the ascending elevator, noting the room number on the little paper wallet. He had been in that same room so many times before, but, again, always with her, and once more he was reminded of how alone he was without her. Yet he had not wanted to spend this, the first wedding anniversary since her death, in the house that they had once shared. He wanted to do as they had always done, to commemorate her in this way, and so he made the call and booked the room – this junior suite that was so familiar to him.

After a brief struggle with the electronic lock – what was so wrong with metal keys, he wondered, that they had to be replaced by unappealing pieces of plastic? – he entered the room and closed the door behind him. All was clean and neat, anonymous without being alienating. He had always liked hotel rooms, appreciating the fact that he could impose elements of his own personality upon them through the simple act of placing a book on a nightstand, or by leaving his shoes by the foot of the bed.

There was an easy chair in a corner beside the window, and he sank into it and closed his eyes. The bed had tempted him, but he was afraid that if he lay down he might not be able to rise again. The journey had exhausted him. It was the first time that he had traveled by plane since her death, and he had forgotten what a chore it had become. He was old enough to remember a time when it had not always been so, and there was still an element of glamor and excitement to air travel. On the flight down he had dined off paper, and everything that he ate and drank had tasted faintly of cardboard and plastic. He lived in a world composed of disposable things: cups, plates, marriages, people.

He must have slept, for when he opened his eyes the texture of the light had changed and there was a sour taste in his mouth. He looked at his watch, and was surprised to see that an hour had passed. There was also, he noticed, a bag in his room, perhaps brought by the bellhop while he was napping, but the bag was not his. Silently, he cursed the young man. How difficult could it be to bring up the correct piece? It wasn't even as if the lobby had been very busy when he checked in. He got to his feet and approached the offending item. It was an unopened red suitcase, and it lay on a stand beside the closet. It struck him that perhaps he might have missed it when he entered the room, wearied by his trip, and it had been there all along. He examined it. It was locked, and there was a green scarf tied around the handle to help distinguish it from similar items on airport carousels. There was no name on it, although the handle was slightly tacky to the touch where the airline label had been removed. He glanced into the trashcan beside it, but it was empty, so he could not even use the label to identify its owner.

The telephone in the bathroom was closer than the phone on the other side of the bed, so he decided to use it to call reception. He was about to do so when he paused and looked again at the bag. He experienced a brief surge of fear: this was a big hotel in a large American city, and was it not possible that someone might deliberately have left this item of baggage in one of its rooms? He wondered if he might suddenly find himself at the epicenter of a massive terrorist explosion, and saw himself not disintegrate or vaporize, but instead shatter into pieces like a china statue dropped on a stone floor, fragments of his being littering the remains of the room: a section of cheek here, an eye, still blinking, there. He had been rendered fundamentally flawed by grief; there were cracks in his being.

Did bombs still tick? He could not say. He supposed that some – the old-fashioned kind – probably did. Just as he had relied upon his wind-up alarm clock to wake him for his flight that morning (he lived in fear of power cuts when he had a plane to catch, or a meeting to make), then perhaps there were times when only a straightforward, tick-tock timepiece with a little keyhole in the back would do the trick if failure was not an option.

Carefully, he walked over to the bag, leaned in close to it, and listened, holding his breath so that any telltale sounds would not be masked by his wheezing. He heard nothing, and instantly felt silly for even trying. It was a forgotten case, nothing more. He would call reception and have it taken away.

He stepped into the bathroom, hit the light switch, and stopped, his hand poised over the telephone. An array of toiletries and cosmetics had been carefully lined up beside the sink, along with a hairbrush, a comb, and a small vanity case. There were moisturizers, and lipsticks, and in the shower stall, a bottle of green apple shampoo alongside a container of jojoba conditioner. There were blonde hairs caught in the hairbrush. He could see them clearly from where he stood.

They had given him an occupied room, one that was already temporarily home to a woman. He felt anger, on both her behalf and his own. How would she have reacted had she returned to find an elderly man snoozing in the armchair by her bed? Would she have screamed? He thought that the shock of a woman screaming at him in a strange bedroom might have been enough to hasten his mortality, and he was momentarily grateful that it had not come to such an eventuality.

He was already composing a tirade in his head when he heard the main door open, and a woman stepped into the room. She was wearing a red hat and tan mac, both of which she discarded on the bed along with two shopping bags from a pair of chichi clothing stores.

Her back was to him, and her blonde hair was tied up loosely at the back of her head, held in place by a leather clip. Now that the coat was gone, he saw her lemon sweater and her white skirt, her bare legs and the tan sandals on her feet.

Then she turned and stared straight at him. He did not move. He felt his lips form a word, and he spoke her name, but she did not hear him.

No, he thought, this is not possible. This cannot be.

It was her, yet not her.

He was looking not at the face of the woman who had died barely a year before, her features heavily lined by old age and the depredations of the disease that had taken her, her hair thinning and gray, her body small, almost birdlike, where she had shrunken into herself during those final months, but at the face of another who had lived by that name in the past. This was his wife as she once was, as she had been before their children were born. This was his beloved as a young woman – thirty, perhaps, but no more than that. As he watched her, he was taken aback by her beauty. He had always loved her, and had always thought her beautiful, even at the end, but the photographs and the memories could not do justice to the girl who had first entranced him, and about whom he had felt as never before or since about a woman.

She walked towards him. He spoke her name again, but there was no response. As she reached the bathroom he stepped out of her way, performing a neat little dance that left him outside the room and her inside. Then the door closed in his face, and he could hear the sounds of clothing being removed and, despite his astonishment, he found himself walking away to give her a little privacy, humming a tune to himself as he always did in moments of confusion or distraction. In the short time that he had been asleep, the world appeared to have changed once again, but this time he had no understanding of his place in it.

After a minute or two, he heard the toilet flush, and then she emerged, also humming the same tune. She cannot see me, he thought. She cannot see me, but can she somehow hear me? She had not responded when he called her name, and yet now here she was, sharing a song with him. It might have been coincidence, and nothing more. After all, it was one of their favorite pieces, and perhaps it was hardly surprising that, when she was alone and content, she would hum it softly to herself. He had, by definition, never seen her alone. True, there were times when she had been unaware of his presence for a time, allowing him to watch her as she moved unselfconsciously through some of the rhythms and routines of her day, but such occasions were always brief, the spell broken either by her recognition of his presence or his realization that there were important matters to which to attend. But how important had they truly been? After she died, he would have given up a dozen of them – no, a hundred, a thousand – for another minute with her. Such was hindsight, he supposed. It made every man wise, but wise too late.

But none of this was relevant. What mattered was that he was looking at his wife as she had once been, a woman who could not now be but somehow was. He went through all of the possibilities: a waking dream, a sleeping dream, a hallucination brought on by tiredness and travel. But he had smelled her as she passed by him at the bathroom door, and he could hear her now as she sang, and the weight of her footsteps left impressions on the thick carpet that remained visible for a moment before the strands sprang back into place.

I want to touch you, he thought. I want to feel your skin against mine once again.

She unlocked her suitcase and began to unpack her clothes, hanging blouses and dresses in the closet and using the drawer on the left for her underwear, just as she did at home. He was so close to her now that he could hear her breathing. He spoke her name once more, his breath upon her neck, and it seemed to him that, for an instant, she lost her place in the song, stumbling slightly on a verse. He whispered again, and she stopped entirely. She looked over her shoulder, her expression uncertain, and her gaze went straight through him.

He reached out a hand and brushed his fingers gently against the skin of her face. It felt warm to the touch. She was a living, breathing presence in the room. She shivered and touched the spot with her fingertips, as though troubled by the presence of a strand of gossamer.

A number of thoughts struck him almost simultaneously.

The first was: I will not speak again. Neither will I touch her. I do not want to see that look upon her face. I want to see her as I so rarely saw her in life. I want to be at once a part of, and apart from, her life. I do not understand what is happening, but I do not want it to end.

The second thought was: if she is so real, then what am I? I have become insubstantial. When I saw her first, I believed her to be a ghost, but now it seems that it is I who have become less than I once was. Yet I can feel my heart beating, I can hear the sound my spittle makes in my mouth, and I am aware of my own pain.

The third thought was: why is she alone?

They had always arrived together to stay in this hotel to celebrate their anniversary. It was their place, and they would always ask for this room because it was the room in which they had stayed that first night. It did not matter that the decor had changed over the years or that the suite was, in truth, identical to half a dozen others in the hotel. No, what mattered was the number on the door, and the memories that those numbers evoked. It was the thrill of returning to – how had she once put it? – "the scene of the crime", laughing in that low way of hers, the way that always made him want to take her to bed. On those rare occasions that the room was not available, they would feel a sense of disappointment that cast the faintest of shadows over their pleasure.

He was seeing her in their room, but without him. Should he not also be here? Should he not be witnessing his younger self with her, watching as he and she moved around each other, one dressing while the other showered, one reading while the other dressed, one (and, in truth, it was always he) tapping a foot impatiently while the other made some final adjustment to hair or clothing? He experienced a sensation of dizziness, and his own identity began to crumble like decaying brickwork beneath the mason's hammer. The possibility came to him that he had somehow dreamed an entire existence, that he had created a life with no basis in reality. He would awake and find that he was back in his parents' house, sleeping in his narrow single bed, and there would be school to go to, with ball practice afterwards, and homework to be done as the evening light faded.

No. She is real and I am real. I am an old man, and I am dying, but I will not let my memories of her be taken from me without a fight.

Alone. She had come here alone. Or alone, for now. Was there another coming, a lover, a man known or unknown to him? Had she once betrayed him in this room, in *their* room? The possibility was more devastating to him than if she had never existed. He retreated, and the pain inside him grew. He wanted to grasp her arms, to demand an explanation. Not now, he thought, not at the very end, when all I have been waiting for is to be reunited with her at last or, if there is nothing beyond this place, to lose myself in a void where there is no pain, and where her absence can no longer be felt, merely absorbed into the greater absence beyond.

He sat down heavily in the chair. The telephone rang, but whether in his world or hers, he did not know. They were layered, one on top of the other, like twin pieces of film, just as in old movies an actor could play two parts in the same scene by being superimposed beside an earlier image of himself. His wife, her shoes now discarded, skipped across the floor to the bed and picked up the receiver.

"Hello? Hi. Yes, everything's fine. I got here okay, and they gave us our room." She listened. "Oh no, that's too bad. When do they think they'll be able to fly you out? Well, at least you won't miss the *entire* weekend." Silence again. He could hear the tinny voice on the other end of the line, and it was his own. "Well, it makes sense to stay at an airport motel, then, just in case. It won't be as nice as here, though." Then she laughed, sensual and throaty, and he knew what had been said, knew because he had said it, could almost remember the exact words, could recall nearly every minute of that weekend, because now it was coming back to him and he felt a flurry of conflicting responses to the dawning knowledge. There was relief, but there was also shame. He had doubted her. Right at the end, after all of their years together, he had thought of her in a way that was unworthy of him, and of her. He wanted to find a way to apologize to her, but he could not.

"I'm sorry," he whispered, and to acknowledge his fault aloud gave him some relief.

He went through his memories of that weekend. Snow had hit the airport, delaying all flights. He had been cutting it pretty tight that day, for there were meetings to attend and people to see. His was the last flight out, and he had watched the board as it read "delayed", then "delayed" again, and finally, "cancelled". He had spent a dull evening at an airport motel so that he would be close enough to catch the first flight out the next morning, if the weather lifted. It had, and they spent the next night together, but it was the only occasion on which they had found themselves apart in such a way on their anniversary, she in their room and he in another far away, eating pizza from a box and watching a hockey game on TV. Recalling it now, it had not been such a bad night, almost an indulgence of sorts, but he would rather have spent it with her. There were few nights, over the entire forty-eight-year history of their marriage, that he would not rather have spent with her.

There was something else about that night, something that he could not quite remember. It nagged at him, like an itch in his mind demanding to be scratched. What was it? He cursed his failing memory, even as another emotion overcame him.

He was conscious of a sense of envy toward his younger self. He was so brash then, so caught up in his own importance. He sometimes looked at other women (although he never went further than looking) and he occasionally thought of his ex-girlfriend, Karen, the one who might have been his wife, who went to a little college in the Midwest with the expectation that he would follow, when instead he went elsewhere, choosing to stay closer to home. They had tried to make it work at a distance, but it had not, and there were moments in the early years of his marriage when he had thought about what it might have been like to be married to Karen, of how their children might have looked and how it might have been to sleep each night next to her, to wake her in the dark with a kiss and feel her respond, her hands upon his back, their legs slowly intertwining. In time, those thoughts had faded, and he had dwelt in the present of his choosing, grateful for all that it – and she – had brought him. But that young man, carefree and careless, would arrive the next morning, and he would take his beautiful wife to bed, and he would not yet understand how fortunate he was to have her.

She hung up the phone and sat on the bed for a time, running her fingers across the stone of her engagement ring and then tracing circles around the gold band that sat above it. She stood, finished unpacking, and then, as he remained in his chair, aware now of flurries of snow falling outside, she drew the curtains, turned on the bedside lamps so that the room was lapped by warm light, and began to undress.

And it was given to him to be with her that night, both distantly yet intimately. He sat on the bathroom floor as she bathed, his cheek against the side of the tub, her head resting on a towel, her eyes closed as the radio in the room played an hour of Stan Getz. He was beside her as she sat on the bed in a hotel robe, a towel wrapped around her head, painting her toenails and laughing at some terrible comedy show that she would never have watched had he been with her, and he found himself laughing along with her as much as with it. She ordered room service – a Cobb salad, with a half-bottle of Chablis – and he saw the fingerprints she left upon the chilled glass. He followed the words on the page as she read a book that he had given to her, one that he had just finished and thought she might like. Now he read along with her, the contents of the book long since forgotten, so that they both discovered it anew together.

At last, she removed the towel and shook out her hair, then took off the robe and put on a nightdress. She climbed beneath the sheets, turned out the light, and rested her head upon the pillow. He was alone with her, her face almost luminescent in the dark, pale and indistinct. He felt sleep approach, but he was afraid to close his eyes, for he knew in his heart that she would be gone when he awoke, and he wanted this night to last. He did not want to be separated from her again.

But the itch was still there, the sense that there was an important, salient element to this that he could not quite recall, something linked to a long forgotten conversation that had occurred when he had finally found his way to this room. It was coming back to him; slowly, admittedly, but he was finding more and more pieces of that weekend in the cluttered attic of his memory. There had been lovemaking, yes, and afterwards she had been very quiet. When he looked down at her, he saw that she was crying.

"*What is it?*" he had asked.

"*Nothing.*"

"*It can't be nothing. You're crying.*"

"*You'll think I'm being silly.*"

"*Tell me.*"

"*I had a dream about you,*" she had replied.

Then it was gone again. He tried to remember what that dream had been. It was relevant, somehow. Everything about that night was now relevant. Beside him, his young wife's breathing altered as she descended into sleep. He bit his lip in frustration. What was it? What was he failing to recall?

His left arm felt numb. He supposed that it was the position in which he was resting. He tried to move it, and numbness became pain. It extended quickly through his system, like acid injected into his bloodstream. He opened his mouth and a rush of air and spittle emerged. He groaned. There was a tightness in his chest, as though an unseen presence were now sitting astride him, constricting his breathing and somehow compressing his heart so that he saw it as a red mass grasped in a fist, the blood slowly being squeezed from it.

"*I dreamt that you were beside me, but you were in distress, and I couldn't reach you. I tried and tried, but I couldn't get to you.*"

He heard her voice from afar, the words returning to him as an echo. He had held her, and stroked her back, touched by the strength of her feelings yet knowing in his heart that he thought her foolish for responding to a dream in this way.

She moved in her sleep, and now it was he who was crying, the pain forcing tears from the corners of his eyes.

"I dreamt that you were dying, and there was nothing that I could do to save you."

I am dying, he thought to himself. At last, it has come.

"Hush," said his wife. He looked at her, and although her eyes were still closed her lips moved, and she whispered to him: "Hush, hush. I am here, and you are here."

She shifted in the bed, and her arms reached out and enfolded him in their embrace. His face was buried in her hair, and he smelled her and touched her in his agony, his heart exploding deep within him, all things coming to an end in a failure of artery and muscle. She clasped him tightly to herself as the last words he would ever utter emerged in a senseless tangle.

Before the darkness took him.

Before all was stillness and silence.

"Hush," she said, as he died. "I am here…"

My god, I love you so.

"And how you are here," he replied.

Hush. *Hush.*

And he opened his eyes.

MY LIFE IN POLITICS
M. R. Carey

Tonight, after supper, Mum tried out her speech on me and it was really good. It made me cry. She said Mr Peverill – Tom – was a great man and a great politician, and that his name will shine out like a beacon for all time to show what people can do when they've got vision and moral courage. I clapped when she'd finished, and said "Encore! Encore!"

Mum didn't like that. "Don't be doing that tomorrow, Denise," she said. "You'll make an exhibition of yourself. Oh my God, I think my nerves will go."

Mum has trouble with her nerves. I think maybe I do, too, although we get different medicine so it's not the exact same thing. It's just sometimes I get anxious if people want me to do something and I don't know what it is, and then I get confused and I don't always follow.

That's how Dad says it. "Try to follow, Denise," he says, "for Jesus Christ's sake." When we're watching *Days of Our Lives* or *General Hospital*, and I ask who that one is, or what he meant when he said that, or whether she knows he loves her. And I do try to follow, but sometimes I can't.

It's a big honour that they asked Mum to do the eulogy. Dad thought it should be him because he's been the Treasurer of the Constituency Association for seventeen years, but Mum is the Chair, which is more important.

It was thanks to Mum that I got to work for Tom, before he got to be an MP, when he was just our local candidate. And then after he won and he went to the House of Commons to represent all of Coddistone, I carried on working for him but not in the Palace of Westminster. Just here, in the constituency.

It was a good job and I was happy, although not as happy as I was when I worked at Costella's Café. At Costella's, Shamin let me take home Cornish pasties that weren't the right shape or got burned, and if I worked on Saturday I got an extra ten pounds that didn't go into the brown envelope but Mr Costella put it in my hand.

"You can't go wrong with ten pounds in your hand, now can you?" he always said. And I used to keep it tight in my hand all the way home, pretending it was magic. And once a boy who was skateboarding on the pavement really fast stopped dead right before he hit me, as if he'd hit a wall I couldn't see, but I don't know if that was the ten pounds or not.

After Tom – Mr Peverill – went to the House of Commons, I didn't see him as much, even though I was still working for him. He was writing his bill and then he was getting people to vote on it and that took up most of his time so he didn't come back to Coddistone very much.

Until that last day when he came back to make his speech on the Town Hall steps. I wish that hadn't happened. Any of it. I wish he hadn't come. I wish Mum hadn't made him a briefing pack. And I wish she hadn't told me to drop the briefing pack off at his house. Whenever I remember it, I think my nerves will go.

The only time I saw Tom before I went to work for him was when I was still in school. I was in year eleven and he came to Bishop Laud on prize day. He gave the science prize to Angela Brereton, but before he gave it to her he made a speech about moral courage. He said moral courage was about doing what was right even when everyone was telling you it was wrong. He said if you lived right and followed your own vision, no man or woman could reproach you.

It was a very inspiring speech. I wrote an article about it for the school newspaper and Miss Charles said it could go into my coursework folder. "You need something else besides your weird little fantasy pieces, Denise," she said. "This looks like it will do very nicely."

I got an A in English, in the end – nearly an A star – and I think that article was the reason. It was the best thing I ever wrote. I used FOLLOW YOUR VISION as the headline, and I put a photo of Tom next to it, looking up towards the ceiling and off to the right. It was a photo that Mum took for his campaign posters.

English was my only A. I got Cs in Art, Religious Studies and Geography, and the rest were Ds. My mum went into school to talk to Mr Nuttall. She said I should be allowed to stay on and do A-levels because an A that's nearly an A star is outstanding. I'd shown what I could do if I got the chance.

I dream, sometimes, what I could do. Like fly in places that aren't even places, and scoop up the shiny stuff that makes the stars and press it all against me until I'm shiny too. Sometimes I used to write the dreams down, and that was what Miss Charles called my fantasy pieces, but in the dreams it felt real and anyway I only put down the parts I could find the words for. Some of it was just feelings.

Mum got her way, like she usually does. Mr Nuttall said I could do English and Geography A-levels and retake my Maths. But then I got sick with my appendix and I missed a lot of time. My mum said, "You've just got to apply yourself, Denise, that's all." And she got the school to send homework packages for me every day I was in hospital, but I was very tired and very sore after the operation and I couldn't apply myself all the time even though I really tried.

Part of that was because I just hated being in the hospital. My room was small and dark, and sometimes when I was there by myself it got smaller and darker. I heard one of the nurses say they were scared to come in there. She said she thought the ward was haunted. It wasn't though. I never saw any ghosts there.

I got Ds in the Christmas exams and they weren't even good Ds. Mr Nuttall suggested I should take the rest of the year off and start the course again in September. "A clean slate," he said. My mum and dad said no; I didn't need a clean slate. I could make up the lost time in the spring. And I promised I would, and I did try to, but for a lot of reasons it didn't happen. So I left at the end of year twelve and got a job at Greggs in the High Street and then at Costella's Café.

My mum didn't like that. She thought working in a café was beneath me, and that I was shaming the family. She talked about it with my dad a lot, late at night when they both thought I was asleep. Some of the talk was about which side of the family I took after and whose fault I was, but some of it was about finding a better job for me to do that wouldn't shame anyone.

Then one day my mum went to a Constituency Association meeting and came back very happy and excited. She said Tom Peverill had got the party's nomination to stand for Coddistone in the next general election. A local man! Mum was especially proud because she went to school with Tom Peverill's wife, Violet, who I had to call Auntie Vi when she came to visit, so Tom was almost one of the family. "And that's good news for you, my lass," she said to me. "I had a word with Vi and she had a word with Tom, and what do you think? You're going to work in his office!"

I was sad to leave Costella's. Mr Costella said there would always be a job there for me if I changed my mind. Shamin told me don't look back, just do it. "There's more things in life than taking meat pies out of a sodding oven." And she hugged me, which was a bit of a surprise but very nice. Mum doesn't do hugs. She says she's never been one to get all touchy-feely and she doesn't trust people who do.

So I went to work at Tom's office, which was in Holland House behind the Co-op, in the same building as the Constituency Association. In fact, it was a room they rented as a storeroom, and everyone's first job was taking all the boxes out of it and putting them on the landing where they stacked up all the way to the ceiling.

After that I did stuffing envelopes, and printing out fliers and putting them through doors. There were seven different fliers, depending on which part of town we were going to. They all said Tom Peverill will protect local interests and keep Britain for the British, but then there was a list of other things he would do that were different. If you lived in the centre then it said he would get tough on noise and drunks when the clubs let out. If you lived in the flats by Wilding Park it said he would repair the footpath and the bridge. I forget the others, but they always said things that were about where you lived. And they always had Tom's face, looking up and to the right, and a Union Jack, which is actually a Union Flag unless it's flown at sea.

Some of the people who worked in the office also did what my mum called doorstepping, which was talking to people about what a great man Tom was and what he would do for Coddistone, but they didn't make me do that. I was glad, because I'm not good with people. What I did do, sometimes, was carry extra boxes of fliers out to the doorstepping teams if they ran out, and once I was in a van with loudspeakers on the roof, handing out fliers while my mum said, "Turn out tomorrow and vote! Vote For Peverill! A vote for Peverill is a vote for security!"

Sometimes Tom came into the office, which was always quite exciting. Everyone stopped work to cheer and clap their hands whenever he came into the room, and he would clap his hands too, pointing at us to say that we were the ones who deserved it.

Tom gave speeches and held meetings, too, and when he did those things I went with him and did stuff outside the speech or the meeting. Sometimes I took people's coats and gave them tickets with numbers on, and sometimes I gave out fliers to people when they came into the room.

I wasn't usually inside the room when the speech or the meeting happened, but one time I was. That one was a candidates' debate, and Tom won it hands down. Especially the part where the audience got to ask the candidates questions. This was when Africa was getting too hot to live in, and all the boats were coming, and the question from the audience was: what should we do with the boats. Tom said the Royal Navy should blockade the English Channel so no boats could get in. One of the other candidates, I think the green one, said that was inhumane, and Tom said hands up everyone if you would want to have a refugee from Africa living in your house. Only a few hands went up.

"Congratulations on playing to the lowest common denominator," the green lady said.

"You have contempt for your constituents," Tom said. "And that is why you can't represent them in the House of Commons." I don't remember the exact right words, but it was something like that. And my mum punched the air and whispered, "Yes!"

Then it was election night, which was the most exciting night of my life. My mum and dad had a party for the people from the Constituency Association, and the food was Marks & Spencers. It was really lovely. My dad said at least the Jews were good for something.

Coddistone was one of the last seats to report, so I got to stay up really late. I was eighteen by this time, so really I could go to bed whenever I wanted, but I was living in Mum and Dad's house so mostly I couldn't. At ten o'clock, or half past, Mum would say "Denise" and look at the clock, and that would mean I had to go to bed. Only that night she didn't say it. I don't think she remembered to. She was sitting on the sofa from midnight to two o'clock, hardly saying anything, just watching. We knew the party was going to win, because they were fifteen points ahead in the polls, but Mum desperately wanted Tom to win too. And when the returning officer said, "Thomas Peverill, eighteen thousand seven hundred and six," she screamed. But it was a happy scream, not a scared one. My dad got a bottle of champagne out of the fridge and popped it, and we toasted Tom and the party and the next five years. I had lemonade to toast with, of course, not champagne. "We don't want to set you off, do we?" Dad said.

I wondered as I sipped my lemonade whether we would all go to London and work for Tom there. That would be amazing! We didn't, though. He had a London office, but it had London people in it and we stayed where we were.

Nothing much changed in the office apart from Tom not coming in there anymore. I still printed fliers and delivered them. Sometimes I got to write them, too, although it wasn't really writing. It was cutting and pasting text from the party's website and then dropping in quotes from Tom, taken from our database of his speeches and interviews.

We saw him on the news sometimes. Almost always he was talking about the refugee situation. Most European countries were taking some refugees by then, because Africa had suffered what they called a complete ecological meltdown. At least the bit in the middle had, and all the people there were going north and when they got to the coast they got into boats and sailed across the sea.

Tom said they shouldn't do it, and we shouldn't encourage them to do it. He was drafting a bill that was about not having to let the refugees in when they got here. It kept him very busy, so he didn't get to come up to the constituency very much at all, and when he did he mostly didn't come into the office. Mum said constituency business was still really important to him, he just had to prioritise right now.

There were people in the Association who weren't happy, though. They said Tom was still working for Coddistone and how could he do that if he never came to any Association meetings or even talked to the committee?

That was when Mum had the idea of the briefing packs. Every time we heard that Tom was coming back to Coddistone, someone would go to his house first and drop off a briefing pack, which was all the minutes of all the meetings he'd missed and all the important news from around the constituency. Mum would stay up late typing everything out and then it was usually me or Lucy who took them over.

"It's okay if he's not there," Lucy said to me once. "I wouldn't want to be alone in the house with him, would you?"

"Why not?" I asked her.

She raised both her hands and wiggled her fingers. "You know," she said. "Wandering hands. Wandering everything, Eileen Franklin told me." She winked, and I laughed, but I was only pretending to understand. I knew that Eileen Franklin had gotten expelled from the Association for inappropriate behaviour. I didn't know what wandering everything meant.

Tom's house was really nice. It had three floors and six bedrooms, and the living room was so big it took me twenty-three steps to walk from one end of it to the other. It had a chandelier, too, with all these glass leaves hanging down that tinkled when you opened the door or when there was a gust of wind.

There was also a statue at the front next to the driveway of a man with goat legs playing a pipe. I used to pretend the goat man could talk, and I would ask him on my way into the house to play some music for me. I would say, "Play it, Sam," like Humphrey Bogart in *Casablanca*, and point my finger at the goat man on my way into the house. And sometimes I would hear the sound of pipes playing when I was inside, but it was just one of my fantasies or maybe the radio in the house next door.

One time Tom came back to the constituency because a ship, the *Wayfarer*, had gone down in the English Channel and it was full of refugees. "The bloody media are all over him," my mum said. "As if it was his fault they piled two thousand people on a ship that could only hold five hundred! He can't get a moment's peace down there."

She gave me a briefing pack to take over to Tom's house, and also a fruit loaf that she had baked for my dad, with a card saying *Best Wishes from All in the Association*. I took them over and left them on the kitchen table the way I usually did. And then I went into the living room and walked from one end of it to the other, listening to the sad sound of the goat man's pipes.

It was such a big house! And Tom lived in it all on his own ever since Auntie Vi left him and took the kids away with her (I wasn't allowed to talk about her after that). It seemed sad to me, and a waste, that most of the time that lovely house was empty.

I pretended I was talking to the refugees who drowned when the *Wayfarer* sank. They had two thousand voices, so when they talked it was more like music than it was like ordinary talking. They said it was sad that they had got so close to a new country and then hadn't made it to shore. "That is sad," I agreed.

And we lost our ship, the refugees said. *We can't find our way into the next world without a ship. We're lost, Denise. And we're so unhappy. But because we're at the bottom of the sea nobody can hear us crying.*

"You should live here," I said, "in Tom's house. There's plenty of room. And maybe you can build a new ship, or maybe I can find you one. But in the meantime, you should stay here."

Thank you, Denise, the refugees said. *We will.*

The goat man smiled at me when I left the house and gave me a nod as though he thought that I had done a good thing. It was just one of my fantasies, of course. The whole thing was.

As it turned out, Tom didn't get that briefing pack. He didn't come back to the constituency after all. He went to a place called Martinique and he stayed there for two weeks. My mum said it was for a fact-finding mission but I don't know what facts he found.

Then Tom's bill got its final reading, with a big debate in the House of Commons. A lot of people talked about the *Wayfarer* ("Bleeding hearts!" my mum said. "Hypocrites and bleeding hearts, the lot of them!") and Tom said it was a tragedy but it wasn't *our* tragedy. "It was made in Africa," he said, "and it should have stayed there. It was no business of ours to intervene in it. It is sheer vanity to suggest that we can solve the world's problems when we have so many problems of our own."

When the House voted on the bill, it passed by thirteen votes. The *Daily Mail*'s front page the next day was just a photo of Tom with the single word VICTORY. Mum photocopied it thousands of times for a flier that we put through every door in Coddistone.

Then Tom got his cabinet seat and we didn't see him at all. Mum was doing the briefing packs regularly now, every week, and mostly it was me who dropped them off. I always got Sam to play for me and I always said hello to the refugees. They were still sad, and they still talked a lot about not having a ship.

You said you would find us one, Denise, they said.

"I said I'd try," I told them. "But I don't know where to look. Please don't be angry with me."

We're not angry. But it's very dangerous to lie to us.

"I'm really sorry," I said. "I'll do my best." And I did look up to see how close the canal came to Coddistone but it was thirty miles. And canal boats can't even go on the ocean, let alone into the next world, so I didn't know what I was going to do and I wished I hadn't promised.

I said we didn't see Tom anymore, but of course we did. He was on TV all the time. He was still talking about refugees but also about things like compulsory registration and prison sentences and patriotism and how free speech is a paradox because it comes at a high price. "People talk more about their rights than about their duties," he said, and he said that had to change. The *Daily Mail* had his picture again, this time in Parliament Square with Big Ben behind him, and the headline was TIME FOR CHANGE.

"He's going to go for it," my mum said when she saw that headline.

"He'll get it too," my dad said. "And he'll make us proud. By God, he will."

They hugged each other, and then they both hugged me, and we did a little dance together in the living room. It was nice. I didn't know what Tom was going to go for, but I was sure that he would make us proud.

That week's briefing pack had a letter my mum wrote. It was supposed to be private and I got all the way to the house without reading it but then I couldn't help myself. You carry all our hopes and dreams, it said. Everyone in the Association and in the whole town is proud of you. I didn't read any more than that because the refugees came and all the lights in the room got darker.

Where is our ship? they asked.

"It's coming," I said. "I'm sorry. It's coming soon." I almost wet myself. I hadn't done anything since I looked up where the canal went. I got out of the house quickly. I even forgot to thank Sam for playing for me.

I had my twentieth birthday three weeks after that. My present from Mum and Dad was a coat. It had a wide collar and two rows of buttons and I liked it a lot. I remember it because I was wearing it the next time I went to Tom's house.

I was going to say it was the last time I went to Tom's, but it wasn't. It was only the last time I went inside.

It was a Tuesday, exactly one month after my birthday. I was at the office and I was adding some more of Tom's interviews to the database when the phone rang and my mum answered it. It was Tom's PA, Lionel Gates. He said Tom was coming to Coddistone that night so he could have a press conference the next day on the Town Hall steps. "Thank you, Lionel," my mum said. "Can I take it he's going to announce?"

When she put the phone down everyone in the room was watching her. She didn't say a word for a long, long time. Then she said, "That's a yes," and everyone shouted and cheered.

"What's he going to announce, Mum?" I asked her. She just looked at me and shook her head. She said, "In a world of your own half the time, aren't you?"

Eileen told me that Tom was going to run for leader of the party now that Maura Voss was standing down. I remembered then that there had been a thing on the news about Maura Voss, so it was probably that. If Tom won the leadership it meant he would be our next prime minister, because the party didn't lose elections anymore.

Mum got busy making up a briefing pack. It was like her usual briefing packs except that it had a bottle of champagne as well as all the papers and the USB drive. Actually, it was different in other ways too. She went online and got all the opinion polls from the last year and made graphs and charts out of them to show Tom which people liked him for which things. It took ages to do and we all had to stay late helping her find the figures for the charts. She wanted it to be the best briefing pack ever. I think she wanted Tom to remember her, and the Constituency Association, and how they had always helped him right from the earliest days when he was an MP and before that when he was in the council.

She asked Lucy if she could drop the pack off on her way home. But Lucy wasn't happy about having to stay in the office until after seven o'clock and she said no. "Sorry, Mrs Tanner. I'm going to Rosehead to pick my mum up from her physio, and I'm late already. I'll be driving in the opposite direction."

Mum turned to me. She didn't look happy. "It will have to be you, then," she said. "Put your new coat on. Make yourself presentable, in case he's there already. And if he is, you call him Mr Peverill, not Tom."

"Okay," I said.

"Well, what are you waiting for?" Mum said. "Off you go."

It was already dark when I left the office. There was a moon, but there were clouds too, and mostly you only saw the edge of the moon behind the cloud. But it came out when I got to Tom's house and the goat man shone like he was a light bulb.

"Play it, Sam," I whispered as I went past him.

I was going to go in through the kitchen door, the way I usually did, but then I saw there was a light on in the living room. Tom must already have arrived from London, like Mum thought. So I rang the doorbell and after a moment or two the door opened.

Tom looked tired. He was wearing a suit and a tie, but the tie was undone and hanging down. And his hair wasn't combed properly, so it was sticking up a bit at the front. He didn't recognise me at first, until I said hello to him. "Oh," he said then, and he seemed to relax. "Denise. Right. What is it?"

I showed him the stack of papers I was holding. "It's from the Constituency Association, Mr Peverill," I said. "Your briefing pack. My mum spent all afternoon on it."

Tom laughed and rolled his eyes. "My briefing pack," he repeated. "Of course." Then he saw the champagne bottle, which was wrapped in gold paper with a red ribbon on it. "Is that from the Association, too? Shit, you should have led with that. Come on in."

I went inside and he closed the door. "Living room for that lot," he said. "I'll take the bottle."

The living room was the same as it always was except for a little suitcase with its handle still sticking up that Tom must have brought with him. I put the briefing pack on the biggest of the coffee tables and as I was doing that I heard the pop of the champagne cork from the kitchen.

A few moments later Tom came in holding two glasses full of champagne. "The party never stops," he said, and he laughed again. "Here you go."

He held out one of the glasses to me. There were all bubbles in it, and it looked as though some of the bubbles were bursting in the air over the top of the glass. It was really beautiful. "My mum and dad don't let me drink alcohol," I told Tom.

"They're not here, though, are they?" Tom said. He put the glass in my hand and I took a sip before I even thought about it. It was the fizziest thing I had ever tasted, fizzier than Coca-Cola when you drop the can but you open it anyway. "It's really nice," I said.

"More where that came from," Tom said. He tilted the glass when I took my next sip, so I drank more than I was going to and got the hiccups a bit.

I could hear goat man Sam playing his pipes in the garden. It was a sweet, mournful sound.

"Let me top you up," Tom said. And then, "Do you want to take that coat off? It looks ridiculous indoors." And then, "Let's sit down. Over here. Come on. I won't bite."

I was starting to feel dizzy. I don't think I did sit down, but I was on the sofa somehow. On the arm of it and then half onto the seat, with Tom's hands on my shoulders and Tom's face up close to my ear. "I really feel like I ought to have taken the time to know you better," he said. And then he licked my ear.

It was so gross I yelled out, "Ow! Stop!" as though

it hurt me. It didn't hurt me; it just surprised me. I dropped my champagne glass so I could put both hands up to push him away. But he wasn't going away, he was putting his arms around me and one of his hands was on my bum. When I tried to move it he grabbed my wrist tight with his other hand. "Just relax," he said. He sounded angry with me and I didn't know why. I wasn't hurting him; he was hurting me.

"I want to go home," I said.

Tom didn't answer. His face was moving up and down against mine. He was trying to make his lips be where mine were so he could kiss me, but I kept turning one way and then the other way so he couldn't.

"I want to go home," I said again, louder.

Goat man Sam stopped playing. *Is he hurting you?* he asked me.

No, I said. *But I think he's going to. I'm scared, Sam! Can you help me?* I knew he couldn't. It was just one of my fantasies, and I needed help that was real. I knew enough about what happened when a man is with a woman to know what Tom was going to do to me, and I didn't want him to do it.

No, Sam said sadly. *I can't help you. I'm out here in the garden and I can't come into the house.*

All right, then, I thought. I'll lie down on the sofa and then when Tom tries to climb on top of me I'll bring my knee up between his legs. But he was sort of slantways on top of me, not properly on top of me, and I couldn't get my leg free.

Well now, the refugees said. *It's about time you woke up to your obligations*. The music of their voices came out of nowhere, from all directions, filling my head.

Please help me, refugees! I said. *Tom is going to rape me.*

You must give us permission, the voices said. *In the old words and the old cadence. Do that, and perhaps we will be able to solve each other's problems.*

I don't know the old words or the other thing you said, I said. Tom's hand was up between my legs and his weight was all on top of me and it really did hurt now.

Just repeat what we say. But say it aloud, so that all may hear. I gift you this ship, to sail in.

"I gift you this ship to sail in!" I yelped.

To your journey's end.

"To your journey's end!"

"Be quiet," Tom said. "For fuck's sake."

No god, nor man gainsay you.

The words came out one at a time, because of the hiccups from the champagne and because of Tom moving on top of me to try to get inside me.

"No.

"God."

Tom stiffened, and he shook a little bit.

"Nor.

"Man."

Tom got very still again. He made a sound that was like a sigh.

"Gain.

"Say.

"You!"

Tom slid off the sofa onto the floor. His face was white, and when I bent down to listen I couldn't hear him breathing. I don't know how to do that thing where you feel a pulse with your fingers so I didn't do it. Anyway, I could see that he was dead.

Dead, the refugees said. *Yes. He was a bad man. But he will make a fine ship.*

They climbed inside him and sailed away in him. Not in his body. That stayed where it was, except that it looked even deader now. They sailed away in his soul, which they hollowed out so they could fit in it. It was just one of my fantasies but it felt so real.

I grabbed my coat and my handbag and ran out of there.

Is all well? goat man Sam asked me.

It's fine, Sam, I said, as I was running down the driveway. *I'll tell you later.*

The news said Tom had a heart attack. My mum cried and cried as if she was never going to stop. She asked me how Tom had been when I saw him and I said he seemed fine. "He was really happy. He even gave me a glass of champagne so I could celebrate with him."

I had to say that, because the police would have found the two glasses and they would already know I'd been in the house. But there was no sign that anything bad had happened. Tom just died because his heart stopped working, so nobody thought I could have done anything wrong and really I don't think I did. It wasn't my fault if Tom had wandering hands and wandering everything. It was his.

I go back to the house a lot, but I'm really careful not to be seen and I never go inside. Sam and I just meet in the garden. It's lovely there on summer nights when the moon is full and it's just the two of us, but it can be a bit cold at other times of the year. Sam says we should go somewhere else. He knows a place called Arcadia where it's summer all the time and the goat men dance and drink sweet wine as well as playing music.

I think I'll go with him. Politics is more Mum's thing than mine.

FRANK, HIDE
Josh Malerman
(This is for James Henry Hall. Thanks, man)

Oh, to see Lauren again.

Once more. In any way.

Oh, to take care this time, to really see her exactly as she was, so that her true features might finally replace the memory he'd held onto, a memory that had blurred in the six years since her death, as though the tears he'd shed stood like a pane of glass between himself and her.

Frank walked. Out the front door. Out onto the street.

When he experienced guilt of any sort, when he detected it coming, he walked. Out the front door. Out onto the street.

Toward the meadow.

He walked.

Oh, to see Lauren again. To hold up both hands, palms out, to say *hang on, wait, wait a second while I study your face so that when it goes away again I will remember it exactly as it was.* No more of this blurred vision, shaken by guilt, this interior room of darkness. He'd spelled her name wrong in a letter thanking her folks for their help with the funeral. He'd forgotten her name entirely one night, very drunk, while speaking of her. Guilt, yes, for not being able to recall the exact distance from the end of her nose to the curve of her chin. From the sides of her eyes to her ears. Shouldn't Frank be able to recite those numbers to a man much more artistic than himself? And shouldn't that artist then be capable of rendering Lauren exactly as she was?

Guilt. Ugly, indeed.

Frank walked.

Down the street.

Toward the woods. Toward the meadow.

He'd been walking a lot lately. Long walks that required stretching beforehand, a bottle of water during and, often, breaks. He always took the same route; out the front door of the home that had plenty of photos of him and Lauren on the walls, all the way to where Bolton Street ended (of which Lauren had joked, *God didn't like our street, put an end to it*), then over the guardrail and into the woods. To the meadow Frank would go. It burned him up inside, lit up that dark interior room, to recall how bothered he'd been by Lauren's constant prattling about exercise and good food, laughter and sleep. By God, sometimes it sounded like she'd emerged from the nineteenth century, when doctors decided fresh air and water cured all bad things. It was easy to bring back to life the terrible uneasiness he felt every time Lauren saw him on the couch, every time her eyes traversed the length of the living room and settled on him just sitting there, watching a movie, a television show, relaxing. Oh, how she'd look out the window, silently saying, *You're hiding, Frank. From the real world.* Frank often wondered: how might you rename "relaxing" if someone was constantly there to rile it? Lauren was certainly stuck on the healthy stuff. Oh, was she. Jogging. Vitamins. Vegetarian. She felt bad after every time she drank, and made sure to remind a hungover Frank of the many other ways they might've had fun the night before.

Like looking at the stars.

Like giving each other full body massages.

Like playing classical music low and getting into long conversations that could revolve around anything so long as the echoes of progress and philosophy were involved.

It was enough to drive Frank mad.

So he walked. Now. He walked. To the end of the street. Over the guardrails. Into the woods.

Today, despite the flaring anger at her ways, despite the guilt, too, Frank found himself missing the very things Lauren had said so often they'd become little hammers, tapping against his stability, until her good intentions sounded more like howling.

You shouldn't hide from the real world, Frank.

He walked. In the woods now. Hidden, in a way.

Lauren had loved a lot of things when she was alive but none quite so much as the meadow. When she'd returned from walks of her own, as Frank pretended to just be sitting down or just be getting up, the smile she wore, the contentedness he'd seen in her eyes was inarguably due to her time spent in the meadow. And on the days when she hadn't walked, the inverse expression could be seen in her face as well, as she always seemed to be standing close enough to the window to look out through the glass, as though seeing that open expanse of glory, where the bees didn't bother you and they expected the same.

Frank understood now. These days. The meadow was good after all. Lauren had been right. Moving, exercising, getting a good night's sleep.

Oh, to see Lauren again.

Frank walked. As the almost cartoonish nature of the deep dark woods had him thinking of movie sets like *The Wizard of Oz*, where the browns were perhaps too brown and the greens too green, but in the end thank God for *that*, or those same woods might've been a bit scary to traverse. And who could be scared when salvation lay in the Lauren meadow less than a mile away, here on a perfect summer afternoon, a Saturday no less, away from the office, away from the home, and away from the windows of that home, the windows Lauren used to longingly look through as though constantly wanting to be out in the world, out moving and walking, exercising, eating well, breathing fresh air, anywhere but near Frank and the television and a dinner of pizza and fries? Frank got it. Now, these days. In the six years since Lauren's passing, he'd shed some six or seven pounds, eaten more vegetables, taken more walks.

Like this walk.

The walk that brought him to the end of the woods and thus to the sunlight glossing the colorful meadow before him. Oh, to see this meadow reflected in Lauren's eyes: the reds and purples, the whites and yellows and greens. The smell changed, a better smell, the second he crossed the boundary of woods and meadow; a new smell so sudden it was as if he'd been in the meadow all along, as if the woods were morning and this, here, at last, the day.

Ahead, the meadow stretched a half-mile until it faded into a grassy hill that rose to meet more woods. But for the moment, the space looked like forever, open and hopeful.

No guilt out here. Nowhere to hide at all.

But that wasn't entirely so. No. As Frank squinted into the sunlight ahead he saw something that possibly didn't belong. Surely a thing that hadn't ever been in the meadow before. If it was a city sign, he couldn't read it from this distance, rectangular and raised, probably telling people like Frank there would be NO TRESPASSING on a perfect day like today.

Frank didn't turn back, and the closer he got, the less he believed it was a sign. In fact, whatever it *was*, it seemed to reflect the blue of the sky, the meadow itself, so that, from this distance, it looked something like a painting upon an easel, left behind by an artist who had decided a lone widower ought to find it, encounter the reality and the rendering at once. Frank could easily imagine a man or a woman having fallen for the still air, the peaceful quiet, the inherent health and beauty of the meadow. He looked for him or her. The artist. As the unavoidable floor of flowers and tall grass crunched underfoot, he looked for who had left this painting, this picture, this inspiration, proof of a good place that Lauren loved so dearly.

But as he approached, as he continued to out-walk the guilt he'd felt coming, he saw it wasn't only sky and meadow in the frame but a *person*, too.

He raised a hand and waved. The person waved back. That person was himself.

A reflection, then. The back of a metal sign? Reflecting the meadow, the sky, himself?

Frank continued, hands in his pockets now, feeling less alone, more like he was being watched, more like whoever had put the sign up was still here, nearby, close enough that he or she might pop out from behind a tree, say, *hey there, you look like you thought you were alone, you look genuinely surprised.*

You look guilty.

Frank stopped walking. He had to. Because he'd gotten close enough now to see the thing was clearly not a sign, and since it was also not a painting he had to make sense of what it actually was.

A window. Suspended, it seemed, above the meadow.

There was no debating it. The rectangular frame, the chipped wooden crossbar that indicated the split between the panes of glass, the place a person might put their hands to push it open.

Frank laughed. What else was there to do? And how might one rename "sense" if there was something in the way of making it? He didn't doubt it was a window. It was undeniably *so*. So how to explain it? He looked to the far boundaries of the meadow, expecting to see stranger artists than the ones he'd imagined only moments ago, this window being some sort of theater, an installation, performance art, *something*. There was clearly no stand propping the window up and certainly no arching branch above for it to be hung. Yet... there it hung. Unwavering. As though lodged into a house he could not see.

Frank didn't like it. Didn't like the feeling it gave him. As if the window itself was more alone than he thought he'd been. As if, even, someone were looking out from the window, a face on the other side of the glass, not his own reflected.

Frank stepped aside, but there was nowhere to hide in all this open meadow.

A cloud covered the sun, the reflection in the glass slipped away. Frank no longer needed to squint at the houseless window.

What he saw scared him deeply. Space. Room. An impossible, dim-lit depth behind the glass.

An under-exercised part of his mind told him he had two choices and two choices only: go straight home and stay forever afraid of what he'd seen in the meadow, or make sense of this now.

"Hello?" he called. Because he had to. Had to make a sound, prove he was still Frank in the meadow.

A face behind the glass. Maybe. Swallowed by the reflection of the meadow, as the sun shone again.

"Lauren?"

He hadn't told himself *it's her*, hadn't even decided if it was a face at all. But her name came out all the same.

Frank stepped back from the window.

He thought of his dead wife standing by the window at home, thought of her longing to go outside. She did that a lot, especially near the end of things, the days when she grew increasingly sick, as her weight dropped considerably, as she struggled to flash healthy smiles in his direction, Frank still sitting on the couch, smiling able-bodied in return, thinking, *I've been poisoning you for a week. How long does it take?*

Movement behind the glass? Frank stepped back from the window. Again. A little more.

How long, indeed! Perhaps that answer lay in the very method and delivery of the poison, as Frank had slipped it into the one thing Lauren wouldn't mind staying home for, the one thing she enjoyed almost as much as the meadow: good, healthy food.

How torturous those days had been, being forced to sustain a feeling of righteousness, when a single violent motion could've done the trick in seconds or less!

A tapping on the glass? Frank came out of his reverie, his nerves electric with the heat of sudden fear. As if the explanation for the suspended window was about to be given straight out under the blinding sun, clear as the growing guilt.

He stared for a long time at the glass. No tapping, no. Nobody *at* the glass to tap it. Rather, a new cloud had come, lessening the reflection once more, exposing more of the depth behind the impossible glass.

A room, absolutely. A dark room right here in the middle of the blazing afternoon.

Frank ducked, momentarily, looking to the flowers and tall grass beyond the suspended window, as if he might see there an expanse of darkness, a long stretch of an empty room impossibly placed in the meadow.

Life behind the glass? No. Frank didn't think so. Frank refused to think so.

Widower. Window. Window. Widower.

"Go home," he told himself. "Get some sleep. Drink some water."

He turned his back on the glass. Saw movement, new colors emerging from the woods.

A man in blue?

Two.

Frank, he thought. *Hide*.

But where? The woods were too far. The flowers and tall grass too out in the open.

Frank imagined the men pointing at him on the meadow floor.

That's him. Guy who poisoned his wife's vegetables. His wife who meant no harm. His wife who was right. Walks are good. Water and fresh air. Get up off the couch. Don't hide from the real world, Frank.

Frank looked to the sky, as if there might be a rope

ladder, something to remove him from the meadow.

He looked to the window.

To the darkness beyond the glass.

Then, incredibly, he was placing his hands upon the chipped wood of the lower pane's frame, pushing the window open.

He heard the men talking as he lifted his leg through the nothingness beneath the window. As he planted a shoe on the sill. As he climbed into the suspended, foundationless frame.

On the other side, his nose to the glass, he watched the men approach. Their strong forms testing the stitches of their uniforms. Frank ducked to the side, watched them by way of peering, leering, imagining them pointing to the window, saying, *It took us six years but we found him. He's in there. In that room. Hiding from the real world.*

They were in range of the window now. Must have been able to see it. But neither pointed. Neither squinted. Neither said, *What's that suspended in the meadow?*

Instead, they talked. Nodded to each other's words Frank couldn't hear.

Or could he? Certainly he'd heard *something*. Words indeed. Words from the dark room he stood in.

He turned. Saw life in that darkness. No. Saw death. Saw a ghost and poisoned food.

Oh, to see Lauren again.

Frank tried to open the window. Pounded on the glass.

"HELP!" he cried. "LET ME OUT!"

The men in blue were so close now. Weapons at their hips that could so easily shatter the glass. Hands that could so easily open the window.

"HELP!"

Frank's hands were wet from the glass. As if the pane were made of tears.

More words from the darkness. Movement, too.

One officer looked in the direction of the window as they walked, his eyes and nose less than a foot from the glass. Frank pounded. The man in blue seemed to look through the glass, straight through the room itself, tilting his head, briefly, as if perhaps hearing the almost undetectable sound of poison being sprinkled into a bowl of soup. Then he was nodding again, walking past the window, in step with his fellow officer. Frank heard their muffled words, heard them loud enough to understand them, as a cloud covered the sun again, bringing to life a reflection here, inside, this side of the glass.

"How it should be," one officer said, "in the end."

"You believe in that?" asked the other. "After what we've seen?"

But Frank couldn't see them anymore, as they'd passed from view, as the whole of the meadow was replaced with the dim-lit reflection of the room.

And a face, too. Over his shoulder.

Coming to look out the window.

Oh, to see Lauren again.

Oh, to see Lauren.

Oh.

THE CHAIN WALK
Helen Grant

*A*t *any rate, I wasn't cruel to her*, Fraser said to himself as he stared down into the open grave.

He could feel the first drops of rain on his face. Scottish weather was always unpredictable, especially along the coastline. Sunshine had been forecast, but now fat raindrops were running down his cheeks like the tears he was unable to produce. Fraser felt mildly irritated with himself for having forgotten to bring an umbrella; there was something melodramatic about standing bareheaded in a downpour at the side of a grave. Mostly, however, he wondered about the coffin.

It's what she would have wanted – that was a phrase that had been bandied about rather a lot while the funeral was being planned. Ishbel had been into nature and the environment; even in the last stages of her illness, she had loved to sit by the window, watching the birds on the bird table and the changing colours of the sky. Cremation wasn't for her, nor confinement to a solid wooden casket. A biodegradable coffin, that was what she would have wanted – an ecologically friendly burial that would allow her to dissolve naturally into the earth's embrace. Fraser had gone for cardboard, which coincidentally was inexpensive too.

Now he looked at the coffin with its printed pattern of leaves and flowers and wondered what would happen if it got really wet.

The rain was getting heavier; his hair would soon be plastered to his head. He blinked against the water running into his eyes, and the blurry mourners on the other side of the grave swam back into focus. Ishbel's sister Kirsty was weeping so hard under her umbrella that her mascara had run. Black was bleeding down her plump face, marring skin surfaced to perfection with foundation. She was pitiable in her grief, Fraser knew that. He couldn't wait for the funeral to be over.

He looked down into the grave again and saw that the coffin was now sitting in a centimetre or two of rainwater. The lid was shiny with it. He imagined the water rising, rising, until the coffin was floating, bumping gently against the sides of the hole like a boat straining at its moorings. Or would the cardboard begin to disintegrate before that happened? He didn't know.

Lost in thought, it took him a few moments to realise that the ceremony was over. Kirsty was turning away, leaning heavily on her brother. The mourners began to drift towards the waiting cars, eager to get out of the rain, to get to the wake where the comfort of food and drink awaited.

Fraser was in no hurry to follow them. It meant at least another hour of talking about what had happened and enduring the condolences. He wouldn't have dared to say to anyone: *It's a relief.* All the same, he didn't want to hear anyone say how very sorry they were. He particularly didn't want anyone to squeeze his shoulder, making a happy-sad face at him to show their sympathy.

He glanced down once more at the coffin, and then looked about him, orienting himself in this new, Ishbel-free world. A flash of yellow caught his eye: discreetly positioned behind a tree, a small digger waited to fill in the grave. Fraser supposed he had better follow the others. He didn't want to watch clods of earth splashing down into the open hole.

The wake was a short drive away in Elie, Ishbel's hometown. Kirsty had never moved away, so her house was the obvious place to hold it. Kirsty hadn't done any of the catering, though. Her sister-in-law Catriona had made platefuls of unappetising sandwiches, egg mayonnaise or ham between dog-eared triangles of plain bread. There was plenty of weak tea, and not nearly enough whisky. She handed these things round, and Kirsty sat on the overstuffed sofa with a handkerchief pressed to her face and the panda eyes of grief. "I'm sorry," she kept saying. "I'm sorry."

Fraser endured it as best he could. After a quarter of an hour, he went and stood by the patio doors, looking out at the garden and hoping that people would have the sense to leave him alone. The glass panes were still spotted with raindrops, but the sun was already coming out. It was Scottish weather altogether: sodden one moment and radiant the next. Fraser remembered a hillwalking trip long ago, when he had experienced rain, snow and blistering sunshine all in one day. Today was almost as extreme; soon he saw a faint vapour rising as the patio stones and the neat square of lawn dried out.

Fraser wanted to turn his mind to the future. His life was entirely his own now, after all; it was not unreasonable to plan. In fact, it was healthy.

I did the right thing, he said to himself, and indeed, he did have the sense that he had achieved something. *I stayed when other men would have left. She never knew*, he told himself. *She thought I loved her, right up to the end.*

After that, he deserved what he had earned: the small inheritance, the future freedom.

She died happy, Fraser said to himself.

Still, he couldn't make his thoughts stay on his own prospects; they kept turning back to the falling rain, the wet hole in the ground, the water soaking into the printed cardboard. In his mind's eye, he saw the clods of earth dropping from the bucket of the digger; he saw how thick and sticky they were from the saturating rain. He imagined them thumping down onto the damp cardboard lid, buckling it. It would be like covering the coffin with wet cement. If Ishbel had lain there alive, she would soon have been so compressed that she could not have expanded her chest to take a single breath. But Ishbel was never going to take a breath again.

Watching the sunshine, and the vapour rising from the garden outside, he wondered if the same heat was making tendrils of steam rise from the freshly covered grave.

When someone laid a hand on Fraser's arm, he started violently.

"Fraser," said his brother-in-law, a slight slur in his voice; it seemed he had made the most of the limited whisky supply – or brought his own. He peered into Fraser's face, which must have been etched with the shock of the sudden jump, and interpreted the expression as grief. "A terrible thing, Fraser," he said. "A terrible thing."

"Yes, Callum," said Fraser, "it's a terrible thing."

He made up his mind to leave then, before Callum poured out any more of his maudlin whisky-fuelled condolences on him. He thought there was a very real risk he might put both hands on Callum's chest and shove him away as hard as he could. So he shook his head to indicate that the wicked mysteries of Fate were beyond him, and slipped past his brother-in-law, making for the front door.

In the hall, he met Catriona carrying a plate of biscuits.

"I need a wee bit of air," said Fraser, doing his best to look tragic. He opened the door and escaped.

It was warm in the sunshine and he couldn't wait to get out of his funeral suit; the stiff new shirt and sombre tie were irritatingly restrictive. He walked back through the town to the inn where he had taken a room. As soon as he was alone with the door closed, Fraser ripped off his formal clothes, leaving them scattered all over the bed.

Thank God it's over. He didn't examine that thought too closely.

He briefly considered taking a shower, but the memory of the water pattering down into the open grave was still too fresh. Instead, he pulled on jeans and a sweater and flopped into a chair. He supposed that later he would go downstairs and order a meal and a large Scotch, but for now he would do nothing at all. It would be a luxury. When he looked back at the last days, weeks, months – years even – he saw nothing but an unending stream of obligations. Appointments, waiting rooms, meetings, household chores, letters, test results, handholding, and talking, talking, talking. The memory of it made him want to put his hands over his ears. All that talking, and yet it hadn't brought him closer to Ishbel. The things she had wanted to say had seemed to take her further away from him; they were radio signals from a foreign country. And now there was silence.

He sat in the chair for a long time, looking out through the window, towards the sea, where the sunshine sparkled on the moving water. After a while, he dozed, and when he woke the light had changed; the brilliant sunshine had been replaced with a soft greyness, and the sky was full of clouds.

Fraser's watch told him it was late afternoon. He went downstairs to the bar and ordered a steak and chips. It wasn't really dinnertime, but he had only himself to please, after all. While he was eating, there was another squall of rain; the windows rattled as it passed over. By the time he had finished, however, the rain had stopped.

As the day waned, Fraser thought he might go out and stretch his legs for a bit. He would be travelling for most of the following day, after all. The wake must have finished by now; there was no way that he could reasonably be expected to go back. If he ran into anyone, he could intimate that the whole thing had been too much for him to bear.

It was not quite twilight when he followed the path that ran across the links and down to the beach. The shadows were long and the light had that high degree of contrast that one sometimes sees around an eclipse. The tide was coming in and much of the beach was covered, but it was still possible to walk along the strip of sand that was left. Fraser went west, increasing the distance between himself and the town. He picked his way over rocks, skirting pools and slippery piles of seaweed. He would never come back to Elie after this; he might as well take a good look at what he'd never see again.

At the end of the beach, a worn and winding path ascended to the rocks. Fraser saw a square of white standing out against the stone: a noticeboard. He remembered that the chain walk began around the corner, out of sight of the beach.

The chain walk was a peculiarity of the location. Originally constructed in about 1920, it was composed of sections of steel chain strung along the most inaccessible parts of the rocks, over a distance of about half a kilometre. By clinging to the chains and using additional footholds cut into the stone, people could make their way along the entire distance. *Why* they would want to do such a thing was a mystery to Fraser. He had done the chain walk a couple of times in his younger days – once to impress Ishbel when he had first met her – and he couldn't recall anything particularly useful about the route. It didn't lead to anything and you couldn't safely bathe from the rocks there. Certainly, it didn't rouse enough nostalgia to tempt him to try it now. He turned away, thinking that it was time to walk back to the inn.

For the first few paces he was climbing over rocks, keeping an eye on his footing, but as he raised his head and looked east, towards the town he saw something that made him stand still.

Someone was coming along the beach towards him – and he thought he knew who it was. Fraser was filled with dismay.

Kirsty.

She was too far away for him to see her face clearly, but he was pretty sure it was Ishbel's sister. The robust figure, swathes of black clothing hanging like drapes from the upper slopes of her ample chest; the big bun of hair perched like a knob on the top of her head; the arms swinging in a determined manner as she walked towards him: yes, it had to be Kirsty. And she was pissed off at him, he could tell that at a glance. She had Things To Say, and she was determined to say them.

She probably had a right to be angry, Fraser knew. He'd left the wake indecently early, without saying all the things she'd have wanted him to say, about Ishbel's beautiful personality and kind heart and all the rest of it. Since then, she had quite possibly drowned her grief in a few glasses of wine, removing any inhibitions she might have had about reading her sister's partner the riot act. There would be no stopping her.

Except he didn't have to stand here and listen. With the tide this far in, and the beach narrowed to a thin strip of sand, there was no hope of getting *past* Kirsty, but he could still get away from her if he went the other way. If he went along the chain walk.

Kirsty wouldn't manage it; he was sure of that. A sedentary person, she wasn't very nimble at the best of times, and she had hobbled herself further with stacked heel shoes. There was no way she could follow him along the rocks, even with the help of the chain.

Fraser was confident he could manage it himself, though. He turned his back on Kirsty, pretending he hadn't spotted her at all. It was possible that she called out his name, but the word dissolved into the sound of the waves unfurling on the shore; it could safely be ignored. He projected nonchalance as he walked away from her, weaving his way with ease between the rocks.

In a short time, he had reached the point at which the path – such as it was – turned a corner around the rocks, disappearing out of the view of anyone on the beach. He glanced briefly at the noticeboard with its warning to proceed with care, and then it was behind him and he was clambering over the pitted grey surface of the rocks.

The first thing that struck Fraser was that the chain walk was more intimidating than he remembered. He was older, of course, than he had been the last time he had attempted it, and less fit, but also the tide was in. The waves were rolling into the first inlet with some force, the grey-green water lapping at the footholds cut into the rockface. He didn't think he'd done the chain walk when the water was this high.

He stared at the roiling water, considering his options. If he went back, he would have to face Kirsty. The phrase "the devil and the deep blue sea" had never had such urgent meaning for him.

In the end, he waited for perhaps five minutes, hoping that his pursuer would give up, and then he made his way carefully back to the corner and peered around it.

Kirsty was making her way over the rocks towards him. She was moving slowly – much more slowly than Fraser had – with her arms out to steady herself. But she was still coming. It was really impossible that she could attempt the chain walk in those boots, but it was equally impossible for Fraser to go back the way he had come without confronting her. He ducked back behind the rock, cursing under his breath.

There was nothing for it. He clambered over the rocks again, steeling himself for the unnerving step onto the chain walk. The steel links were, at any rate, reassuringly thick and heavy, and the bright gleam of the metal showed that they were fairly new and well maintained. He grasped the first part of the chain and began to climb.

The first short ascent felt alarmingly exposed. The chain ran almost vertically up a rocky outcrop, close enough to the corner of it that the empty air and the dizzying drop to the surging water below were always at his shoulder. When he got to the top he crouched on the rock, not trusting himself to stand up. His palms were sweating.

From here the chains descended a little and ran horizontally along the side of the inlet. The level section looked straightforward enough, Fraser saw with relief. He started along it with renewed confidence.

Very quickly, he realised his mistake. The rock bulged outwards and the chain was just a little too low and a little too slack: with his feet on the holds and his hands on the metal links he was leaning too far backwards to balance properly. The constant crash and ebb of the waves below him kept distracting him from watching where to put his hands and feet. He couldn't stop looking down and wondering whether the next swell of water would be high enough to wash him right off the rock.

He took another clumsy step to the left, and as he

did so a wave swept into the inlet, foamed over the rocks at the end and then ebbed as swiftly. As the water seethed through the multitude of pebbles on the floor of the inlet, Fraser heard a single word, pronounced with lingering sibilance amongst the hissing of the waves.

Fra-s-s-s-er.

His foot slipped, his leg swung out into thin air, and for a sickening instant he thought he was going to fall right into the water, his body cringing at the imminent plunge. He grappled with the chain, hanging on by sheer panic, fists and elbows hooking over the slick-wet metal. The links dug painfully into his triceps. He grunted, arms shaking with the effort of taking his entire weight.

When he had recovered enough balance to stand on the footholds again, he took a moment to catch his breath. His gaze kept sliding to the green-grey water that sucked so greedily at his heels.

I imagined it, he said to himself. *Nobody said my name. It was just the sound of the waves. Or it was that silly cow Kirsty calling from the other side of the rocks.*

All the same, it had rattled him. He couldn't risk another shock like that. He fought his way to the end of the inlet, where the section of chain ran out, and hopped down onto the rocks. Here it was possible to walk across the gap without going into the water. After that, he would have to climb onto a large ridged rock and from there step onto the rockface on the other side, where a new section of chain would guide him up and round the rocks.

Fraser paused on the ridged rock before he stepped across. It wasn't a *big* step. He wouldn't have thought twice about it in most circumstances. It was just that the water slopping back and forth below him kept snagging his gaze. He felt irrationally nervous about falling in. *In and out*, went the waves, *in and out*, like breathing. The movement of the water was deliberate but uneven, organic, as though it was the motion of a living thing.

He was committed now, though. He took a deep breath and stretched one foot out across the gap. When it touched stone on the other side, he moved his weight onto it and grabbed the tail end of the chain, which dangled from the first bolt. A second later he had both feet on the rockface and both fists tight around the metal links. He climbed rapidly, putting distance between himself and the seawater.

When he got to the top, Fraser sat down on the rock. He looked back towards the beginning of the chain walk. He could not see Kirsty from where he sat.

He had better make up his mind whether to keep going forward or go back and risk meeting her. The sun was low in the sky. He couldn't imagine trying to complete the chain walk once it became dark. He hauled himself to his feet, turned towards the setting sun and set off across the rocks.

After scuttling crab-like across another outcrop cut with footholds, and tackling an uncomfortable climb over some large stones, Fraser followed the route along a stretch of shingle beach. He kept well away from the water's edge.

Once, a great wave came rolling in and broke against a rock. For a few moments, the air was full of sparkling droplets, before they pattered down onto the pebbles. The falling water disturbed Fraser, though he could not have said why. He moved a little further up the beach. The air had a moist tang of salt in it, and he licked his lips as though he had tasted something repellent.

The next section of chain, which ran up a wall of stone and down the other side, led onto a strange open plain of jagged rocks and shallow pools choked with brown weed. In the dying sunlight, it looked alien, a scene from another planet. Fraser started across it, taking care to keep his shoes dry. Was that the end of the chain walk? No; he spotted another length of steel links dangling from a rocky saddle ahead of him. A metal post marked the highest point of the chain.

As he walked towards it, amongst the distant susurration of the sea, he heard his own name whispered.

Fra-s-s-s-er.

He broke his stride for an instant, stiffening, and then he put his head down and walked on.

Nothing, he said to himself. *Nothing but imagination.* His throat was tight and his heart thumping. He kept moving. To react visibly would be to accept.

It was a relief to reach the bottom of the chain and begin the ascent. Every metre – every *centimetre* – that he put between himself and the level of the water eased the feeling of urgent repulsion he had towards it. In spite of the growing weariness in his limbs, he went up as fast as he could. When he got to the top, he clung to the metal post, panting.

Imagination, Fraser told himself again. *If you are a suggestible person, the hissing of the surf can sound like any word with a sibilant in it. Any word at all.*

But as he sat there, something else suggested itself – something that insinuated its way into his thoughts in spite of all resistance.

The rain pouring down into the open grave, surrounding the cardboard coffin, saturating it. The wet soil heaped onto it, covering it: everything so sodden – a slurry, really. In his mind's eye the sun came out and scorched the newly turned earth, and from the grave there rose thin exploratory tendrils of water vapour, curling towards the sky until they evaporated. Water droplets, invisibly small, drifting into the sky.

He thought of air cooling, of clouds forming, and at last, rain falling. Which way had the wind been blowing that afternoon? Fraser didn't know; he had been indoors the whole time. He supposed it didn't matter; the rain that came down along the coastline here would end up in the ocean anyway. He pictured the burn in St Monan's, the next settlement east of Elie, running straight down into the sea, the fast-flowing water carrying—

Carrying what? Fraser asked himself fiercely. He realised he was thinking of something for which he could find no better word than *contamination*. He rested his forehead on the cool metal of the post, closing his eyes briefly. *This is crap. This is stress – or some kind of a minor breakdown.*

He decided that when he got back to the inn he was going to pack up and leave. He didn't care about paying for a night's accommodation he wouldn't be using, nor about the long drive home. If he had to, he could stop somewhere in one of those cheap travellers' hotels that studded the motorway network like carbuncles. Anything to get away from Elie – and Ishbel's family. It served them right that he had left the wake early; he didn't deserve this persecution.

I wasn't cruel to her, he thought to himself once more. *I did more than most men would have.*

His hands were becoming chilled from contact with the chain's cold metal and the cool evening air, and he could already feel stiffness setting in from the unwonted exertion. Time to move.

He looked down the other side of the rocky saddle and his heart sank. It looked like the longest section yet; the height was enough to make him feel slightly vertiginous. The first part had rough steps hewn into the rock; after that, the chain descended vertically almost to the level of the water. He could have wept. He bit back a curse.

There was nothing for it, though. Much as he would have liked to put off climbing down, the longer he left it, the more difficult it would be. If his fingers actually became numb, there was a real risk of falling off. Fraser grimaced. He forced himself to get up, turned to face the rock and began to descend, gripping the chain tightly.

Below him, at the bottom of the rockface, there was another inlet, bigger than the first. Along this channel, the seawater also foamed and sucked, and in the shivering of a thousand tumbled pebbles Fraser heard his name whispered over and over again.

He paused halfway down the chain, fighting back dread. He was determined not to hear it. He *would not* hear it. There was no other option but to go on; if he went back he would have to face the other inlet, and he was tired now. His confidence in his ability to haul himself along that first section without slipping off was all but drained. Doggedly, he continued to descend.

At the bottom, his limbs trembling, he clambered over a rocky bulge and found another horizontal section of chain. Below the carved footholds, the water slopped and surged. The dying light of the sun made strange patterns on its surface; frail arabesques like handfuls of fine hair turned on the current.

I cannot, said Fraser to himself as he looked at the chain stretching ahead of him. *But – I must.* He almost wept.

He grasped the cold links and stepped onto the first of the footholds. A wave came rolling up the inlet, and for a moment he froze. He squeezed his eyes tight shut for a second, cringing, and then opened them again. The water had passed within centimetres of his heels, but his feet were dry. He inched to his left with painful slowness.

Before he had gone far, he spotted the end of the chain. There was a cavern beyond it, a high but narrow opening like a doorway set into the cliff. Its inner recesses were deep in shadow. The effect was undoubtedly sinister, but it was not the dark heart of the cave that filled Fraser with cold horror. It was the water washing gently back and forth across the entrance of it. It was not deep enough to drown him, he could see that. But he would get wet, and that he could not bear. He would have endured anything, anything at all, rather than let that glossy moisture suck at him. His flesh shrank from it.

Fraser stopped moving along the chain. He tried to think clearly about what to do, but his thoughts shimmered and danced like raindrops on water.

Fra-s-s-s-er, sang the waves that moved sinuously against the rock below his shoes. A swell of water more daring than the others rose up and washed over his feet and ankles.

Cold. So cold. His wet feet were instantly numb, so numb that they might have ceased to exist altogether; he had no sense of them. He was afraid to look down, thinking he might find that he was *un-becoming*, dissolving into the briny water.

With no sensation below his lower calves it was hard to maintain his position. He could feel his knees scraping against the rough surface of the rock but below them nothing; his feet were as useless as the dead white feet of a corpse. Since he could not feel them, he could not draw them up out of reach of the water when the next wave came up and took them off at the knees. With horrible inevitability, he slid off the foothold.

He still didn't fall into the water; his hands clung desperately to the chain. He fought to put his elbows over it. He was still clinging there, grunting and sobbing and fighting with the chain, when a great wave came, a glossy protrusion of water that overtopped the high tide mark on the rocks and swamped him easily. He lost his grip on the metal links; the scream was drowned in his throat, sound converted to bubbles.

An observer – there was none – might have thought that the upswell of the water lingered too unnaturally long on the face of the rock, clinging to it in a languorous, almost gelatinous manner. Then it subsided gracefully, and the metal links clinked softly back against the rockface. Tiny rivulets of seawater ran down the bare stone. The figure that had clung to the chain was gone.

A little later, Kirsty came puffing and panting along the cliff path above the chain walk. If she could not follow Fraser along the chain walk, she was determined to meet him at the other end. She found without difficulty the place where a worn track led down to the end of the chain walk, and there she waited, hands on hips. But there was no sign of Fraser at all, not then, nor ever after.

THE ADJOINING ROOM
A. K. Benedict

"**W**ill you be wanting *two* keys, Madam?" the receptionist says, his voice flexing on "two" almost as much as his right eyebrow. Behind him, a clock tocks against wood panelling.

"No, thanks. It's just me," I say.

"Have two anyway," he replies, leaning closer as he hands me the white plastic cards. There's a slant to his smirk and a grey edge to his teeth that matches the uneven flagstones. "You never know, you might get lucky."

I laugh. I've only shared a bed once at a conference, and that was with a type of mite. Left me with an unscratchable rash on my back. I take the keys anyway. He's right, you never know.

"You're in room 535," he says. "Lift to your left. Do you need help with your bags?"

I hold up my small suitcase. "I'm fine. Travelling light."

He nods, eyes already sliding to the person behind me. "Enjoy your stay, Dr Phillips."

I'm sure I will. I like it when conferences are held in old places. Identikit box hotels may have better beds but they lack stories and atmosphere. It also takes longer to get drunk in them, as if the air-conditioning sucks up alcohol fumes as well as fun.

This hotel was grand, once. It's there in the name and the ghosts of gold leaf on the mouldings. I walk straight past the birdcage-style lift to the staircase. I got stuck in a lift once and haven't been in one since. Anyway, it's good to take the stairs – keeps my step count up.

My room is at the very end of a long corridor. I've definitely had worse rooms: the bed doesn't sink in the middle; my knees fit under the desk; and the art deco bathroom, patched with brown grout, is clean. Best thing is the sea view. Cagoule-grey waves and parka-hood spume.

Suitcase open on the bed, I unpack. As I hang up my suit, I hear sobbing. It's coming from the room next door. The cries are muffled but I recognise them. They're the kind that give sound to the searing that's going on inside. The kind that tear. I hover by the locked door that links our rooms. I want to say something, but know it wouldn't help, would embarrass them. Last thing they need is knowing someone can hear them.

Downstairs, welcome drinks are being set up in the ballroom. Conference-goers gather for free glasses of wine. It is already too loud, voices rebounding off mirrored walls. I walk past, head down, towards the revolving doors. I'm not in meeting people mode yet.

The wind greets me as I step onto the seafront. It pushes back against me, as if wanting to spoon, but I walk through it and over the road. Beyond the railings, the sea kicks against the shore. I breathe in. My lungs fill with salt-baked air and, as I exhale, the whole journey, and all of last year, empties out onto the sand. They're dragged back in again on the inhale, but a few memories are left, bladder-wracked, on the beach.

I walk on, past dog walkers, shuttered shops, a bandstand waiting for a band. The rain is at a slight angle, like cold commas aiming for my face.

Back over the road, a café is still open. Light bleeds through steamed-up windows. I could go in. Sit with a chipped mug of tea. Read yesterday's paper. Decide I don't want to deliver the keynote speech and go home.

I should get back to the drinks, though. The opening ceremony will take place soon and I'm supposed to be there, shaking hands and smiling. I turn, and this time the wind pushes me in the small of my back, speeding up my feet until I round the promenade and see the off-white edifice of the hotel.

At dinner, I'm sat next to a man who can't stop talking about ellipses. He's already delivered half of a lecture on them that he's going to give tomorrow when I interrupt.

"And here would be a perfect place for an ellipsis," I say.

"That way I get to keep the mystery going till tomorrow."

He laughs. Continues his lecture. A woman on the other side of the table rolls her eyes.

Face aching from fake smiling, I get away before the after-dinner speaker starts, claiming that I want to go over my speech. The carpet swirls as I climb up to the fifth floor. I stop by room 534 but can't hear anything. They must've gone out, or cried themselves to sleep.

As my key bleeps me into my room, I feel the relief of being alone. Make-up removed, pyjamas on, I slip into bed. The sheets are so cold they feel damp. Or so damp they feel cold. It's quiet. The sea seems a long way away. I turn the telly on to hear voices: just because I want to be alone, doesn't mean I don't get lonely.

A Friday night panel show is on. Comics discuss the merits of pork pies.

I lie on my side, the spare pillow pressed behind me (in theory, to support my back; in fact, to give the impression that someone's there), close my eyes and wait for the room to spin. I've had enough wine for it to cartwheel but it stays put. In my head, I start to recite my speech on "Asyndeton and Contemporary Disconnection".

It's half three when I wake. In the next room, a woman is shouting. She bangs on the walls, screams at someone to get out.

I wrangle the blankets off the bed, stumble across the room. "Hello?" I call out. "Do you need help?"

The shouting stops. All I can hear is a faint, low hum, and the sound of someone breathing, inches from me, on the other side of the door. "Please. Help me." Her voice is so close she can whisper.

"I'll call reception," I say.

"There's no point. They won't believe you."

"'Course they will. Stay there."

She says nothing, only laughs the kind of laugh that says nothing's funny.

I pat across the wall for the light switch, blink until I can see, pick up the phone on the desk. Dial 0 for reception.

"Good morning, Dr Phillips. What can we do for you?" the voice says. It's not the same receptionist. This one has a deeper voice, seems annoyed at being contacted.

"There's a problem in the room next to me, 534. Someone's asking for help."

A pause at the other end. A muffled voice, as if a hand has been placed over the receiver. Then removed. "Thanks for letting us know, Dr Phillips, we'll look into that immediately. Our apologies for your disturbance." The line clips closed.

Behind the door, the woman moans. "You've got to help me."

My hand goes to the lock of the linking door, and stops. It's the middle of the night and I'm thinking of going into a stranger's room, into an unknown situation. I step away. Coward. "They're on their way," I say.

"You don't understand."

Footsteps down the hall. Stop just before my room. Knock on another door. "Hello? Can you open up, please? We've heard there's a disturbance."

I run to the peephole. I can't see, the angle's wrong. I open my door an inch and look through the gap.

A security guard stands outside room 534. He knocks again.

The door opens. A man comes out, tying a hotel bathrobe. His hair is pillow-fuzzed. He blinks, adjusting to the light. Maybe she's had a breakdown and he slept through it? That can happen. "What is it?" he says.

"A guest contacted us, says there's a problem in your room, sir," the guard replies.

"You've got the wrong room. I've been asleep," he says. He sees me. Scowls. His mouth seems huge, lips striped with red wine stains.

"Can we just have a look around?" the guard says. "Check everything's okay?" He moves forward slightly. It wasn't a request.

The guest huffs then retreats into his room. The guard follows. I can't see anything without stepping right into the corridor.

"There," the guest says, coming back into view. His arms are folded. "Satisfied?"

"Very sorry for the inconvenience, sir," the guard says, re-emerging.

"I'll be wanting a discount for this."

I want to barge into the room, fling open the wardrobe, whip back the shower curtain. She's in there, hiding.

Hurting. It's what people in her position do. Whereas people like me, in my position, lurk behind doors, listening.

"Talk to reception, sir." The guard glances at me and looks quickly away, as if he were a guilty child, and strides back up the corridor.

My neighbour turns to me. "Had a good look, did you? Enjoy your little trick? Pathetic bitch." His artificially red lips stretch into a sneer. I can almost hear them cracking.

I step back, close the door. Put the chain on. I move across to the other door, place my ear close to the wood. I can hear him moving across the room, very slowly, dragging his feet. She's whimpering.

"I'm sorry," I whisper to her.

"Leave me alone," she says.

Breakfast next morning. I load up my plate with pastries, sit in the corner window. Outside, waves pay no attention to railings. They land on the promenade and on surprised passers-by. The dining room is full of draughts and hungover delegates. The coffee, though, is good. I peel layers from a croissant but do not eat them.

"Can I join you, Dr Phillips?" Henrik Villiers says, gesturing to the empty chair at my table. He is a lecturer at Queen's, whose thesis on the em dash causes a surge in the pulse rate of punctuation pedants. I nearly got up the courage to talk to him in Vienna last year on the pretext of discussing his paper, but I turned away at the last minute. And now he's here. He has kind, seventies-brown eyes behind his glasses and, for a moment, I feel seen.

"I was just leaving, I'm afraid," I say, standing up and brushing pastry flakes from my trousers.

"That's a shame," he says. We stand for a moment, facing each other, like a pair of square brackets. "I'm looking forward to your keynote later. It'll be fascinating."

"Let's hope so."

"See you in the bar after?"

I nod, stride off as if I know where I'm going.

The day is so crammed with events and lectures, punctuated by hallway meetings with people only seen in other conference hallways, that I don't return to my room till late afternoon. I have one hour before my speech. Time enough to make a cup of tea and go through my notes. My heart punches like unending ellipses. I've never been the keynote speaker before. I hope it doesn't show.

I angle one of the armchairs so that I can see the sea, place my laptop on the little table. As I open the presentation, a fist hits the adjoining door.

"Open it," the woman screams. "Help me, please." Her words blur, plosive "p"s missing.

I go straight to the phone. Dial 0.

"Yes, Dr Phillips?" It's a different voice again.

"It's Room 534 again. A woman says she needs help."

That pause. Muffled voice. The feeling that I'm not hearing everything I need. "Room 534 is empty, Madam. The previous guest left this morning, after an unnecessarily disturbed night."

"The woman is still in there. In pain. I think she needs medical attention."

The receptionist sighs. "The room was cleaned an hour ago. The maid would have noticed anyone inside the room, and tonight's guests have yet to arrive."

"But she banged on the adjoining door, less than a minute ago. Calling for help."

The pause is long this time. "You are mistaken, Madam. There are no adjoining rooms in the hotel."

"I'm looking at it now." The door is right in front of me, bolted.

"That is not true. If you would like an adjoining room then our sales team would be delighted to talk to you about one in our sister hotel?"

"I. Don't. Want. Another. Hotel." I'm shouting. Punching the words.

"We are glad you are satisfied, Dr Phillips."

The line dies.

I let out a screech of frustration. Slam the wall with my palm.

"Told you," the woman whispers from behind the adjoining door. "They wouldn't. Believe you." Her words emerge slowly, as if they're hurt.

"How did you know?"

"I've been. Where you are."

"And where are you?" I unbolt the adjoining door. Reach for the handle.

"Don't," she says. "Don't open the door."

"I don't understand."

She is silent for a while, then says, "I'm sorry. I shouldn't have asked. You to open. The door."

I press my face against the frame, whisper into the crack. "Why? You need help."

"I'm past that."

She whimpers. "No," she shouts. "I won't. You can't make me."

"Who's in there with you?"

But she doesn't reply. Behind her whimpers, the low, revving thrum gets louder.

My keynote comes out on autopilot; I don't even feel the words in my mouth. The audience laughs in the right places, claps in others, gets to its feet at the end. After, I shake hands and take business cards without hearing anyone's names.

Henrik walks over. "That was brilliant." He holds out a gin and tonic. I take it.

"Thanks," I say. "I don't remember saying most of it."

"Well, you had this lot in the palm of your hand." He gestures to the room of flush-faced delegates.

"Helps that they were already pissed."

He laughs. "They weren't for my paper on terminal

points this morning. Two people fell asleep and one left in the middle. Clearly gripping."

"I'm sorry I missed it," I say.

"I'll send it to you."

"I'd like that."

We're smiling at each other. Proper grins, top lips stuck to gums. We find a table, tucked around the corner, and, for the next hour, we talk. We talk about everything other than full stops: David Lean, broccoli, our relatives, our exes… Possibility passes between us. For a moment, I think of us going through life together, of us being old, bent over like guillemets, on either side of the family portrait.

And then I remember the adjoining room.

"What is it?" Henrik says, brows meeting, voice dropping.

"What do you mean?"

"Your face changed," he says. "Like you tasted something that had turned."

"I had a difficult night. Not a great day, either."

"Do you want to talk about it? I'm a good listener. Secrets stop with me."

"It's not easy to say."

"Say it anyway," he says, turning his back on the crowd.

I test the words in my mouth before letting them out. When I do, they rush at him. "There's something wrong in my room I don't know what's going on I need to show you please help me."

He doesn't even flinch. "Of course. Do you want to go now?"

Cuban heels spit against parquet. "This is where you're hiding, Lisa," Mark, the conference administrator says, grabbing me by the elbow. He is tall and thin with a small, round head, like an upside-down exclamation mark. "People want their guest of honour."

Henrik watches as I'm wheeled off to meet and greet – is still watching when I crane back to where he's standing.

I'm dragged off to talk semi-colons with one group, next year's conference with another, and then it's dinner. The room is filled with clinking and clattering and high-pitched laughs. Even the smells are loud – peas, cleaning fluid and gravy. I'm told stories by those next to me. I know by their teller's tone when to show concern or make my mouth upturn, but their words fall away. I keep thinking about what I said to Henrik. I've got two options: tell him to forget everything, or let him in on what's happening. Not sure which is the braver.

Conversations go on around me; chicken cools on my plate.

Before they serve the desserts, I get up to go to the toilet and, on the way back, stop at Henrik's table. I still don't know what choice I'm going to make.

"How's it going?" he asks when I crouch next to him.

"Not great. Though everything'll look better after the sticky toffee pudding."

He nods, making a show of taking this very seriously.

I laugh. Eyes swivel in our direction.

"What would you like to do, later?" he asks, his voice soft and low.

I open my purse and palm one of the keys. "I've got to do the rounds after dinner," I whisper. "But I'll meet you in my room after eleven. Room 535." I hand him the key. At this point, I don't care who sees. Gossip needs nourishment and will be well fed tonight.

It's only half ten when I get to my room. I take off my shoes and lie on the bed. The ceiling spins, taking me with it. I sit back up again, it's the only way to make it stop.

Knock, knock.

It's not Henrik. It's from the other side of the adjoining door. The knocking comes again, along with a sound that reminds me of scales being ripped from a fish.

"HELP ME!" she screams. Her voice is metallic and stretched as if squeezed through a pipe. "OPEN THE DOOR."

I can't wait for Henrik. I have to help.

I grab the handle. It doesn't turn at first. I have to keep forcing it, trying to block out her sobs. I can't stand her pain anymore.

I open the door and step inside. The adjoining room is white and striped with shadows.

The woman lies on the floor. At least, I think it's her. She is a skinless thing, curled-up like a comma on the tiles. Red and raw. Her eyes cannot blink. I try to move towards her but can't. I'm paralysed. Through a lipless slit, she says, "I'm sorry."

Her arm lifts, sinews shining. She points.

Someone is standing in the corner of the room. It wears her skin like a shroud. Breathes into her flensed breasts.

I try again, to move, to run. Nothing happens.

It shrugs off her skin, slowly. I see it for what it is.

The woman rises. She takes up her skin, throws it over her like a cloak. The scalp flaps back like a hood. She walks out, slick feet sticking to the tiles. Slams the door.

I can't get back.

I can't look at the presence in the corner, but I know what it wants. It will let me out only if I trade places with the one in the adjoining room, as the woman did with me.

An hour later, the door to Room 535 bleeps. I hear Henrik's steps. His tentative, "Lisa?"

And I can't say anything back.

I'm in the Adjoining Room. There is one window. Sometimes it shows the sea.

It has my skin and will only let me go when I let someone else in. I have two options. I'm not sure which is the braver.

I can't do it, though – offer someone else up to what lies in the corner. I've been close to it, I admit. I keep the bolt on my side of the door in place. It's safer.

In room 535, people come and people go. Some are alone. Some argue, some fuck. Most are alone while doing both. I talk, but the majority cannot hear. Those that can are already lost, but I still don't ask them to open the door. Maybe they can find their way back.

Henrik comes back to the room, once a year, every year, on the anniversary of my disappearance. Calls out to me when awake and asleep. Can't say I live for his visits, for this isn't life, but he's all I have. I hear him breathing in there, right now. Don't know how many years it's been, but he wheezes. I hear the thud of his stick as he walks round the room. Hear it bang against the door.

"Lisa," he says. His voice is deeper, cracked. "This is the last time I'm coming here. If you're there, now is the time."

There is silence as well as walls between us. Enough.

"Henrik," I say. The word feels jagged.

The bed creaks. He walks slowly to the adjoining door.

"I knew you were there," he says. "Let me in."

"No," I reply.

"I'm not leaving till you do."

"No."

"There's nothing for me out here, not anymore. We've got things to catch up on. Now let me in."

Pain shrieks through my nerves as I unlock my side; he unbolts his. Opens the door.

If anyone asks, we're in the Adjoining Room. There is a window. Sometimes it shows the sea.

THE GHOST IN THE GLADE
Kelley Armstrong

There's a ghost that plays in an empty glade, in the woods behind my house. She tells me she's lonely. She tells me she's sad. She begs me to stay and cries when I leave and wants me to join her. To play with her forever. To lie alongside her under the earth, in eternal sleep and eternal play.

Mother used to say my father cursed those woods tucked in the midst of our crops. When I was little, I thought that meant he'd actually cursed them, the way a witch does. Perhaps that idea should have made me steer clear. Instead, it drew me like a magnet.

What I found in those woods was not a cursed land, but a magical one. An oasis in our desert of fields, those ugly scars that sprouted endless, backbreaking toil. When I had to spend all day working the fields, I'd sneak into the woods for respite. There, I became a forest nymph, dancing through the trees and tramping through the stream, freer than I ever was outside them.

I also ran into the forest when my father told me to go play. To me, alone, without brothers or sisters, those adventures were play. Then I went to school, and I learned that play meant games. Play meant rules. Play also meant interaction with other children, who mocked my dirty fingernails and patched dresses and lunches wrapped in handkerchiefs.

One day, when I was ten, I was supposed to be inspecting the crop for weevils. I did until my vision blurred and my head ached. Then I slipped into the forest to clear my head with the rich scent of pine and spruce.

I wandered through the woods, eyes half-closed and resting, making my way by memory. I was nearly to the stream when I caught a glimmer of movement in the trees. I went still, hoping to spot a fawn I'd seen the week before. Instead, a flash of pink and white whirled through my fairy glade.

I didn't mistake the creature for a fairy. I knew there was no such thing. My mother was very, very clear on that. When she caught me reading a book of fae lore I found in the village shop, she threw it into the fire. Wicked words, she said. A good girl needed nothing but Scripture.

I managed to rescue my book after my parents went to bed. Yet I knew Mother would notice it missing from the fireplace, so I replaced it with the only other book we had in the house: the Bible. I burned it beyond recognition and left it there, a changeling child for my fairy tome, which seemed appropriate. I had no illusions about the severity of what I'd done, but if reading about fairies made me wicked, then one must expect me to do wicked things. It took a month for my mother to notice the Bible missing, and even then she only thought she'd left it at church.

After that, I kept my fairy book hidden under the floorboards. Most of the pages were scorched but intact, and I reread it often. I understood, though, that the mysteries contained within its blackened covers were mere stories. Calling the clearing my "fairy glade" amused me. I knew it didn't contain actual fairies. But on that day, it did contain something that should have been equally impossible.

It contained a ghost.

From the moment I saw Amelia Carter pirouetting around my fairy glade, I realized she was a phantasm. The sun shone right through her pretty pink dress. Her white Oxford shoes danced inches above the ground. Otherwise, she looked as perfect as always. Even in death, her cheeks glowed, and her dark hair hung in ringlets that twirled out as she spun.

She noticed me and stopped mid-twirl.

"Hello!" she called. "I see you behind that tree. Come and talk—" Her pretty face twisted, as if she'd bitten into an unripe apple. "Oh, it's you."

I walked over, staying in the shadows to hide my filthy work dungarees and my cousin's oversized boots. Her lips still made that grimace I knew well.

"Aren't you ever clean?" she said.

I wanted to shoot back that I was always clean. I probably bathed more often than she did. The difference was that a lawyer's daughter didn't need to dig in fields after school. She didn't need to do anything except dress her dollies in pretty clothes and whisper hateful things about other girls.

Last month, Amelia Carter had disappeared from a church picnic. For a week, the entire town searched for her. I'd wanted to join. Even if Amelia never had a kind word for me, it seemed only right to help find her. My father refused to let me. I'd overheard my parents talking about what they thought had happened – that a traveling laborer had stolen Amelia and done terrible things to her. My father feared what horrors the searchers might find, and so he refused to allow me to join them.

I heard other talk, too. People saying that whatever horrors befell Amelia Carter, they came from much closer to home.

Tommy Lyons. That's the name they whispered. Tommy was fourteen and lived on the farm beside ours. At the picnic, he'd been overheard telling Amelia how pretty she looked in her pink dress. He'd been seen walking with her. Whispering with her. After she disappeared, the searchers combed his parents' property, but they found no sign of Amelia.

Soon, the story changed, and people started saying someone passing through must have snatched her. She was such a pretty child that some poor childless rich woman could not resist her, and now Amelia was living like a princess in a big city. That's what people wanted to think. But her ghost in this glade told a very different story.

"Where am I?" Amelia asked, looking around.

"On our farm."

Her face screwed up. "This doesn't look like... Oh, it's that horrible forest. My father came to see your mother again, didn't he? To get his darning done. He has so much of it." She rolled her blue eyes. "We'd best get back to the house. He'll want to leave as soon as she's done."

"Your father isn't there. Do you remember... anything?"

She flounced down on a log.

"Amelia?" I said when she didn't answer.

I waited, and finally, she whispered, "I think something's wrong."

"What do you remember?"

She ignored the question and said, "I can't leave."

I inched closer, careful to stay out of her reach. I knew much of fairies, but nothing of ghosts, and I feared what she might do if I came too close.

"What do you mean you can't leave?" I asked.

She pushed to her feet and strode toward the edge of the clearing. The moment she reached it, she bounced back, as if she'd struck a wall.

"What's wrong with me?" she asked.

I moved farther into the clearing. Ahead, I could see a spot where the soil had been disturbed. A hole dug and filled in, the turf laid back over it. A spot big enough for the body of a twelve-year-old girl.

Amelia marched over and planted herself in front of me, hands on her hips. "I asked you a question."

When I didn't reply, she sniffed and spun on her heel. "Never mind. I don't want to talk to you, anyway. I only ever do because Daddy makes me. I keep telling him I don't want to. You're boring. Stupid, boring and dirty."

I started to leave.

"Wait!" she said.

I stopped just past the edge of the clearing. I didn't turn around. I just stood there as she sniffled.

"Something's wrong with me," she said. "I can't remember how I got here, and now I can't leave. I'm sorry I called you stupid. You aren't. You're the smartest girl in class. If anyone can figure this out, you can."

I turned to see another familiar look on her face, one she'd get whenever she needed my help with her homework. She'd tell me I was clever and beg for my assistance, and I'd do it, but that never changed anything. She'd still whisper about me behind my back. Not always *behind* my back, either.

I looked back at the place where the soil had been disturbed. I didn't like Amelia. I might even hate her. But whatever she'd done, she didn't deserve this.

Did she deserve the truth? To know she was dead? Not if she couldn't change that. Not if it wouldn't help.

"It's a fairy trap," I said.

Her face scrunched up again. "What?"

"You must have come here to see the fairies." I settled onto a stump. "One time, when you came with your father, you followed me out here, and I told you about the fairies," I lied. "Do you remember that?"

She shook her head.

"Well, I did. You must have come back to see them. Only they've trapped you. That's what they do. They play music, and when you follow it, you get trapped in the dance. You were dancing when I walked by. Do you remember that?"

She nodded.

"Why were you dancing?" I asked.

"Because I was bored."

"No, you were dancing because you heard the fairy music. You just forgot it."

"So how do I get out?"

I told her I didn't know, but I'd find out. I had a fairy book, and I'd look for the answer, and when I found it, I'd come back.

I didn't return for almost a month. I thought by then she'd be gone, that her ghost was only temporarily stuck here, and a gate would open, and she'd go... wherever. She didn't. I went back, and Amelia was right where I'd left her.

To my relief, she'd forgotten my promise. She didn't even remember I'd been there. I found her dancing, and we repeated the whole conversation, as if for the first time. Again, I promised to find the answer. Again, I stayed away for a month. Again, I returned to find her ghost still in that glade, still trapped, still forgetting why.

It wasn't long before people stopped looking for Amelia. Two years passed, and her parents had another baby, a little girl. They named her Amy, in memory, as if even *they'd* given up hoping to find Amelia.

Soon, the town seemed to forget about Amelia altogether. As she faded in their memories, so her own memories faded. The ghost in the glade forgot who she was. She forgot where she was. She forgot that she'd had another life before this and that another life existed beyond her glade. She stopped asking me to help her escape. The glade became her world, and she danced and played it in endlessly.

She forgot me, too. That is, who I'd been to her when she was a creature of flesh and blood. I became her best friend. Her only companion.

"Come play with me," she'd say.

"I'm too old to play."

"No one's too old to play. Come. *Come*."

I tried to play with her. I didn't quite do it right, but she no longer seemed to mind. She was like a child desperate for attention. Always desperate. Always lonely. Always alone.

"Don't go!" she'd say whenever I had to leave.

"I have chores. And schoolwork."

"You don't need that. Play with me. Stay with me."

"I can't stay. Remember? We've discussed this. I don't live here."

"But you could. It's nice here, in the sunshine. No chores. No school. We could dance and play forever."

"I don't want to dance and play forever."

I don't want to be like you, dead and rotting beneath the soil.

Sometimes, I thought of telling her the truth, so she'd understand why I couldn't stay. But I didn't. I feared it wouldn't matter.

No, I feared she already knew. That she'd realized why she was trapped there, and she knew exactly what she was suggesting when she asked me to join her.

As I grew older, I visited less frequently, going only once a month, as I had in the very beginning. As much as I dreaded those visits, I owed her that much.

Soon, I turned fifteen and had to drop out of school. My mother said I'd had enough education. It was time for other things. Time to move on with my life, whether I wanted to or not.

I didn't tell Amelia that I'd be leaving home soon. That would've been cruel. So I played with her, and I listened to her. One day, when I was nearly ready to go, something caught her eye, and she spun, saying, "Who's there?"

I looked over quickly. The forest seemed empty. Amelia ran to the edge of her glade and shaded her eyes.

"I saw you," she said. "Come out and play with us."

No answer. Then, off to my left, twigs crackled underfoot.

"Who's there?" I called as I strode toward the noise.

A figure stepped from behind a tree. Tommy Lyons. My future. That's what my parents said. Tommy and I were to wed when I turned sixteen. Our families and our farms would join. That was my future. My fate. Standing in front of me.

"Who were you talking to?" Tommy asked.

"You."

"Before that. I saw you in that clearing. I heard you talking to someone."

"Myself," I said as I brushed past him.

He grabbed my arm, hard enough to hurt. "Only crazy people talk to themselves. You aren't crazy, are you?"

I considered telling him that I was. Maybe then he'd refuse to marry me. That wouldn't help, though. If Tommy rejected me, I'd never wed, and I'd be trapped here with my mother's endless chores and Amelia's endless pleas.

"I'm sorry," I said. "It won't happen again."

He peered at the clearing. Then at me, his eyes narrowed. I tried to shake free, but he only tightened his grip and marched me back toward the house, saying, "Stay away from there."

After Tommy warned me to stay out of the woods, I went there even more often. I couldn't help it. I used to flee my chores. Now I fled my life.

"You aren't happy," Amelia said, spinning through the glade. "I can tell."

"Am I usually happy?"

"No, but you aren't sad, either. You're sad now. And I know how to fix it."

I didn't reply.

She kept dancing until she was right in front of me. She still looked exactly as she had at the town picnic, in that pretty pink dress with her face scrubbed clean, hair in perfect ringlets. Forever twelve years old. Forever playing. Forever dancing.

"Join me," she said.

She spun around me, her skirt billowing. "Join me. We'll dance, and we'll play, and you'll be happy."

"No, *you'll* be happy."

She only smiled. "I will. If you join me, I won't be alone anymore. I hate being alone. It gets cold when you're gone. Cold and dark."

"I'm sorry."

"Don't be sorry, just say—"

She shrieked as a figure appeared at the clearing's edge. I turned to see Tommy.

"I thought I told you not to come here," he said.

I backed into the forest. "I just wanted—"

"You knew I was coming over for dinner. You deliberately snuck out here to provoke me."

"What? No. I forgot."

"You forgot? That's your excuse?"

I kept moving backwards, away from the clearing. Amelia screamed, but he couldn't hear her. Couldn't see her. He advanced on me, his face twisted with rage.

"I'm not sure what's worse," he said. "The fact that you forgot I was coming, or the fact you snuck out here behind my back *because* you forgot."

"I'm s-sorry."

He lunged and grabbed my arm. "You're going to be my wife, and you still act like a child, running around the forest and talking to yourself." He pulled me so close I smelled ale on his breath. "Or are you communing with the fairies?"

"Wh-what?"

He jerked his thumb at the clearing. "That's a fairy glade. My gran told me about them. She told me about girls who commune with the fairies. Wicked girls."

"N-no. I'm not—"

He pulled me to him and hiked up my skirt, one sweaty hand on my thigh. "Are you a wicked girl?" he whispered in my ear. "Do you dance naked with the fairies?"

I scrambled away. He grabbed at me. I stumbled and fell on all fours. He dropped on me and flipped me over, and his hand dove under my skirt again.

"We're almost married," he said. "Then I can do whatever I like." He smirked down at me. "So you might as well start getting used to it."

I fell back, whimpering. He fumbled to push my skirt up. As soon as he looked away, I reached over my head and grabbed the stone I'd left there. I swung it against his head. It hit with a satisfying crunch. I'd heard that crunch before. On the day Amelia Carter chased me here all the way from the town picnic. She chased me and grabbed me and told me that her father did *not* come to get his socks darned. She told me what he did do – that she'd seen it. She called my mother a whore. Called me one, too. I said I wasn't the one who let Tommy Lyons kiss me behind the schoolhouse. That's when she attacked me. I grabbed the rock and hit her on the head. I only meant to make her stop. That's all I wanted. To get free and run away. But when the stone struck Amelia's temple, she fell, and she didn't get up again.

Tommy *did* get up. He tried, at least, dazed and blinking. I hit him harder, and I kept hitting him until he lay as still as Amelia had, all those years ago.

When I was sure he wouldn't rise again, I returned to the clearing with the spade I'd hidden earlier. Amelia said nothing. She only watched as I dug. Then I dragged Tommy's body to it, and she clapped in delight as I laid him in the hole.

There's a ghost that plays in an empty glade, in the woods behind my house.

But she isn't lonely anymore.

THE RESTORATION
George Mann

Rae has always believed in magic.

Not the elaborate trickery of stage performers, nor the twee tales of childhood, whispered by a soothing mother into her childhood ear: talk of healing kisses and mischievous sprites, hidden portals in the back of wardrobes and faerie folk at the bottom of the garden.

No, this is magic of an earthly kind; the sort made real by the scratch of pencil upon paper, the gentle sliding of a brush across a fresh canvas – a spell wrought in indigo and ochre, in crimson and gold.

As a child, the faces that peered out at her from the walls of the National Gallery had entranced her – windows into other lives, fragile snapshots of long-forgotten worlds. Once, when she had been no more than five years old, a guard had caught her leaning too close, her nose almost brushing the encrusted surface of a winter scene. Rather than admonish her, he had lowered himself beside her on creaking knees and whispered that she must be careful, lest she trip and accidentally fall in.

She'd looked at him, wide-eyed and amazed, imagining herself tumbling into the snowy landscape before her, splashing through the vibrant colours, right into the heart of the frigid scene. One of the boys would abandon his snowball fight to help her up, and together they would galumph through the drifts, up to the warmth and safety of the old stone cottage on the hill. There she would be welcomed by the grinning woman in the window and given hot soup, before being sent on her way again, back into the real world.

The guard had tapped the side of his nose, his eyes gleaming, as if to say: "Of course it's all true, every bit of it, but you can't let on, you can't ever tell anybody else."

To this day, she never has, and even now, as she walks amongst the stacks of musty canvases and worm-ridden frames, she cannot help but imagine what role she might play in each of the paintings she sees – a handmaiden, a farmer's wife, a worshipful peasant, a blood-doused murderess. This is how Rae's life plays out – a succession of paintings, lived through and experienced, each one another chapter in her unfolding story.

She feels cold in the gallery of the old house, and hugs herself, drawing her cardigan tighter around her shoulders. She's been brought here by the promise of undiscovered gems, masterworks long abandoned, in need of her caring touch. This is her forte, her purpose – she stirs the dead back to life. As a conservator, she coaxes new life from old, repairs flaking memories, excavates stratified layers of over-paint in search of treasure. She seeks beauty in forgotten things.

Today, she is part of a restoration project in a tumbledown old house on the South Downs, a wind-whipped Jacobean manor – dark and bleak and half-buried under the accumulation of years. She's charged with sifting through all the peeling portraits in search of anything that might be saved.

There's nothing here of real value, of course. The estate has already been picked over by auctioneers and dealers, its main assets stripped and sent away for sale. Now the estate has fallen into the hands of a trust, and Rae's job is to salvage what she can from the remnants, to help make the place attractive for future paying visitors. No doubt there'll be a gift shop, she muses, and a café selling cream teas and fancy cakes. That, she thinks, is what people have come to expect from old houses such as these – as if the servants that once filled its halls had all been waitresses and volunteers, and were judged to have done well in their vocation if nobody got lost and the carrot cake passed muster.

She strolls along the gallery, her eyes flicking over broken frames and ageing panels, half-lost faces and shadowy figures, their lustre lost beneath layers of gloomy varnish. She hears a sound – one of the trustees, perhaps, entering the gallery behind her – but when she turns, there is no one to be seen. She shrugs and continues, knowing that it's just a symptom of passing years – that houses creak and ache the same as people as they age.

Her eye is drawn to the portrait of a bearded man,

propped against the skirting board amidst a stack of water-damaged frames. She crosses to it, drops to her knees. She'll be filthy by the time she's finished here, so she doesn't worry too much about the dust that clings to her knees.

She carefully lifts the painting from the stack. It's faded and cracked, and the man's skin tones have taken on a rich yellow hue. He stands with one hand on his hip, encased in armour plate that once shone bright with polish – immaculate and unsullied by battle. The man has a coquettish look about him, a knowing twinkle in his eye. She studies the frame. There's no obvious attribution, for artist or sitter, although it's clearly seventeenth century from the style.

Rae thinks she might have found her first project from the old manor. The workmanship lacks finesse, but the sitter's expression holds a certain charm. It would be a relatively simple matter to clean it, too, to strip back the layers and reveal the artist's true intent beneath.

She stands, propping the painting against the wall while she turns up the collar of her cardigan. One of the ancient windows must be warped and ill-fitting; the breeze on the back of her neck is cold.

She stoops to reclaim the portrait, but stumbles, her heel catching on an uneven floorboard. She puts out a hand to steady herself, sending three tatty frames crashing to the floor. Hurriedly, she gathers them up – a landscape of the gardens at the back of the house, blocky and ill-observed; a scene of austere childhood in a bygone nursery, the child's face stern and unhappy; and the portrait of a woman, once beautiful – as evidenced by the full lips, the curve of the jaw – but now so marred and blemished as to be almost unidentifiable.

Something in this last portrait gives her pause. She straightens herself and then carries it over to the window, where the afternoon light slants in through the syrupy panes. She blows on it, gently, stirring the patina of dust. It's in poor condition. The paint has become brittle, and there are areas around the woman's face that have been completely lost, leaving behind an incomplete jigsaw, its pieces scattered throughout the centuries. She knows she should put it back, abandon it to its fate on a spoil heap; it's too far gone. The work involved in restoring such a thing…

Yet there's something in the surviving strokes that excites Rae. This is the hand of a true craftsman: that playful smile, the sweep of the velvet drapes behind the sitter, the way the woman's hands are interlaced upon her lap. This deserves investigation.

She glances back to the picture of the armoured peacock and then makes up her mind. She's taking the woman's portrait back to her workshop, where she can assess it properly. Somehow, it just feels *right*.

To her, his studio was a place of darkness and flickering candlelight, of dancing shadows cast by the glow of a warm fire.

She only ever visited him at night; his habit was to rise late, and to entertain his wealthy patrons in the afternoons, working until the light went, polishing their likenesses until their portraits shone like beacons of unreality.

He'd always said he was a liar; his work was not to seek the truth but to weave fictions for gold. If he painted his clientele as he truly saw them – he'd told her this one night, as he stroked her milk-hued thigh, his eyelids heavy with the dulling effect of the wine – he should paint them as mouldering corpses, for their souls were too rotten to bear.

She'd laughed at such nonsense, and consoled him in the only way she knew how.

His words, however, had marked the onset of a malaise, and in the weeks that followed he had moped about the place, lacking all enthusiasm for his work. He feared that he had doused his own flame, that he no longer retained any passion for his art. In every person, he saw only the dull and the grey. Life had lost its colour – and no one, he claimed, wished to look upon paintings of that.

His only consolation was the time he spent with her. To him, she was the one thing left alive in a world populated by the shambling dead, the only thing that stirred him from his fugue. And so, laughing, she had thrown off her nightgown and posed for him in the moonlight, challenging him to paint *her* instead, to abandon his lifeless clients and stoke what passion he had left before it ebbed away entirely.

It had worked, too. That night he had filled sheaf after sheaf with charcoal sketches, working until the candles had almost shrunk down to stubs. Before long, he had eschewed all others, deferring even the most highborn of clients to make way for what he now claimed would be his masterpiece: a study of her, Ariadne, a portrait that truly captured the magnificence of her soul.

Their time together became that shared by artist and sitter, and she feared that she had inadvertently placed herself upon a pedestal, that he had begun to worship her for her form, to come to see her as something other than she was. She told herself that the fervour would pass once the work was complete, and took solace in his renewed enthusiasm. Perhaps, when this was done, he would return to his other clients with more vigour. Perhaps, too, he would finally take her as his bride, a marriage forged in charcoal and oils.

For now, though, there was only the painting. He had eyes for nothing else.

Rae sits at her desk in the studio, hunched low like a crooked finger, absorbed in a world of microscopic veins and arteries – the cracks running haphazardly across the surface of the portrait like the scatter-brained map of a nervous system.

She's been studying the picture for three days, scribbling notes on a pad beside her arm, absorbing every facet, every inch. She feels as if she's beginning to build an understanding of the portrait, to develop a sense of the artist's original work. It's going to take hours of labour and further investigation, not to mention the repair work she'll need to carry out, but the painting has got under her skin, now. It often happens that way – that a particular work has a way of speaking to her, drawing her in. This time, though, there's more to it than that. She's not sure why, but she feels the need to look this woman in the eye, to help her re-emerge from the folds of time where she's been hidden. To see if she can uncover the truth behind that secret smile.

"Your scans are ready."

This is Margot, a fellow conservator with whom Rae shares her studio. Rae has often reflected that Margot is an odd name for a woman in her early thirties – particularly one who seems so effortlessly stylish. For Rae, the name conjures images of different times, of middle-class housewives taking tea and scones in House of Fraser, but she knows this is wrong of her, a preconception caused by watching too many sitcoms from the '70s. She has her boyfriend to blame for that.

"Thanks, Margot. You want tea?"

"Oh, go on then," she replies, as if Rae were tempting her with some illicit treat. She bustles off to her table in the corner, where she's mixing pigment for a restoration job of her own.

Rae rises from her chair and stretches her weary limbs. She crosses to the small kitchenette on the other side of the room and fills the kettle.

She's still struggling to establish the identity of the artist – there's no signature in evidence on the canvas – although her research so far suggests it matches the style and period of William Foxley, a little-known portrait artist working in and around the court of King Charles I. Only a handful of his works survive, and all of them are portraits of courtiers, merchants and clergymen. Yet the woman in the painting here seems to lack the nobility or means of Foxley's typical sitters. At least, so far as Rae has been able to tell.

The kettle boils and she makes the tea. She deposits one mug on the edge of Margot's desk and carries the other over to the computer. A few brief keystrokes and she brings up the x-ray image of the painting on the screen.

She always loves this bit, the moment when the veil is lifted, when secrets are revealed. She leans closer, rubbing her neck, peering into the picture. It's as if she's peering into its soul, seeing past the artist's façade to everything that lies deeper.

She's not disappointed.

Beneath the layers of flaking paint, there's a drawing so exquisite that she gets up from her chair and walks across the room. She takes a deep breath and then slowly lets it out. She realises she's digging her fingernails into her palms. She stops, and drums them on the work surface of the kitchenette. Then she returns to the computer, sits down and pulls her chair in close.

The line work is phenomenal. It's been sketched in swift, confident movements, each stroke tracing the contours of the woman's body. The face peering out at her is a thing of beauty: slender, with high cheekbones and a gentle, curving jaw. It's almost as if the woman is looking straight at her, here and now, peering out from behind all that damaged paint to meet her gaze. Rae leans closer to the screen, and for a moment the reflection of her own features seems to line up with those of the nameless woman within, eyes meeting eyes, lips meeting lips. She feels a kind of kinship with this lonely survivor, as if they're both somehow adrift, yet orbiting one another through the painting. It joins them, somehow, like a tether, an anchor.

"…for all the ages."

The sound pulls Rae from her reverie, and she sits back from the computer screen, feeling somewhat dazed. "I'm sorry, Margot. I missed that."

"Missed what?"

Rae twists in her seat to look at her friend. "What you said. I was lost in my painting. Sorry."

Margot laughs. "You must be hearing things. I didn't say a word."

Rae frowns and then shakes her head. "Maybe you're right," she says, sipping her tea. But she feels a momentary pang of disquiet.

Still, now that she has the drawing, she has the map of what she needs to do. She'll start by cleaning back the last of the varnish and dirt, and then she can – slowly, carefully – begin to wake the woman who lies beneath.

* * *

Days became weeks became months.

Every night she would visit his rooms, and every night he would be waiting for her: the battered stool set out by the window, the canvas propped and ready on its easel, the scarlet gown upon the bed.

She'd learned to hate that gown. It was all he would have her wear – all he could see now when he looked at her. When she filled the gown, she existed.

He'd barely touched her for weeks. She'd tried provoking him flirtatiously, but his disinterest manifested in other ways, and they'd both been disappointed; he for the time he had lost, dragged away from his canvas, she for the intimacy that no longer existed between them.

William had found a different sort of intimacy, of course; he worshipped her with his brushes, teasing her every curve, tracing his fingers around the shape of her breasts, the pout of her soft lips. For him, this was more than enough. He had his muse, and it was all that he could think of. It occupied his every waking thought, and she knew that she could never live up to the perfection he sought in her image. To Ariadne, the painting had become a prison. In freeing William, she had confined herself.

And yet… she loved him still, and so she sat in the tallow light while he worked, and longed for the day when she might be free.

"At least let me see it," she pleaded, late one night, beyond the witching hour, when he finally downed his brushes. There was a look of quiet contemplation on his face.

"It's not ready," he replied dismissively. "It's bad luck. It'll ruin everything."

At this she'd thrown the gown off and stormed out indignantly, slamming the door behind her and eliciting cries of outrage from the family in the neighbouring rooms.

She'd thought twice about returning the following night, but something – perhaps habit, perhaps the hope that her outburst might have stirred some reaction from him – led her back to his door.

Sure enough, he was waiting for her, pacing the room, his hands clasped behind his back, the stool by the window, the gown repaired and waiting on the bed.

Why she didn't turn and flee, she did not know. Wordlessly, she had entered the room and closed the door behind her. He had met her gaze, the relief evident behind his eyes. And then she had donned the dress, and taken her place on the stool as before.

This, then, became her life. The days belonged to her – days filled with long walks along the river, household chores and gossip – and the nights belonged to him. Summer slid slowly into autumn into winter. Still, the work continued.

Now, though, William had begun to indicate that he was entering some penultimate stage in the painting's development, for his excitement was palpable. He'd swapped his earlier brushes for smaller, more intimate ones, and he'd abandoned shaving – or any sort of personal grooming – sprouting a wiry auburn beard and a wild, dishevelled look. When she arrived each night, he'd already be lost in the midst of his work, and he'd barely glance at her as she undressed by the side of the bed. Where once his eyes had lingered on her with such longing, now they barely strayed from the painting, and his appetite was only for the woman there, this new, alternate version of Ariadne that she was yet to see – the unwelcome interloper in their affair.

This alteration in William's temperament coincided with a similar alteration in Ariadne's health. Whether it was a symptom of the changing seasons, or something more insidious, she could not say, but the days sapped her strength, and she felt a weariness creeping into her bones that she could not shake. She grew pale, and dark rings formed beneath her eyes, yet William barely seemed to notice, as if his vision of her was unshakeable. In attempting to paint the reality of her, he had succeeded only in rendering the real Ariadne a fiction.

Yet still, she persevered. He was so close now, and they had come so far. There'd be time to rest once it was done.

The work is progressing well. It's late on a Friday evening, and Rae is supposed to be out with her friends, but she's made her excuses and remained at the workshop, hunkered down over the painting, unwilling to break away from the complex task at hand. She hasn't even stopped to make tea for the last few hours, not since Margot left for the weekend. Outside, in the street below the workshop, she can hear drunken people falling about and laughing, the vocal track to the deep, thudding beat emanating from one of the nearby clubs. She has no idea what time it is, but it's irrelevant; she's already decided to work through the night.

Her boyfriend is concerned that she's working too hard, returning home weary, skipping meals, barely exchanging two words with him. She knows he's right, but the work has become too important to her, and he'll still be there when it's finished. Just another few days and she'll be done.

More than ever, she feels what she's doing here is somehow vital. The woman is slowly beginning to emerge from the painting, brought back to life with every dab of paint. This is more reconstruction than restoration – she recognises that – but it's almost as if she can feel the original artist guiding her hand, ensuring the placement of every brushstroke. She thinks if she were to stop, her hand might well continue of its own volition, urged on by that spectral link to the past.

It's almost as if she can sense the woman's impatience, her need to be remembered; as if the original sitter is present in the workshop, watching over Rae's shoulder, urging her on and on, desperate for the work to be completed.

Rae knows that she's imagining this – she's never been one to believe in such tales – but she finds the thought strangely comforting. She's felt a connection with this forgotten woman since the very moment she first saw her, back at the manor house, up in the dusty gallery. It's as if, in excavating her from beneath the layers of blistered paint, Rae is somehow revealing some secret truth.

The woman in the painting, Rae is now convinced, is not some typical client of Foxley's. She's studied photographs of his known works online, and while she lacks the provenance to prove her theory, she's certain that the work is his. This portrait, though, feels somehow more personal than the others; in the way that Foxley forgoes the typical trappings of his other work – the overblown sense of drama, the finery, the polished gleam. It's clear those other portraits were intended to flatter, whereas this feels more real, more alive. This is not simply a portrait – it is a study, a window into a woman's soul. It feels dangerous and exciting, like no painting Rae has encountered before.

She quickens her pace. In her mind's eye, she can see the finished work, resplendent, beautiful. She can sense the woman's smile, the peace that follows its completion. It's almost like setting her free.

Rae flexes the muscles in her neck, issues a long sigh. She's so tired, and so cold. And yet she cannot stop. Not until it's done. Then she can rest.

The cold had crept into her bones and settled, and no amount of blankets or logs upon the fire could banish it. She knew now that this was no mere ailment, to be treated by rest, or herbs, or doctors. This was something far deeper, a malaise of the soul, from which she could never recover.

She was bedridden, too weak to even leave the confines of William's rooms. She craved the sight of the pale sky, the kiss of the breeze, the pungent smells of the river.

William remained with her, day and night, and yet his attentions were perfunctory, a symptom of necessity. He brought her soup and water and propped her up against the pillows. From time to time he sat with her while she ate, saying nothing, all the while thinking of the painting. She could tell this from the way his eyes flicked continually to his easel and his hands fidgeted nervously, by the way he grew agitated when he was separated from it for too long, and would hurriedly clear away her bowl the moment she indicated she was finished.

These last few days he'd seemed almost resentful, as he hurried to splash the thin, tasteless gruel into the wooden bowl. He'd worked through the nights, snatching only an hour or two of sleep before returning to the canvas. The place reeked, and she knew that sour smell was the scent of her own impending death. Yet still she held on, clinging to the last vestiges of her life – waiting for the painting to be completed.

It had become the centre of their existence. Their world had shrunk to contain just these paltry few rooms and each other, and their only purpose was the completion of the work. She longed to be free of it.

So it was that, with the crowing of the birds one morning in the early spring, William threw down his brushes and issued a heartfelt cry of triumph that threatened to wake the entire neighbourhood.

Ariadne – so weak now that she could barely stir – opened her eyes with startled surprise, forcing herself up on one elbow. "It's done," she said, her voice brittle and dry, like the rasp of barley husks in the wind.

"It's done." He paced to the window, and then to the door, and then back to the easel, as if suddenly lost, or excited, or uncertain. "It's everything I hoped it would be. A portrait for all the ages. You shall be preserved here for all time, a thing of beauty and wonder."

She breathed deeply, and then let it out, steadying her nerves. In all this time, she had seen nothing of the work, not a single glimpse. She almost did not want to see it, for she knew what it represented, what it meant to them both. Yet she had to be sure it had been worth it. She had to know. "Let me see."

He nodded, reaching for the easel. His hands paused upon the frame, as if, even now, he remained hesitant to share it with her. But then he lifted the easel and turned it to face her, and she saw that, for the first time, he had succeeded. He had achieved everything he had set out to do. He had painted the truth.

The woman in the painting was *her*. Not a mere expression of her, not a facsimile rendered in oils; the woman staring back at her was more real than she was. He had captured her essence, painted with the medium of her soul. He had taken everything she was and placed it upon that canvas, and now she, herself, was an empty husk. There was nothing more of her left. He had given her an immortality she had never wanted, a prison made of paint.

"Now I can be with you forever," he said. He crossed to the bed, sat down beside her. He took her hand in his. His skin felt warm. There was no sadness in his eyes. "It's finished, now. You can rest. We both can."

Ariadne wanted to rage at him, to beat her fists upon his chest, to demand he destroy the thing, but the light was fading, and she could no longer muster the strength. Her mind drifting back to that moment, all those months ago, when she had first posed for him in the moonlight, and he had sketched her body, and she had felt truly alive.

She closed her eyes, and quietly slipped away.

It's nearly finished now.

Hours have rolled into days. Time passes in a blur, and if she stops to consider it for too long, she grows nauseous, as if she's suffering from motion sickness like she did as a child, watching the world flit by from the rear seat of her dad's car. She can focus on nothing but the painting.

She hasn't slept for days. There have been moments where she's blacked out, her head lolling forward, unable to continue any longer, but then she's come round again to find herself still sitting at the easel, her hand frantically darting back and forth across the canvas, the brush still firmly gripped between her fingers.

Before her, the woman looks out from the depths of the canvas with a devilish smile, and for the first time, Rae notices that there's something vaguely sinister in the curve of the woman's lips, something knowing, expectant. Where before Rae had read only serenity, amusement, warmth – now she reads desire. It is as if the expression has changed as she's worked, and the closer she's got to completing her work, the more determined the woman's expression has become.

She realises it's time to stop. She's been working too hard, for too long. It's as if the painting has somehow been tightening its grip upon her, and she needs to step away, to break its spell.

She knows this is only tiredness at work. Her mind is beginning to imagine things that aren't there, to read intentions into things that can have no intent. And yet, when she tries to pull away, she feels a soft pressure at her back, encouraging her to stay.

Disturbed, she attempts to put down the paintbrush, but her hand seems to ignore her command, continuing its jaunty dance across the painting. Frowning, she tries again, and this time the pressure is more firm, more insistent – as if someone is leaning on her shoulders, pressing her down into the stool, forcing her hand to keep on working. A cool breath on the back of her neck makes her skin crawl.

She feels panic flare.

"Margot? Margot!"

But Margot isn't there. It's the weekend. There's no one else in the building.

Rae screams, trying urgently to drag herself away from the easel. But she's feeling so weak, so tired, so *cold*, and this other presence, this other person, is so insistent, so strong. She doesn't have the strength to fight back.

She glances up at her hand. The brush is darting around the portrait's eyes, her hand operating under the volition of this *other*. She realises that she's no longer even working with oils; the pigments on her palette must have run out hours ago, yet still colour flows from the tip of the brush, reinvigorating the picture before her eyes. What, then, is she dabbing onto the canvas?

And now she sees what she has missed. The woman in the painting – it's Rae. Somehow, in her delirium, she's lost track, she's missed the moment when the change occurred, when she started to paint *herself* into the portrait.

She doesn't understand what's going on, how all of this is happening to her.

"For all the ages," a woman's voice whispers in her ear.

She knows then that the voice belongs to the woman in the painting – a woman so desperate to be free, to be remembered, that she has coerced Rae into taking her place.

The light is growing dim. Rae feels her hand drop away from the easel. She slumps forward, suddenly released.

But this is no release.

* * *

The woman is looking straight at her, lips curled in an amused half-smile – a smile that is terribly familiar.

Rae stares back, unable to avert her gaze. She's sitting on a stool in a workshop. It's dark, and silvery moonlight slants in through the window behind her. She's wearing a scarlet dress, her hands folded neatly on her lap.

The woman leans closer. "Thank you," she says.

Rae tries to speak, to implore the woman to help her, to not leave her like this – but no words are forthcoming. All she can do is watch.

The woman turns and walks away, and Rae stares after her, a silent scream forming on her unmoving lips.

ONE NEW FOLLOWER
Mark A. Latham

"Here you go, one pint of lager." Dave put two glasses down. Foam dripped over the sides.

"Hmm?" Kyle said, tearing his eyes reluctantly from his phone screen. He frowned a little when he saw that Dave hadn't bothered with a beer-mat. Frowned fully when it finally registered what was in front of him. "I was on ale," he protested, feebly.

"Asked you three times." Dave shrugged. "Glued to your phone, weren't you? Had to make a best guess." He winked at Steve.

"What's so interesting, anyway?" Steve asked, tearing open a bag of salted nuts. "You've barely said a word tonight. *Again.*"

Kyle took one last look at the screen, pressed SEND, and closed the app, shoving the phone back into his jeans pocket. "Alright, alright," he said. "I'm all yours."

"No, come on, don't be all mysterious," Steve pressed, through a mouthful of half-chewed snacks.

"It's his photography app," Dave interrupted. "New obsession." He gave Kyle a knowing smirk.

"It's a bit more than that," Kyle said, slurping the head off his pint. "It's called 'ViewFindr', you know, 'finder' without the 'e'."

"Like Grindr?" Dave asked. Steve snorted lager out of his nose.

"Look, it's a photo app, but it's also a social media platform. No daft filters, no forced crops... It turns your smartphone into a proper camera. Or, rather, it makes your phone act like an artist's sketchbook for getting your compositions right. You just find a subject, go snap-happy, and it auto-uploads to your online workspace. Then your friends offer critique live and raw. Help you perfect the shot."

"*Friends*." Dave sniggered.

"Sounds like a bloody nightmare," Steve said. "Too many cooks..."

"You would say that," Kyle laughed. Steve was an architect, and he was a notorious perfectionist. If anyone so much as glanced at his drawing board when they were in his studio he'd tense up. Offering an opinion before he was finished was strictly *verboten*.

"Anyway," Dave said, "what you're saying is you've got a bunch of virtual mates on your phone who're more interesting than your actual mates. Who you hardly ever see these days, I might add."

"Yeah, yeah." Kyle held up his hands. "Guilty as charged. Look, the phone's away now. I'm all yours."

"Never will understand why you moved to that little village, city boy like you."

"Well, it's for work, innit? Thought it might inspire me." He didn't want to admit that he'd needed a change of air after Cassie had left. He'd moved to a little cottage about fifteen miles outside the city, although it'd had such an impact on his social life it might as well have been a hundred.

"And has it?" Dave asked.

Kyle laughed. "Not really, no. Actually, I'm off out for a proper nature walk tomorrow, so hopefully I'll get some good shots for an exhibition. Found out about it on ViewFindr, as it happens."

As one, his friends rolled their eyes.

Kyle trudged down a narrow footpath, wellingtons caked in mud. His dog, Bertie, ran through the muck gleefully, legs like black socks. It was good to see the old boy happy, but Kyle didn't relish the thought of bathing him later.

He hadn't picked the best day for it. The sky was the colour of tired linen, and fine, gauzy rain drifted from the heavens, settling on Kyle's waterproofs, dripping from the brim of his hood in oily beads. He told himself it was a scouting mission – he'd find some good shots, upload them to ViewFindr, and come back when the light was better for the final photos.

He was hoping that some desolate, melancholy subject would present itself. A pile of rusting farm machinery;

a lightning-blasted tree; a deer carcass half-chewed by a fox. The kind of thing his friends would poke fun at him for, but that would complement his long-unfinished series. His friends, come to think of it, had never understood his work, no more than they'd understood his house move. Steve and Dave looked and sounded like jack-the-lads down the pub, had done ever since the three of them had been thick as thieves at uni, but in real life, they were successful professionals; Steve was a partner in his architect's firm and Dave was a solicitor. They had matching canal-side flats in the city centre, within walking distance of work and their favourite bars. Proper townies. Steve couldn't even drive.

The track ahead narrowed, and sloped inwards in a "v", causing Kyle to take toddler steps as his feet slipped awkwardly in the mud. He couldn't even go off-road: the undergrowth was thick and gnarled and full of thorns. Bertie was having a field day, sticking his head into every bush, prompting the occasional rustle as he disturbed some creature or other.

Kyle checked his phone, covering the screen with a hand to protect it from the rain. He'd been walking for a grand total of thirty minutes from his front door. There was good 4G coverage. He could still just about hear the main road traffic over the wind and the rain. Despite not being far from civilisation, and the footpath being clearly marked, he hadn't encountered another living soul. The random guy on ViewFindr had said hardly anyone ever came here. That morning, Kyle had asked the newsagent, Mr Booth, if he ever came here with his dogs, and the old fellow said he'd never heard of it. Stranger still, this particular walk, although fairly long, didn't seem to have a name on any maps Kyle could find online.

He entered an overgrown field with the whisper of a narrow track winding through it. In the distance, through the grey haze, Kyle could make out the shadow of some buildings, maybe a barn, and a tall mobile phone mast – that explained the coverage. Either side of the field, the undergrowth gave way to neat rows of saplings, their trunks encased in plastic tubes and chicken-wire – maybe Kyle would get some deer photos after all, even if they were live ones.

By the time he made it to the top end of the field, Kyle's legs were burning; the incline was steeper than expected and the mud was only getting deeper. He reached a large gate and leaned against it to take a breath. He was out of shape. Bertie bounded over, looking pleased with himself. The big lab was nine years old but still acted like a pup. Kyle opened the gate, let the dog through first, and followed.

He emerged onto a much wider, somewhat waterlogged track. In front of him was the wall of a massive barn, so Kyle assumed that he must be standing in a tractor lane, although he doubted it was still in use. There were two ways to go: down the hill, presumably back towards the village; or uphill, where the track vanished around the far side of the barn. The way back to the village was tempting. He was wet and hungry. He hadn't seen a single subject worth photographing. Kyle's right foot was ice-cold. He thought maybe his wellie was leaking and muddy water was seeping into his sock. Bertie looked up at him, panting expectantly.

"In for a penny, in for a pound. Come on, boy." Kyle turned right and headed up the slope alongside the barn. It could well be a dead end, in which case he'd head back.

The guy on ViewFindr – what was his handle? BokehBuddy? Something like that – had said the tracks were all interconnected, so it was impossible to get lost. The only thing Kyle had to worry about was trudging too far in the cold and wet with a leaky boot. Still, he had a log-burner and a bath back home, which would seem all the sweeter after his trek.

Kyle marched up the hill, now facing the rain, the wind catching under his hood until all he could hear was it whistling around in his ears. When he rounded the corner of the barn, he stopped dead. This was promising.

Beside the barn was another structure, hidden from view until now. It only had two walls, and a large pitched tin roof supported by tall girders. The floor was concrete, and covered in rubble, lengths of old cable, rubbish, and ripped tarpaulin weighted down with bricks. Kyle wasn't sure what he was looking at – hay storage maybe? It was certainly disused, like the rest of this land. His photographer's eye took in the more unusual details. Graffiti was painted large on the interior walls: LISA + JONO in yellow letters, four feet tall, the usual stuff. All except one piece. A black figure, abstract and blocky, with spiked hair, large round, white eyes. A noose around its neck, the painted rope stretching all the way up the wall until it disappeared into the shadows under the eaves. Nearly twenty feet high? How was it painted? He didn't want to think the words "voodoo doll", but they prised their way into his mind regardless.

And beside that black figure, which Kyle increasingly disliked, was a smaller structure, tucked into the corner. It was a cube, with crumbling walls, covered in scrawled graffiti. The walls were maybe eight feet high, and it seemed to have a flat roof. There was a large door in the centre of the wall facing outwards, ajar, around eight inches thick. The handle was hanging half-off. There were thick electrical cables trailing between the nearby barn and the top of this structure, and they hung down loosely, vanishing into the roof of the cube before him. It looked like a big walk-in freezer, like you'd find in an abattoir – Kyle shuddered as he remembered that day spent photographing in the slaughterhouse.

Kyle noticed for the first time that he couldn't hear anything but his own breath, which frosted in front of his face. He couldn't even hear the rain pattering on the tin roof. He specialised in the macabre, and yet he hadn't seen much that unnerved him like this weird little farm building did. He couldn't take his eyes off the crack in the door, and the darkness behind it.

Kyle forced some rational thoughts into his brain. This was probably a tractor port, and if that little room was powered, it had likely been a workshop. Maybe the farmer had mothballed this place when the phone mast went up, and simply rented the space out to the telecoms company. He was just on edge because the outbuilding had obviously been used by the local colour, and maybe recently. There were cigarette butts and crushed cola cans on the ground; for all he knew there could be druggies or lager louts here every night, and that in itself made him feel a little unsafe. Yes, that was it.

But as it was daylight and he hadn't seen another soul, he'd probably be okay. He stepped over the threshold, onto the concrete. As soon as he set foot on the hard ground, the wind seemed to get under his jacket, and he shivered as though someone had dropped an ice cube down his back. He paused for just a moment, cursed at his own silliness, and stepped closer. Kyle took out his phone – still 4G, excellent. He opened ViewFindr. The in-app camera was better than the one on his phone sometimes. If this place unsettled him, it'd make for some great interactions. He took a snap of the cube-shaped structure.

Uploading.

He went closer and took another.

Uploading.

He heard a low rumble behind him. He turned round and realised it was Bertie. Head bowed, hackles up, growling.

"Christ, Bertie, don't do that," Kyle said. But the sound of his own voice spooked him, because what if there was someone behind that door? Some wino, or some glue-sniffing kid with a knife?

"Stupid," Kyle muttered, now finding it reassuring to say it out loud. "It's not the big city, mate."

His phone buzzed in his hand, making him jump.

One new follower.

"That was quick." He clicked on it, welcoming the distraction. No username. Avatar just a black circle. "Weird." Kyle frowned. He didn't think it was possible to have a blank username.

He turned back to the structure, trying his hardest to ignore Bertie. The old boy wasn't always the sharpest tool in the box, although he wasn't easily spooked. Unlike his master, apparently.

Kyle took a breath, marched up to the door, and swung it open.

The door creaked with the rust of ages, the grinding metal making far too much noise for Kyle's liking. Foul air rushed out of the room, blowing around Kyle's hood like a rasping breath. His stomach lurched, like he expected to see something horrible behind the door. But no one leapt out at him. Not a creature stirred within. It was just a dark, square room that smelled of damp and piss. The walls were covered in large tiles, probably asbestos, which bloomed with black mould. The ceiling was intersected by steel joists, from which a broken lamp hung by a chain. The room was no more than ten feet across. Light from the broken roof filtered in weakly, but was reluctant to illuminate the far corners, which remained stubbornly shrouded in darkness.

He took three shots, uncharacteristically imprecise, really not wanting to linger more than necessary. To get the best composition, he took another couple with the flash on, and found himself looking away when the flash went off, like he was scared of what he might see.

"Pity's sake," he hissed to himself. "Man up, Kyle."

With that, he swung the door to, as he'd found it, flinching again when the closing door revealed the voodoo graffiti. From where he stood, it was like it was looking at him.

Bertie barked.

"Yeah, you don't have to tell me twice," Kyle said, as the dog took two steps backwards. Kyle tramped away from the barn, back onto the grass and mud, pressing "Upload All" as he went.

It took Kyle another hour to complete the network of paths and tracks, and although the weather brightened a little, his heart wasn't really in it. Everything seemed more still and quiet than before. Kyle couldn't hear any birdsong, or scurrying animals – all those sounds that he'd taken for granted before passing by that barn. Bertie no longer rooted about in the bushes, instead plodding along at Kyle's side. The old boy must be tired.

Although the rain hadn't stopped, Kyle felt compelled to pull his hood back, acutely aware of his lack of peripheral vision, and he had a growing sense that there was someone following him. Or, at least, watching.

Definitely watching, like eyes burning a hole in the back of his head. But of course, every time he stopped and looked around, there was no one.

Not a living soul.

By the time Kyle had bathed the dog, had a soak himself, and got the fire going in the lounge, he felt unusually tired. It was early evening, already dark, and he'd got the heebie-jeebies so bad earlier that the usually cosy cottage wasn't the slightest comfort. Kyle sank into his favourite armchair with a cheeky whiskey and picked up his phone. But he didn't open ViewFindr. Something gave him pause. He had to admit to himself that he didn't want to review the photos he'd taken. Maybe he'd do it later; or, better still, tomorrow morning, when it was light. He put the phone down again.

Kyle realised he felt very alone in the quiet old cottage, even with Bertie curled up by his feet. He turned the TV on to inject a bit of life into the room. Even when his phone pinged to tell him his photos had received a new Like, he didn't open the app. He took a few sips of whiskey, tried and failed to concentrate on the game show on TV, and before he knew it he felt his eyelids droop, his breathing grow heavier.

Must be all the fresh air, he thought. *A little nap won't hurt.*

* * *

Kyle felt something cold and wet on his skin. He tried to open his eyes, but they were gummy with sleep, his eyelashes sticking together, sight blurring. It was dark. He was moving.

Half-asleep, panic gripped him, rising in a wave. He felt ice-cold wind on his legs, his arms, his back, all over. His feet slid through damp grass, the blades tickling his shins, toes digging into sucking mud. Something was closed tight around his wrists: bony fingers. Several pairs of hands. He was being dragged.

He fought to open his eyes, tried to move his sluggish limbs, eventually managing to dig his feet just a little deeper into the soft earth. This resistance was met by tightening grips and painful yanks that threatened to tear Kyle's arms out of their sockets. His head felt heavy. He tried to raise it, but it lolled about on his neck like a dead fish. He saw mud-caked shoes poking from under black skirts. Or robes. He couldn't speak. Couldn't cry out.

A sudden pain at his ankles jarred him to lucidity. His feet bashed against something hard and then scraped along rough ground. There was concrete beneath him, strewn with rubbish. The footsteps of his captors rang out on the hard surface.

Kyle tried again to look up, catching sight of a thick, metalled door set into a crumbling wall. His head flopped down again. Rusty hinges groaned. And then he was yanked hard forwards, into pitch darkness. His feet slipped on slime. His nostrils filled with decay, and something fouler. He managed to babble at last, "Wh... what are you doing? Who are you?"

There was no reply but for the rustle of robes in this dreadful place of stillness and quiet and dark.

Something was slipped around his neck, tightening painfully. He knew it was a noose even before it began to drag him upwards, raising his body from the hard floor. He opened his eyes now, but it was so dark it did him no good. There was a shaft of moonlight beyond the heavy door, but it couldn't find its way inside. Not in here.

Kyle started to choke. All he could do was claw at the rope around his neck. Bile rose in his throat but had nowhere to go. His thoughts were a jumble; he wanted to think of a way out, but all he could do was wish he could scream as his feet left the ground and he was hoisted up, up, into black.

The barking dog jolted Kyle awake. Whiskey sloshed from the glass in his hand onto his trouser leg.

Kyle's heart pounded in his chest. His thoughts were fogged. The room was dark. But as his breathing slowed, he realised he was in his cottage, in his chair. The fire was out. Bertie barked once more, then whined. The dog was looking at the floor, where Kyle's phone blinked and vibrated.

"What a nightmare..."

The lounge was cast in a cold, greyish light that streamed in around the edges of the blinds.

"Shit!" Kyle clicked on a lamp, set his tumbler down, and retrieved the phone that must have fallen off the chair arm as he'd slept. The phone's lock screen displayed 6:57 AM. He'd slept for over twelve hours. "Impossible…"

He swiped open the phone.

ViewFindr: 127 notifications. Alright, that was unusual.

It was with some trepidation that Kyle opened the app, and the first thing he saw was the message board.

Is this for real?

FFS, sicko.

Nice Photoshop, but not really suitable for ViewFindr.

This isn't a horror site!

Blocked and reported.

"What the hell?" Kyle tried to type a reply, but was met only by a message:

This function is temporarily suspended while we investigate a breach of our terms and conditions. Thank you for your patience.

Kyle scrolled up to his gallery, and his blood ran cold.

His last three shots in the series were motion-blurred, hastily composed, and entirely unexpected. Each showed, in varying levels of detail, a dead woman, hanged from a steel joist. She was naked, her body bruised and filthy. Her eyes bulged. Her lips were cracked and blue.

Kyle shook uncontrollably. Bile rose in his throat. He held his head in his hands. He couldn't work out what was happening. Had he been hacked?

He stood up, his legs like jelly.

A bang on the front door: three loud raps. Kyle almost screamed.

He threw the phone into the armchair and staggered over to the window, opened the blind slowly, no longer certain of anything. When he saw a police uniform he didn't know whether to be relieved or even more afraid. A second man, with two-day stubble and a cheap suit, held up an ID card to Kyle's window. His expression was not reassuring.

The door of the gloomy interview room opened, and DI Stein entered, carrying a stack of folders and evidence bags. He took his seat on the other side of the table.

"Look," Kyle said, wearily. "I've been here all day, and there's still no charge. You must know I haven't done anything. How many times do we—"

Stein held up a hand, and Kyle shut up at once. Without saying a word, he opened a polythene bag, removed Kyle's phone, and slid it across the table.

"It's your lucky day, Mr Watson," the detective said, his voice almost a growl. "Digital forensics back up your story. The original images on your phone do not match the indecent images uploaded to the app."

"Told you!" Kyle said, with a mixture of relief and anger. He looked uncertainly to his court-appointed solicitor, who said nothing. "So… I can go?"

"Not so fast. We still need to finish examining your computer, to make sure the photo-editing wasn't done by you."

"Of course it wasn't! I uploaded those shots from my phone, I told you a thousand times."

"Yes, and then went to sleep, and woke up this morning to find you'd been hacked. Convenient. Tell me, Mr Watson, what made you visit Dewberry Farm yesterday?"

"I didn't even know it was called Dewberry Farm. Someone online told me about the walk. Thought it'd be good to take the dog, maybe get a few photos. I'm a professional photographer; that's what I do."

"And you maintain that you don't know the history of the place?"

"I haven't lived in the village very long. I don't really know much about anywhere around there yet. All I know is it's a nice, quiet walk."

"Do you know why it's so quiet, Mr Watson? It's because, less than ten years ago, a woman was found hanged in that tractor shed you found. More specifically, in the workshop you photographed. This woman." Stein opened a folio, and passed three photographs over.

Kyle could barely focus on them. He saw bulging eyes, pallid, naked flesh, dark lips, lank hair. He turned away, queasy.

"That was Amanda Bartlett, aged twenty-eight, resident of Dewberry Farm, just four miles from where you live. Left her home in the middle of the night, later found hanged in the workshop. Official verdict was recorded as suicide, despite various strange circumstances. Her brother, Mr Thomas Bartlett, maintains that she was coerced into killing herself by a weird cult that she joined on the internet. Nothing substantiated. I like to think of it as unsolved. But that's not the strangest part, Mr Watson."

Kyle looked at Stein uncertainly. The detective was impassive.

"Those are coroner's photographs from the scene," Stein went on. "They're the only images in existence of Amanda Bartlett's body, or so we thought. The pictures uploaded to your account on the ViewFindr app are a definite match for the victim. But they aren't the same photographs. They're different, as though someone else took photos before the coroner got there, and saved them, just for this."

"I... I hadn't even heard of this village ten years ago," Kyle said. "I was living down South. I can prove it."

"The other strange thing," Stein said, ignoring Kyle entirely, "is that your photographs—"

"They're not mine!"

"—Your photographs aren't scans. They're original, digital photographs, probably taken with a mobile phone camera at the scene. Now, the backgrounds match your originals, so the figure of Miss Bartlett must be superimposed. But the positioning is congruous with the angle of the shots in every photo. Forensics say it's the best fake they've ever seen. Almost like the pictures were carefully staged. By a professional."

"Check the metadata. That'll prove it."

"It's been stripped." Stein gave Kyle that stony look again.

Kyle twitched a little. "Well… it's easy enough to erase metadata. There's an app for it."

"Interesting that you know all about these things, Mr Watson."

"Look… Like I said, I wasn't here ten years ago. I'd just graduated from uni. I was working for a local paper… Maybe they can verify where I was."

"I'll be sure to check."

"My client has a point," the solicitor said, making a rare contribution. "It seems more likely that someone with local knowledge used my client's photographs to play a joke, in rather poor taste. Perhaps you should be looking into the users of this photography app."

"We are. But your client can't prove he hasn't obtained these images from someone else," Stein said. "When forensics have finished with his computer, we'll know for sure."

"And how long will that take?" Kyle groaned.

"As long as it takes."

* * *

It took the rest of the day. Kyle returned to a dark, empty cottage, tired and hungry. He'd first had to call round, shame-faced, to the elderly neighbours he hardly knew, to retrieve Bertie from his emergency accommodation. Apparently, the old boy had been "no trouble at all", which was something. And Kyle struggled to get away from the woman who wanted to know what had happened at the police station.

Much as he wanted to forget everything, Kyle felt the strands of a mystery tugging at his mind like a jacket sleeve caught on an old nail. He didn't have his computer, and so he looked to his phone, ignoring the notifications flashing for attention on ViewFindr. He found scant information on Amanda Bartlett, just a quote from her brother, Tom, from years ago.

"Our lives were never the same after she met those people on the internet. Sending her messages day and night. And then one night she got something that rattled her. I'll never know what it was – they never found her phone. But those people, whoever they were; maybe they didn't kill her, but they might as well have. I'll not rest until I've found out the truth."

Kyle checked the phone book. No Bartletts in the village, unless they were ex-directory. He wasn't sure what good tracking them down might do anyway, except upset a bereaved sibling. Instead, he called Steve.

Half an hour later, he was on the bus into town, feeling guilty about leaving Bertie once more. Half an hour after that, he was in a pub, taking as much comfort as possible from the chatter of regulars, garish lights, modern décor. He told his story to Steve as best he could, leaving out only those parts that made him sound neurotic. Or worse, a coward.

"So, what… are you a suspect?" Steve looked grave.

"Maybe. I don't know. They kept my computer and my external drive. Five years of work on there; if they mess up those image files I'm screwed."

"So you and I both know that someone's messing with you. Hacker? But it has to be someone who knows you live in the village, right? Someone who knows the crime scene, and might even have taken those photos ten years ago."

"Shit, that's right. What if… what if the person that did it killed her?"

Steve took a big gulp of his lager. "Let's not get carried away. You said it was someone on that app who pointed you towards the walk?"

"Yeah, yeah… *Bokeh*-something. The police have already been through my account with a fine-tooth comb. God knows what they made of all my weird stuff. I'm probably on a bloody watch list now."

"Focus, mate," Steve said. "This Bokeh fella – he on there still?"

"I'll have a look."

Kyle took out his phone, opened the app – ignoring the unread messages this time – and instead cycled through the notifications, scouring them for the message in question. But he stopped short.

"You alright, mate?" Steve asked. "Look like you've seen a ghost."

"Just... a reminder. When I uploaded the first pictures of the shed, I got a new follower, instantly. It stuck in my mind because it had a blank username, and a black avi. Thought it was a spam-bot, y'know? But it just feels like too much of a coincidence now."

"Okay, can you click on it, see if there's any info?"

"Yeah. Oh... bugger." Kyle had tapped the blank username, and was met with a placeholder profile, and the message: *This user has deleted their account.*

"What's up?"

"They've deleted their account. What if... they're the ones who set me up? They might have even reported it. And now they're gone, anonymous."

"Or it could be a spam-bot like you said. Is there anything you can find out about it? Any info at all."

Kyle tapped on the black avatar and pinch-zoomed. "Huh, I thought this was just solid black, but there's an image here." Kyle saved the image to his phone gallery and opened it up in an editor app. Now he felt sure there was something organic there. Was that the shape of an arm maybe? So what was that above it? He pinch-zoomed as far as he could on some dark grey, pixellated blobs in the middle of his phone screen, clicked on brightness and contrast, and did what he could to bring the shapes into view. If he could just brighten it a little more...

"Fuck!" Kyle leapt out of his seat. The phone flew from his hands, hitting hard laminate with a crunch.

Steve nearly jumped out of his skin at the abruptness of Kyle's reaction; every head in the pub turned to look.

Kyle slid back into his seat. Steve was asking him if he was okay, but he could barely register his friend's words. He shook like a man with pneumonia. His head swam. He thought he might be sick.

Steve picked up the phone. "Crap, mate. You've done a number on this. Completely dead."

"I… I think I should go home."

"What the hell did you see? Was it a message or something? Has someone threatened you?"

"No. I don't know. Look, it's all been a bit weird. I think I might have imagined it. I appreciate you coming out with me… maybe I could call you tomorrow, when I'm not so stressed, yeah?"

Steve frowned. "You don't seem yourself. Why not come and stay at my place?"

"No… I need some time alone, to get my head straight. Besides, the police will probably be calling tomorrow. It'll look suspect if I'm not home."

"Fair enough. Look, don't catch the bus. Let me get you a taxi."

"I… I can't really afford a taxi." That was the first time Kyle had admitted any such thing to Steve. He reddened.

"It's on me," Steve said, without pausing for breath.

Kyle staggered out into the cold air like a drunkard. He felt numb, in shock. Steve helped him into a black cab and gave the driver a twenty.

Kyle just needed tomorrow to come. He wanted

daylight and normality, and then maybe he could work out what the hell to do. When he got home, it was all he could do to drag himself to bed, where he lay awake, trembling, for what seemed like hours, until he grew so tired that even the strangely unfamiliar creaking of the old cottage could no longer keep him from sleep.

The ground slid beneath him, wet and glistening, ice-cold on his bare skin. Kyle felt groggy, his mouth dry and cottony. He felt strong hands around his wrists and forearms; felt them yank at him, and his knees hit concrete and scraped across a hard floor.

Footsteps echoed in darkness. Robes swished. Kyle thought he must be dreaming. It wasn't so bad if he was dreaming. He tried to speak, but his lips were dry and his throat claggy, and no sound came from his mouth except for a phlegmy rasp.

Rusty hinges groaned. The door. He knew where he was. Another yank. He was over the threshold now, where it was so dark he couldn't even see the floor anymore.

Someone whispered. Kyle didn't understand what they were saying.

Then came the noose.

Must be dreaming. Must be dreaming.

The rope pulled tight, pressing on his Adam's apple, making him gag.

His feet scrabbled on the rough ground. He felt himself rise, like he was flying, and he couldn't breathe.

He spluttered a last breath, then no more would come. He couldn't feel the ground anymore. His eyes felt like they would pop out of his head. The whispering stopped. Footsteps receded. He was alone, dying.

When his own grunts ceased and all he could hear was the creaking of the rope, he spun, weightless, on the end of the noose. Turning in darkness.

Turning to see a woman, face-to-face in a sliver of moonlight, hanging, like him. Pale and bruised and dirty.

Her eyelids rolled open to reveal bulging bloodshot eyes. She was dead. But her cracked, blue lips curled into a smile.

All resistance slipped away. He didn't wake up. He just swayed on his rope, and she on hers. Her glassy eyes were black circles, and he thought he saw a shape reflected in them, indistinct and grey. Was that an arm? A face? It was a hanged man. Kyle Watson. That was him, wasn't it? Kyle couldn't think straight.

He'd seen this before, in another life maybe. It had frightened him then, but not now. Now he understood.

They looked at each other until the light went out of his eyes, and there was no one left on Dewberry Farm.

Not a living soul.

A HAUNTED HOUSE IS A WHEEL UPON WHICH SOME ARE BROKEN

Paul Tremblay

ARRIVAL

Fiona arranged for the house to be empty and for the door to be left open. She has never lived far from the house. It was there, a comfort, a threat, a reminder, a Stonehenge, a totem to things that actually happened to her. The house was old when she was a child. That her body has aged faster than the house (there are so many kinds of years; there are dog-years and people-years and house-years and geological-years and cosmic-years) is a joke and she laughs at it, with it, even though all jokes are cruel. The house is a New England colonial, blue with red and white shutters and trim, recently painted, the first floor windows festooned with carved flower boxes. She stands in the house's considerable shadow. She was once very small, and then she became big, and now she is becoming smaller again, and that process is painful but not without joy and an animal-sense of satisfaction that the coming end is earned. She thinks of endings and beginnings as she climbs the five steps onto the front porch. Adjacent to the front door and to her left is a white historical placard with the year 1819 and the house's name. Her older brother, Sam, said that you could never say the house's name out loud or you would wake up the ghosts, and she never did say the name, not even once. The ghosts were there anyway. Fiona never liked the house's name and thought it was silly, and worse, because of the name pre-existing and now post-existing it means that the house was never hers. Despite everything, she wanted it to always be hers.

– Fiona hesitates to open the front door. Go to pg 305 THE FRONT DOOR
– Fiona decides to not go inside the house after all and walks back to her car. Go to pg 333 LEAVING THE HOUSE

THE FRONT DOOR

It's like Fiona has always and forever been standing at the front door. She places a hand on the wood and wonders what is on the other side, what has changed, what has remained the same. Change is always on the other side of a door. Open a door. Close a door. Walk in. Walk out. Repeat. It's a loop, or a wheel. She doesn't open the door and instead imagines a practice-run; her opening the door and walking through the house, stepping lightly into each of the rooms, careful not to disturb anything, and she is methodical in itemizing and identifying the ghosts, and she feels what she thinks she is going to feel, and she doesn't linger in either the basement or her parents' bedroom, and she eventually walks out of the house, and all of this is still in her head, and she closes the door, then turns around, stands in the same spot she's standing in now, and places a hand on the wood and wonders what is on the other side, what has changed, what has remained the same.

– Fiona opens the door. Go to pg 306 ENTRANCEWAY
– Fiona is not ready to open the door. Go to pg 305
THE FRONT DOOR
– Fiona decides to walk back to the car and not go inside the house. Go to pg 333 LEAVING THE HOUSE

ENTRANCEWAY

Fiona gently pushes the front door closed, watches it nestle into the frame, and listens for the latching mechanism to click into place before turning her full attention to the house. The house. The house. The house. Sam said because the house was so old and historical (he pronounced it his-store-ickle so that it rhymed with pickle) there was a ghost in every one of the rooms. He was right. The house is a ghost too. That's obvious. That all the furniture, light fixtures, and decorations will be different (most of everything will be antique, or made to look antique; the present owners take their caretakers-of-a-living-museum role seriously) and the layout changed from when she lived here won't matter because she's not here to catalogue those differences. She'll only have eyes for the ghost house. Fiona says, Hello? because she wants to hear what she sounds like in the house of the terrible now. She says hello again and her voice runs up the stairs and around banisters and bounces off plaster and crown molding and sconces, and she finds the sound of the now-her in the house pleasing and a possible antidote to the poison of nostalgia and regret, so she says hello again, and louder. Satisfied with her re-introduction, Fiona asks, Okay, where should we go first?

– *Fiona turns to her right and walks into the living room. Go to pg 308* LIVING ROOM
– *Fiona walks straight ahead into the dining room.*

Go to *pg 310* DINING ROOM
   – The weight of the place and its history and her history is too much; Fiona abruptly turns around and leaves the house. Go to *pg 333* LEAVING THE HOUSE

LIVING ROOM

Dad builds a fire and uses all the old newspaper to do it and pieces glowing orange at their tips break free and float up into the flue, moving as though they are alive and choosing flight. Fiona and Sam shuffle their feet on the throw rug and then touch the cast iron radiator, their static electric shocks so big at times, a blue arc is visible. Mom sits on the floor so that Fiona can climb onto the couch and jump onto her back. A bushel and a peck and a hug around the neck. The fire is out and the two of them are by themselves and Sam pokes around in the ashes with a twig. Sam says that Little Laurence Montague was a chimney sweep, the best and smallest in the area, and he cleaned everyone's chimney, but he got stuck and died in this chimney, so stuck, in fact, they would not be able to get his body out without tearing the house apart so the homeowners built a giant fire that they kept burning for twenty-two days, until there was no more Little Laurence left, not even his awful smell. Sam says that you can see him, or parts of him anyway, all charred and misshapen, sifting through the ash, looking for his pieces, and if you aren't careful, he'll take a piece from you. Fiona makes sure to stay more than an arm's length away from the fireplace. Of all the ghosts, Little Laurence scares her the most, but she likes to watch him pick through the ash, hoping to see him find those pieces of himself. There are so many.

– *Fiona curls into the dining room.* Go to pg 310 DINING ROOM

– *Fiona walks to the kitchen.* Go to pg 312 KITCHEN

– *This is already harder than she thought it was going to be; impossible, in fact. Fiona doesn't think she can continue and leaves the house.* Go to pg 333 LEAVING THE HOUSE

DINING ROOM

Fiona and Sam are under the table and their parents' legs float by like branches flowing down a river. The floorboards underneath groan and whisper and they understand their house, know it as a musical instrument. Dad sits by himself and wants Fiona and Sam to come out from under the table and talk to him; they do and then he doesn't know what to say or how to say it; her father is so young and she never realized how young he is. Mom isn't there. She doesn't want to be there. Sam says there was an eight-year-old girl named Maisy who had the strictest of parents, the kind who insisted children did not speak during dinner, and poor Maisy was choking on a piece of potato from a gloopy beef stew and she was so terrified of what her parents would do if she said anything, made any sort of noise, she sat and quietly choked to death. Sam says you can see her at the table sitting there with her face turning blue and her eyes as large and white as hardboiled eggs and if you get too close she will wrap her hands around your neck and you won't be able to call out or say anything until it's too late. Of all the ghosts, Maisy scares Fiona the most, and she watches in horror as Maisy sits at the table trying to be a proper girl.

   – Fiona walks straight ahead and into the kitchen.
Go to pg 312 KITCHEN
   – Fiona turns right and walks into the living room.
Go to pg 308 LIVING ROOM

    – *Fiona bypasses the kitchen entirely and goes to the basement.* Go to pg 314 BASEMENT

    – *This is harder than she thought it was going to be; impossible, in fact. Fiona doesn't think she can continue and leaves the house.* Go to pg 333 LEAVING THE HOUSE

KITCHEN

Dad cooks fresh flounder and calls it "fried French" and not fish so that Fiona will eat it. The four of them play card games (cribbage, mainly) and Fiona leaves the room in tears after being yelled at (Dad says he wasn't yelling, which isn't the same as saying he's sorry) for continually leading into runs and allowing Sam and Mom to peg. Mom sits at the table by herself and says she feels fine and smokes a cigarette. Her mother is so young and Fiona never realized how young she is. Sam screams and cries and smashes glasses and dishes on the hardwood floor and no one stops him. Fiona and Mom stand at the back door and look outside, waiting for the birds to eat the stale breadcrumbs they sprinkled about their small backyard. Sam says there was a boy named Percy who was even smaller than Little Laurence. He was so small because the only thing he would eat was blueberry muffins, and he loved those muffins so much he crawled inside the oven so that he could better watch the muffin batter rise and turn golden brown. Sam says that you can see him curled up inside the oven and if you get too close he'll pull you in there with him. Of all the ghosts, Percy scares Fiona the most because of how small he is; she knows it's not polite but she can't help but stare at his smallness.

– Fiona saves the basement for later and walks through the dining room, the living room, and then into the den. Go to pg 315 DEN

– *Fiona backtracks into the dining room.* Go to pg 310 DINING ROOM

– *Fiona goes to the living room.* Go to pg 308 LIVING ROOM

– *Fiona goes into the basement.* Go to pg 314 BASEMENT

– *This is harder than she thought it was going to be; impossible, in fact. Fiona doesn't think she can continue and leaves the house.* Go to pg 333 LEAVING THE HOUSE

BASEMENT

Fiona is not ready for the basement, not just yet.

– *Fiona saves the basement for later and walks through the dining room, the living room, and then into the den.* Go to pg 315 DEN

– *Fiona goes into the kitchen.* Go to pg 312 KITCHEN

– *The idea of going into the basement is enough to make her abandon the tour and leave the house.* Go to pg 333 LEAVING THE HOUSE

DEN

Sam is never delicate closing the French doors and their little rectangular windows rattle and quiver in their frames. Fiona rearranges the books in the built-in, floor-to-ceiling bookshelves; first alphabetical by author, then by title, then by color-scheme. Dad shuts the lights off in the rest of the house, leaving only the den well-lit; he hides, and dares his children to come out and find him, and he laughs as they scream with a mix of mock and real terror. Dad and Mom put Sam and Fiona in the den by themselves and shut the French doors (controlled, and careful) because they are having a private talk. Mom sits on the couch and watches the evening news with a cup of tea and invites Fiona and Sam to watch with her so that they will know what's going on in the world. Sam and Fiona lay on the floor, on their stomachs, blanket over their heads, watching a scary movie. Sam stands in front of the TV and stiff-arms Fiona away, physically blocking her from changing the channel. Mom lets Fiona take a puff of her cigarette and Fiona's lungs are on fire and she coughs, cries, and nearly throws up, and Mom rubs her back and says remember this so you'll never do it again. Sam says there was a girl named Olivia who liked to climb the bookcases in the walls and wouldn't stop climbing the shelves even after her parents begged her not to, and in an effort to stop her, they filled the bookcases with the heaviest leather-bound books with the largest spines that could squeeze into the shelves. Olivia was determined to still climb the shelves and touch the ceiling like she'd always done, and she almost made it to the top again, but her feet slipped, or maybe it was she couldn't get a good handhold anymore, and she fell and broke her neck. Sam says you can see Olivia high up, close to the ceiling, clinging to the shelves, and if you get too close Olivia throws books at you, the heaviest ones, the ones that can do the most damage. Of all the ghosts, Olivia scares Fiona the most, but she wants to read the books that Olivia throws at her.

– *Fiona goes back to the entranceway and to the front stairs. Go to pg 317* THE STAIRS
– *Fiona goes into the kitchen. Go to pg 312* KITCHEN
– *The first floor is enough. Fiona doesn't think she can continue and leaves the house. Go to pg 333* LEAVING THE HOUSE

THE STAIRS

Sam ties his green army men to pieces of kite string and dangles them from the banister on the second floor and Fiona is on the first floor, pretending to be a tiger that swipes at the army men, and if foolishly dropped low enough, she eats the men in one gulp. Fiona counts the stairs and makes a rhyme. Dad falls down the stairs (after being dared by Sam that he can't hop down on only one foot) and punches through the plaster on the first landing with his shoulder; Dad brushes himself off, shakes his head, and points at the hole and says don't tell Mom. Mom walks up the stairs by herself for the last time (Fiona knows there's a last time for everything), moving slowly and breathing heavy, and she looks back at Fiona who trails behind, pretending not to watch, and Mom rests on the first landing and says there's a kitty cat that seems to be following her, and she says that cat is still with her when she pauses on the second landing. Sam says there was a boy named Timothy who always climbed up the stairs on the outside of the railings, his toes clinging to the edges of treads as though he was at the edges of great cliffs. Climbing over the banister on the second floor was the hardest part, and one morning he fell, bouncing off the railings and he landed head-first in the entranceway below, and he didn't get up and brush himself off. Sam says that Timothy tries to trip you when you are not careful on the stairs. Of all the ghosts, Timothy scares Fiona the most, but she still walks on the stairs without holding onto the railings.

— *Fiona walks up the stairs without holding the railing (and actually smiles to herself), and then goes into her bedroom.* Go to pg 319 FIONA'S BEDROOM

— *The stairs make Fiona incredibly, inexplicably sad and Fiona doesn't think she can continue and leaves the house.* Go to pg 333 LEAVING THE HOUSE

FIONA'S BEDROOM

She spies out the window, which overlooks the front door, and being that their house is on top of a hill, it overlooks the rest of the town, and she picks a spot that is almost as far as she can see and wonders what the people there are doing and thinking. Dad reads her *The Tale of Mr. Jeremy Fisher* using a British accent; it's the only storybook for which he uses the accent. Mom takes the cold facecloth off of Fiona's forehead, thermometer from her mouth, and says scoot over, I'll be sick with you, okay? That night Dad isn't allowed in her room and he knocks quietly and he says that he's sorry if he scared her in the basement and he's sorry about dinner and he's making it right now and please open the door and come out, and he sounds watery, and she's not mad or scared (she is hungry) but tells him to go away. Sam is not allowed in her room but he comes in anyway and gets away with it and he smiles that smile she hates. She misses that smile terribly now for as much of a pain in the ass as he was as a child, he was a loyal, thoughtful, sensitive, if not melancholy, man. Sam says that there is the ghost of a girl named Wanda in her closet and no one knows what happened to her or how she got there because she's always been there. Of all of the ghosts, Wanda scares Fiona the most because try as she might, she's never been able to talk to her.

  — *Fiona will go to all of the second-floor rooms in their proper order, waiting until she's ready to go to her*

parents' bedroom. Go to pg 321 SAM'S BEDROOM
   – *The second floor is indeed too much. Fiona doesn't think she can continue and leaves the house. Go to pg 333* LEAVING THE HOUSE

Sam's bedroom

Fiona sits outside Sam's room and the door is shut and Sam and his friends are inside talking about the Boston Red Sox and the Wynne sisters that live two streets over. Fiona finds magazines filled with pictures of naked women under his bed. Dad is inside Sam's room yelling at (and maybe even hitting) Sam because Sam hit Fiona because Fiona took some of his green army men and threw them down in the sewer because Sam wouldn't play with her. Sam lets Fiona sleep on the floor in a sleeping bag (she always asked to do this) because they watched a scary movie and she can't sleep but isn't scared and tries to stay awake long enough to notice how different it is sleeping in Sam's room. Mom hides under Sam's piled bed sheets and blankets and they trick Dad into going into Sam's room and she jumps out and scares him so badly he falls down on the floor and holds his chest. Sam tells Fiona to come into his room and she's worried he's going to sneak attack, give her a dead arm or something, and instead he's crying and says that they aren't going to live in this house anymore. Sam says that there aren't any ghosts in his room and tells her to stop asking about it so Fiona makes one up. She says that there's a boy who got crushed underneath all of his dirty clothes that piled up to the ceiling and no one ever found the boy and Sam never takes his dirty clothes downstairs because he's afraid of the boy. Of all the ghosts, this one scares Fiona the most because she forgot to name him.

– *Fiona goes into the bathroom. Go to pg 323* BATHROOM

– *The second floor is indeed too much. Fiona doesn't think she can continue and leaves the house. Go to pg 333* LEAVING THE HOUSE

BATHROOM

Dad leaves the bathroom door open when he shaves his face and he says there goes my nose and oops no more lips and I guess I don't need a chin. The shaving foam is so white and puffy when Fiona puts it on her face, and she greedily inhales its minty, menthol smell. Sam is in the bathroom for a long, long time with what he says are his comic books. Mom is strong and she doesn't cry anywhere else in the house, certainly never in front of Fiona or Sam, but she cries when she's by herself and taking a bath and the water is running; the sound of a bath being run never fails to make Fiona think about Mom. Everyone else is in her parents' bedroom and to her great, never-ending shame, Fiona is in the bathroom with the door shut, sitting on the floor, the tile hard and cold on her backside, the bath running, the drain unstopped so the tub won't fill, and she cries, and Dad knocks gently on the door and asks if she's okay and asks her to come back, but she stays in the bathroom for hours and until after it's over. Sam says that there was a boy named Charlie who loved to take baths and stayed in them so long that his toes and feet and hands and everything got so wrinkly that his whole body shriveled and shrank and he eventually slipped right down the drain. Sam says that if you stay in the bath too long Charlie will suck you into the drain with him. Of all the ghosts, Fiona finds Charlie the least scary, but she talks to him in the drain.

– *Fiona goes into the hallway and stands in front of her parents' bedroom.* Go to pg 325 PARENTS' BEDROOM DOOR

– *Fiona stays in the bathroom, like she did those many years ago.* Go to pg 323 BATHROOM

– *Fiona doesn't think she can continue and leaves the house.* Go to pg 333 LEAVING THE HOUSE

PARENTS' BEDROOM DOOR

The door is closed. It's the only door in her haunted house that is closed. Even the door to the basement in the kitchen is open. The door is closed. It's a Saturday afternoon and the door is closed and locked, and Fiona knocks and Mom says please give them a few minutes of privacy and giggles from deep down somewhere in her room, and Fiona knocks again and then Dad is yelling at her to get lost. The door is closed because it's almost Christmas and she doesn't believe in Santa anymore but hasn't said anything, and she knows she can't go in there because their presents are wrapped and stacked along one bedroom wall. The door is closed and Mom's smallest voice is telling her that she can come in, but Fiona doesn't want to. Fiona places a hand on the wood and her hand is a ghost of her younger hands. She wonders what is on the other side, what has changed, what has remained the same. Change is always on the other side of a door. Open a door. Close a door. Walk in. Walk out. Repeat. It's a loop, or a wheel. Of all the ghosts, the ones in her parents' bedroom scare her the most because maybe nothing ever changes and even though she's an adult (and likes to think of herself at this age as *beyond-adult* because its connotations are so much more dignified and well-earned than the title *elderly*) she's afraid she'll make the same decisions all over again.

– *Fiona opens the door. Go to pg 327* PARENTS' BEDROOM

– *Fiona returns to the bathroom. Go to pg 323*
BATHROOM
– *Fiona doesn't think she can continue and leaves the house. Go to pg 333* LEAVING THE HOUSE

PARENTS' BEDROOM

Sam and Fiona wrestle Dad on the bed with his signature move being a blanket tossed over their bodies like a net so that he can tickle them with impunity. Fiona tells Mom that Dad shouldn't have hit Sam because she kind of deserved what he did to her for throwing his army men in the sewer. Mom stands in the room wearing only a loose-fitting bra and underwear, and she yells at her clothes, discarded and piled at the edge of the bed, saying nothing she has fits her anymore, and she says it's all just falling off of her. It's Christmas morning and Sam and Fiona sit in the dark and on the floor next to Mom's side of the bed, watching the clock, waiting for 6 a.m. so that they can all go downstairs. Mom is in bed; she's home from the hospital and she says she is not going back. Despite the oppressive heat, Fiona sleeps wedged between her parents during a thunderstorm, counting Mississippis after lightning strikes. Fiona gives Mom ice-chips because she can't eat anything else and Mom says thank you after each chip passes between her dried, cracked lips. Dad sets up a mirror opposite the full-length mirror and takes pictures of Fiona and her reflections from different angles with his new camera (she doesn't remember ever seeing the photos). Mom's skin is a yellow-ish green, the color of pea soup (which Fiona hates) and her eyes, when they are open, are large and terrible and they are terrible because they are not Mom's, they are Maisy's eyes, and her body has shriveled up like Charlie's and pieces of her have been taken away like she was Little Laurence and she says nothing like Maisy and Wanda say nothing, and Sam is standing in a corner of the room with his arms wrapped around himself like boa constrictors and Dad sits on the bed, rubbing Mom's hand and asking her if she needs anything, and when a nurse and doctor arrive (she doesn't remember their names and wants to give them ghosts' names) Fiona does not stay in the room with her family, she runs out and goes to the bathroom and sits on the floor and runs a bath and she hasn't forgiven herself (even though she was so young, a child; a frightened and heartbroken and confused and angry child) for not staying in the room with Mom until the end. Sam says there was a girl named Fiona that looked just like her and acted just like her, and her parents stopped caring for her one day so Fiona faded away and disappeared. Sam says that if Fiona doesn't stop going into Mom and Dad's room that the ghost-Fiona will take her over and she'll disappear, fade away. Of all the ghosts, ghost-Fiona scares her the most, even though she knows Sam is just trying to scare her out of the room so that he can wrestle Dad by himself, and she thinks that there are times when that ghost-Fiona takes over her body and the real-her goes away, and sometimes she wishes for that to happen.

 – *Fiona is determined to finish her tour and she walks downstairs, walks through the first floor, into the kitchen, ignoring Percy, and then down into the* basement. Go to pg 330 BASEMENT

    – *Fiona is still reenacting the night her mother died in her bedroom and she goes back to the bathroom.* Go to pg 323 BATHROOM

    – *Fiona doesn't have to go to the basement. She leaves the house.* Go to pg 333 LEAVING THE HOUSE

PAUL TREMBLAY

BASEMENT

Fiona does a lap around the basement sometimes
holding her hands above her head or tight against her
body so that she won't brush up against the forgotten
boxes and sawhorses and piles of wood and roof
shingles, and careful to not go near Dad's work area
(off limits) with its bitey tools and slippery sawdust, but
she has to go fast as Sam is counting and if she doesn't
make it back to the stairs before he counts to twenty he
kills the light (at some point he'll kill the light anyway).
Fiona follows Mom to the silver, cow-sized freezer and
watches her struggle to lift out a frozen block of meat.
Sam places his green army men on top of the dryer and
they make bets about which plastic man will stay on the
longest and Fiona doesn't care if she loses because she
loves smelling the warm, soft, humid dryer exhaust. Dad
has been in the basement all day and they haven't eaten
dinner and Sam is not there (she forgets where Sam is,
but he's not in the house) and Mom has been gone for
exactly one year and Fiona doesn't call out Dad's name
and instead creeps down the basement stairs as quietly
as she can and the only light on in the basement is the
swinging bulb in Dad's work area, and a static-tinged
radio plays Motown, and Fiona can't see Dad or his
work area from the bottom of the stairs, only the light,
so she sneaks in the dark over past the washer/dryer and
the freezer, and Dad sits on his stool, his back is to her,
his legs splayed out, his right arm pistons up and down
like he's hammering a nail but there's no hammering

330

a nail sound, and he's breathing heavy, and there are beer cans all over his table, and she says Dad, are we having dinner? even though she knows she should not say anything and just go back up the stairs and find something to eat, and he jumps up from off the chair (back still turned to her), beer cans fall and a magazine flutters to the dirty floor (and if it's not the exact same magazine, it's like one of the naked-girl magazines she found in Sam's room) and so do photos of Mom, and they are black and white photos of her and she is by herself and she is young and laughing and she is on the beach, running toward the camera with her arms over her head, and Fiona has always loved those pictures of her Mom on the beach, and Dad's shirt is untucked and hanging over his unbuckled pants and instead of getting mad or yelling he talks like Sam might talk when he's in trouble, a little boy voice, asking what she's doing down here, and he picks up the magazine and the pictures and he doesn't turn around to face her, and then she asks what was he doing, and he slumps back into his chair and cries, and then he starts throwing the beer cans (empty and full) off of the wall, and Fiona runs out of the basement in less than twenty seconds. Sam says that the ghost of every person who ever lived in the house eventually goes to the basement and that some houses have so many ghosts in their basements that they line the walls and they're stacked like cords of wood.

   – Fiona has finally seen all of the ghosts and spent

enough time with them, and she can now leave the house. Go to pg 334 LEAVING THE HOUSE

— Fiona goes back up all the stairs to stand in front of her parents' bedroom door. Go to pg 325 PARENTS' BEDROOM DOOR

LEAVING THE HOUSE

It's colder now than it was when she arrived. Fiona walks to her car and won't allow herself to stop and turn and stare at the house. Even with the visit cut short, she knows the ghosts are not trapped in the house, not bound to both the permanence and impermanence of place, as she foolishly hoped. The ghosts do not follow behind her, in a polite single-file, Pied Piper line to be catalogued, and then archived and forgotten. The ghosts are with her and will be with her, always. It is not a comfort because she will not allow it to be a comfort. How can she? As always, Fiona is too hard on herself, and she remains her very own ghost that scares her the most.

– *Fiona does not forgive herself. Go to pg 305* THE FRONT DOOR

– *Fiona returns to the house. Go to pg 305* THE FRONT DOOR

LEAVING THE HOUSE

It's colder now than it was when she arrived. Fiona walks to her car and won't allow herself to stop and turn and stare at the house. She knows the ghosts are not trapped in the house, not bound to both the permanence and impermanence of place, as she once foolishly hoped. The ghosts do not follow behind her, in a polite single-file Pied Piper line to be catalogued, and then archived and forgotten. The ghosts are with her, have always been with her, and continue to be with her, and maybe that can be a comfort, a confirmation, if she'll just let it. Fiona was ten years old when Mom died from colon cancer. Her father died of cystic fibrosis thirty-seven years later. Dad never remarried and moved to Florida when he got sick and Fiona wrote him letters (he wrote back until he became too weak to do so) and she talked to him every other day on the phone and she spent three of her four weeks of vacation visiting him, and her lovely brother Sam cared for Dad during the last two years of his life. Poor Sam died of pneumonia after suffering a series of strokes five years ago. She doesn't know what to do so she starts talking. She says to her father (who she knew for much longer and so much more intimately than her mother, yet somehow it feels like she didn't know him as well, as though the glut of father-data confuses and contradicts) I'm sorry that we let every day be more awkward and formal than they should've been and I'm sorry I never told you that I don't blame you for anything you did or said in grief, I never did, and I want to say, having out-lived my Marcie, that I understand. Then she says to Mom (who she only knew for ten years, less, really, in terms of her ever-shrinking timeline of memory, and of course, somehow, more) I'm sorry I didn't stay, I wish I stayed with you, and I can stay with you now if you want me to. Fiona cries old tears, the ones drudged from the bottomless well of a child's never-ending grief. And she cries at the horror and beauty of passed time. And she chides herself for being a sentimental old fool despite having given herself permission to be one. As always, Fiona is too hard on herself, and she remains her very own ghost that scares her the most.

   – *Fiona is still turned away from the house and she feels fingers pulling on the back of her coat, trying to drag her back into the house to go through it all again. Fiona still cannot forgive herself for not staying in her parents' bedroom with her mother until the end. She fears her mother's end (all ends, for that matter) are cruelly eternal and that her mother is still there alone and waiting for Fiona to finally and forever come back. Go to pg 305* THE FRONT DOOR
   – *Fiona is still turned away from the house and she feels fingers pulling on the back of her coat, trying to drag her back into the house to go through it all again, or maybe pull her away from everything, pull her away, finally, until she's hopelessly lost. But she doesn't want to be lost either. Fiona walks around the car, tracing the*

cold, metal frame with one hand, to the driver's side door, and gets in the car and starts the engine, which turns over in its tired mechanical way, and she shifts into first gear. The tires turn slowly, but they do turn. Go to pg 337 THE END

THE END

HALLOO
Gemma Files

A voice in the dark, that's how it starts, when you don't even think you're listening – words breathed breathless into darkness, in a whisper, never returned. A voice made from your own blood's secret echo, like waves: that endless hissing surf, the sea inside every shell. They disappear into its open black maw, eaten alive, one by one by one.

> *Hello?*
> Are you there?
> I can't—
> I need to talk. To someone.
> Can anyone hear?
> If you hear me, please say. Please.
> Tell me, please.
> I can't—
> I need to speak. Need to – tell somebody. To tell them, tell them…
> …*what I've done.*

Winter makes you want to sleep all day, even when you've already slept just fine all night – just fine but not enough, obviously. You never feel fully awake. Each time the year turns, the sky just seems to gray out, color draining, and there's a sudden sensation of pressure everywhere at once, pulling you down. Like if you actually bothered to go outside once in a while, you'd fall through the sidewalk and just keep on falling, all the way to the Earth's hollow, kindling core.

"It's just Seasonal Affective Disorder," Mom tells you, dismissively, over the phone. "Lots of people have it; you could go to the doctor for that, get some pills if you wanted." Because: *It's no big deal, Isla – no bigger than anything* else *you complain about, anyhow.*

"She's a bitch," is all Amaya says when she comes home that evening, for neither the first time nor the fiftieth. To which you can barely raise enough energy to agree beyond a hollow-sounding laugh, four cups of strong-brewed coffee notwithstanding.

"Uh huh," you reply. "Me too, so I come by it honestly. And in other news, water still wet, ice-caps still melting, the president still a tool. Plus gravity still sucks."

"You need a vacation, babe."

"*We* need, you mean."

"That too."

But it's not like either of you have that sort of extra money, so the next weekend finds you both still hanging around watching Home & Garden TV in your underwear together, exclaiming once more over the sad fact that every house-hunting couple in North America apparently wants an open-plan kitchen with stainless steel appliances, or hooting at yet another pair of idiots who seem utterly convinced they'll be able to live the rest of their lives in a three hundred square foot tiny house on wheels without killing each other (or their kid, or their dog, or their two kids and two dogs).

Mom rings just as *Flip or Flop Atlanta* comes on. "My Stratford student tenant defaulted," she tells you, without even a hello first. "I need you and Anna—"

"Amaya."

"—that *girlfriend* of yours to go up and check if there's damage. She has a car, right?"

You glance over at Amaya, her eyes still on the TV, trying to figure out a lie Mom might believe: it's in the shop after an accident, she lent it out to friends, it got stolen. But you can't, so: "...yes," you have to admit, at last.

"Well, perfect."

Hardly. But there isn't much to say, not really; the Festival's on, so Mom offers free tickets to *Twelfth Night* to sweeten the pot.

"Plus we can stay as long as we want to, after," you add, as Amaya – no big Shakespeare lover – groans slightly. "If the place isn't too wrecked, I mean."

She frowns. "You expect it to be?"

"Not really. Mom's usually pretty good at picking the Waterloo students who're least likely to hot-box the bathrooms or set up some sort of off-campus brothel, or whatever."

"Except for when they run off without paying rent," she points out.

"Yup."

The Stratford house is always cold; that's what you remember most about it. It was your grandmother's, Nan's, once – the only place she'd ever lived, and ultimately where she died, barricaded against the outside world amidst piles of filth and mail-order delivery boxes full of rhinestone jewelry bought off the Shopping Network. When you helped Mom break the front door down, almost ten years ago, the soundtrack from *Camelot* had been playing on endless repeat from a boom box in the living room. You still remember hearing "If Ever I Would Leave You" coming faintly through the walls, counterpointed by Mom's breathless sobs and the splintering thud of sledgehammer against wood.

The place looks a whole lot better this time around, thank God: no bodily fluid-stained carpet, no peeling vinyl wallpaper, no nicotine-yellowed ceiling paint. Mom's designers have tricked it out in what the HGTV people would no doubt call a "beachy, rustic" sort of color scheme; all light blues, bright whites and sandy accents, hardwood floors milk-washed to brighten the space overall, while mirrors gleam from every corner. Of course, this is the part of the house reserved for theater-going "guests" and seasonal vacationers booked through Airbnb, while the student tenants – and thus, for the time being, you and Amaya – always occupy the apartment in what used to be the basement. Which might have been insulting, if it wasn't just a confirmation of something you've known ever since you told her Amaya's gender: on some level, Mom doesn't really consider you family anymore, let alone guest bedroom-worthy.

"I kicked a hole in this door once, you know," you tell Amaya in front of the kitchen door that leads down to this place you're both supposed to check, clean and (maybe) repair, fishing out the master keys Mom gave you years ago. "Nan was *livid* when she saw; Mom had to pay to get it filled in, and she made me get a second job so I could pay her back. See, right there? You can almost see the seam."

Amaya frowns prettily. "Why would you *do* that, though?"

"God, I don't remember – wanted to get down there for some reason, but it was locked, and I got pissed; I was probably on the rag, or about to be. Story of my adolescence."

"Yeah, yeah; whatever, babe. You're one scary lady, all right."

"You don't even know."

The lock finally yields to the key, and the door opens. The stairwell beyond is black.

There was a time in your life, and not actually all that long ago, when you didn't want anything to do with darkness – you were raised in it, just like your mom, and hers. All of you used to live there, both together and apart, as if it was your shared home address.

They say scent carries memory and vice versa, and that might actually be true. For yourself, there are certain smells you still loathe on contact, smells that fill you with terror: the rose-scented hand cream Mom used during those first few years after the divorce, for example, when you moved into a nightmare-nest of a house three streets over from where she, you and Dad once lived. On its own, it was nothing special, but at the time, its very atmosphere seemed to signify and embody the violent death of everything you'd known up to that point. Even now, you can't help but flinch whenever Amaya slicks her dry, flaking elbows with something squeezed from a tube, at least until the scent (almond, lavender, some combination of the two) reaches you.

You were always "finding things to be afraid of" when you lived there, as Mom used to put it: the grates full of dust, through which distant voices always seemed to be whispering; the upstairs bathroom, with its painted-shut window and its high, cold toilet. The constantly knocking pipes, like Morse code messages sent from behind the walls. Like something trapped in plaster, frantic to find – or make – a way out.

Fear is anger turned inside out, Dr Lavin told you, later on. *And maybe that's where this rage that haunts you comes from, Isla, have you ever thought of that? All these tantrums, these destructive fits, the disassociation afterwards… You want to explode, to go off like a bomb. And then, when you see what you've done, the fear takes over, wiping your mind. Making you forget all about it.*

A lot of people do things they feel bad about, after, you replied. *But they remember them, still; they can't forget, no matter how much they try. Why am I different? What's so special about me?*

She shrugged. *What's so special about any of us? Things are as they are. I'm just here to make sure you understand yourself well enough to forgive.*

She'd never said *who* you were supposed to forgive, though. Yourself, your dad, Nan, your mom – all equally unlikely prospects, in the end.

"That's weird," Amaya says.

You're cleaning out the basement, going through the closet, and amongst all the crap there's a bottle you're *almost sure* you've never seen before. It's pearly, frosted, vaguely translucent – more blue than white. You can't see through it. Raised letters on the side: *Atwood's Jaundice Bitters, Moses Atwood, Mass.* There's a cork in the top, almost rotted through.

"How old you think this is, exactly?" Amaya asks.

You shrug. "Old," you reply. "Like… turn of the century? The twentieth century, I mean."

"'Jaundice bitters.' The fuck are those?"

"Heroin, probably, or morphine. They put that shit in everything."

"Laaaauuudanummm," Amaya intones. "*Abs*inthe."

"It'd be green if it was absinthe."

"Yeah, I guess that's right."

Amaya starts to up-end it, and you suddenly feel the urge to reach out, blurting: *Oh, I wouldn't do that.* No idea why. But you know better than to say shit like that out loud (these days, anyhow), so you don't.

So the last of the cork falls out, hits the floor and skitters, instantly gone. And when you hold the empty bottle back up to blow across the top, trying to make her laugh, the flute-like note it produces is lower than low, so soft it's barely audible, a mere murmur. It hisses.

Like blood in your ear, your inner ear. Like the sea.

Amaya claims to like the bottle, so you stand the open bottle carefully up on what will hopefully become the next student tenant's bedside table, planning to lose it somehow before you leave for home. Then you snap the light off and lie there beside her with eyes wide open, staring into nothing. You're not sure when you fall asleep.

Later that night, though, you dream you're walking down a long, empty beach. Sand squeaks beneath your bare feet, a slippery, volcanic shade of black. The tide is coming in somewhere to your left, the surf a repetitive *shussssh* sound, half lullaby, half warning. Still, you just keep on walking forward, only stopping when you feel something frail about to crack under the sand as you step down.

It's a shell, half-buried. You brush it off, turn for the waves, let one wash it mostly clean; it is nacreous, pale to transparent in places, curled beautifully in on itself like the abandoned home of some long-dead giant snail. You raise it to your ear, and hear—

That *voice*, faintly echoing out of a darkness you can almost see, more red than black; not night, not some windowless room, some *closet*. Interior, in every possible way. You feel it in your chest, your clenched jaw, the delicate facial bones set humming, pulsing, aching. As though, the more you think about it, it's somehow coming from inside...

(*you*)

What I did, I have to tell, please listen—
Are you there? Can you hear me?
Anyone, I need
need
please

It's been too long since you were last here to remember much of the place, so distinguishing what might be theft or damage from what's just age and change is a lot harder than you'd expected. As a result, you still aren't done with the basement apartment by the end of the next afternoon, at which point it's time to get ready for the theater – off to the Avon for the promised *Twelfth Night*. It's excellent, as always.

It's only walking home afterwards you remember how quiet this town is. You're used to sirens, shouts, airplanes, car alarms, never-ceasing traffic, streetlights lining every block. Stratford, Canada, at night in winter, the two of you walking arm in arm past a river already dammed up to prevent freezing damage to its bridges, all icy mud rather than gently flowing water, with the swans, ducks and geese safely housed away until spring… Well, it's not exactly "quiet as the grave," but it's no place you'd ever particularly want to live. Which you know because – as you tell Amaya – you've done so.

"It was back when my nan was still alive," you explain, eyes skewing to keep watch on the pools of shadow bracketing your path. Your breath plumes in the frigid air. "My mom and I had a… thing, and she threw me out, so I didn't really have any other choice – I came up here, got a shit job, paid Nan rent. Just lucky it was between semesters, I guess."

"You *lived* down there?"

"Yeah, for almost three months. So some of that stuff in the closet probably used to be mine." You pause, disengaging to blow on your hands, numb even through thick wool gloves. "I'd have thought she'd thrown it all in the trash by now, considering, but no. Christ, she was an odd old broad."

"How so?"

"Well, things eventually blew up between us, like

348

always. I mean, you could practically time it – there was always something. Like... I listened to music too loud, or I flushed the toilet too many times during the night, woke her up. Or I must've been sneaking up and stealing her food out of the fridge, which I very much was *not* doing, because all she ever ate was shitty casseroles made out of, like, two cans of Campbell's stew mixed with a box of Kraft Dinner, heated up in the microwave. Oh God, the stink of it. It was like living in a greasy-spoon."

"So *she* was a bitch too, is what you're saying."

"A bitch who birthed a bitch, who birthed another bitch in turn. The blood breeds true."

Amaya suddenly stops, turning. "She locked you out," she says, dots connecting visibly. "Your nan. Changed the basement door lock so your key didn't work, with all your stuff inside. *That's* why you kicked a hole in the door. Wasn't it?"

"You got it." A sigh. "She was out, at the Legion Hall – same dance every weekend, all these busted-up human wrecks sitting around listening to swing music and flirting. Used to dress up and everything, like Betty fuckin' Grable."

"But she knew you still had a key to the front door?" Amaya tilts her head. "Wasn't she afraid you'd return the favor? Smash her stuff up or something?"

"She didn't care." You shrug. "On some level, I think she knew everything in her half of the house was total shit... and besides, so what if I wrecked it? She had insurance."

"Wow." A slow, bemused head-shake. "Babe, don't take this the wrong way, but sometimes I'm amazed you're as sane as you are."

Maybe not as sane as you think, you consider replying, then change your mind. Innocent Amaya. Kind Amaya. Who knows so much less than she thinks she does, including about her current topic of conversation.

A swell of love lights your ribcage, and from the back of your mind you hear Viola's speech from tonight's performance repeat itself, those glorious iambic pentameter lines – Viola as Sebastian, a woman playing a man written to be played by a man playing a woman, wooing Olivia the way she wishes unperceptive Prince Orsino would know to woo her. So breathtakingly beautiful, no matter *who* it's meant for.

(*My mother used to recite this to me at night before I went to sleep*, you wanted to tell Amaya in a whisper, earlier. *Gave me* The Collected Works of Shakespeare *for my seventh birthday, so I could read along. She was understudying the part at the time, and guess how many years it took me to figure out I was mostly there to take her on her lines? I mean… actors, right? This is what I got, instead of fairytales.*)

"Make me a willow cabin at your gate
And call upon my soul within the house.
Write loyal cantons of contemned love
And sing them loud even in the dead of night.
Halloo your name to the reverberate hills

And make the babbling gossip of the air
Cry out…"

"Sometimes I'm amazed, too," you say instead, and slip an arm around her waist.

The key is finding a non-destructive way to release stress, Dr Lavin told you. *I promised you when we started this journey together that I wouldn't press you for more than you were ready to give – because I have to tell you, Isla, it's been pretty obvious you've been holding stuff back.* To which you'd said nothing, because there was nothing you could have said without lying.

Which puts us in an awkward position, Lavin went on after a pause, not sounding awkward at all. *You need to express the issue underlying your stress, but you don't have anybody to whom you feel you can do that safely yet. I might become that, eventually, but—*

A shrug. *Fortunately, your subconscious mind isn't nearly as fussy as your conscious. A purely symbolic action may very well help as much as anything more explicit.*

Like what? you asked.

A ritual. Get yourself a container – a bottle, an empty spice tin, a small fabric bag you don't use anymore, so long as it's something unusual and striking. Then tell your story into it, with as much detail as you can, and close it up: cork it, wax it, tie it shut. Put it somewhere you can't get to it again afterwards, and forget about it.

That's therapy? you finally said, once you realized she was serious. *Doc, no offence; that sounds like fucking witchcraft.*

Lavin shrugged again. *A lot of what people called witchcraft is based on exactly these kinds of psychological techniques*, she'd said. *Sympathetic magic, metaphor, whatever – but if it works, who cares?* She leant forward, holding your gaze with hers. *Just promise me you'll try it. Please.*

So you did. You went home, found that huge cowrie shell your dad once sent you from Australia, furled and blushing like a fine-toothed vagina dentata, brought it up to your lips and breathed your worst behavior in, over and over. You didn't get rid of it, though, after. It's at home even now, hung on the wall of the bedroom you and Amaya share in a gold-rimmed glass display case your mother once got you, right next to your other family relics – driftwood and coral, a tiny box full of baby teeth, a bleached-out tin button impressed with a snapshot from 1974 (Mom, Dad, you at maybe six, posing just like a real family on a day out to Toronto's Centreville fun-park, even as your relationship hovers on the ragged edge of dissolving).

Most importantly, however, Dr Lavin's crazy-seeming idea actually did work. Does still. Always has, the shell absorbing your words endlessly, holding your secrets like a cup that never spills over. Because that rage-fire's dimmed somewhat since you were a teenager, but it never entirely dies.

Yet still, as long as you have somewhere to put it all, you're okay.

So far.

Sometime in the very early morning darkness there's *that voice* again, reverberating, setting your skull's shell ringing. Whispering, murmuring—

Did something, oh, I...

—are you there?

...something so terrible, so unforgivable, I

have to tell, must—

Are you listening?

Is anyone *listening?*

Amaya's half out of bed before your posture registers – slumped over, elbows on knees, hands holding up your forehead. "Oh, baby, you barely slept again, did you?" She doesn't wait for an answer before she bounces to her feet. "Give me a few minutes, I'll make coffee."

You listen to her chatter in the kitchenette, wondering how you managed to fall in love with a morning person, 'til your iPhone chirrups. You pick it up and groan. Who else? And you don't dare ignore a FaceTime call this early in the morning; that'll just make it worse when you finally do reply. Pulling up whatever reserves of energy remain after last night, you tap ANSWER.

"Hi, Mom."

Amaya glances at you, instantly silent – she's learned the hard way to stay off your Mom's radar. For her part, Mom seems a little more relaxed than usual: early morning fatigue, maybe.

"Isla. Don't tell me I woke you."

"Nope, I was up already."

"Hmmm. Well, I just wanted to see how things are going—"

"See for yourself," you tell her, sweeping the phone around, grateful and annoyed in equal measure as Amaya skips hastily out of its sightline. "One more day, maybe. The play was great, by the way."

"Oh, I'm sure you earned it. I appreciate that this was an inconvenience…" Mom's eyes narrow, staring at something behind you. "Oh, God. So *that's* where that went."

"What?"

"That horrible bottle you bought at the Weekend Market, the one you used to keep in your room. Smelled like rotten vinegar." She gives an affected micro-shudder of disgust. "I never could tell whether you genuinely didn't notice, or just claimed you didn't; should've guessed it might have found its way up to Nan's. You two always did like that… stuff."

"Antiques?"

"*Old* things. Junk. Like the useless beach trash your father used to mail you every year instead of money, full of all that *muck*—"

A flickering image of ripping brown paper away from a box and opening it teases you, of pouring sand from the cowrie's inner folds back inside its packaging, purest white-blonde and apparently ground from the cracked wrecks of even tinier shells, every grain a new skeleton. As right in your inner ear, meanwhile, you almost think you can hear that most recent dream's voice murmur, telling you to *break it off, don't take the bait for once, just hang up on her, Isla—*

(You'll feel *so* much better if you do.)

"Mom," your mouth says, curtly, "I have to run – still got that last bit of stuff to do, remember? We'll get back to you."

"'We?'"

"Amaya and me. You know, my girlfriend, who I live with? Who's here cleaning out Nan's crap too, for free, just because she loves me?"

Mom frowns, dismissing all of the above with a single flick of her brows: not now, not yet, not ever. "Well, *when* exactly will the two of you—?"

"When it's *done*, Mom; talk to you then. Bye."

A finger stabs hard on red, and the screen goes blank. To your left, Amaya resurfaces from under the kitchenette counter, filter and coffee-tin in hand. "That sounded... different," she says, eventually, to which you simply shrug, spasm-quick.

"I'm done tiptoeing around her," you reply, not turning. "Especially when she keeps pretending you don't exist."

"Huh, well... some people might call that a blessing, considering."

"And some people might call it an insult, ten years'

worth at least, ever since I first tried coming out to that bitch only to have her completely ignore me: *Oh, that's very interesting, Isla. Will you be inviting any of your little college friends home this Thanksgiving? That nice boy Randy, perhaps?*"

"Babe, you're getting yourself all upset—"

Just be quiet, Maya; pour yourself a cup of that fucking awful coffee of yours, and shut up. Don't talk about things you couldn't possibly hope *to understand.*

The same faint whisper, even lower, now barely thrumming through your marrow: *Yes, just like that, that's good, yes.*

(Oh, Isla, *yes*, that's *perfect*.)

"Agree to disagree," is all you say out loud, cool enough to wound. And walk away, back up into what used to be Nan's domain, mounting the rickety steps through a spill of memories let loose, like you're breasting some awful tide, submerged and struggling as the current bears you inexorably back, years peeling away like skin until at last you see clearly what you once thought you'd never have to think about again, *so* clear it hurts—

Should've known that cork was far too fragile to last, shouldn't you? the murmur asks, sweetly. *But the bottle was cheap, at the very least… cheap enough, anyhow.*

You see it, blue-white where a shaft of sun from the door catches it on the edge of one of Mom's favorite Sunday Market tables: lit up from within, what's left of its original glaze gone silvery, come away here and there in patches like glue worn tissue-paper thin. Remember paying for it with a random handful of change, three dollars and four two-dollar coins, the weight of them suddenly so palpable in your palm it makes you start to sweat. It seems frankly impossible you could ever have forgotten – that the bottle belonged to you once, along with anything you might have left inside it. That it still does, and always will.

The frosting, like a bubble, a slow pocket of time. It didn't just appear there, in the closet; you *put* it there, cork in place, certain you wouldn't see it again. And what was it that attracted you to it, in the first place?

Sometimes, things simply suggest themselves, on sight. Objects find their own utility.

Here comes your mother's voice from years ago, meanwhile, overheard through a half-closed office door, younger than you ever recall her and angry in the way only someone terrified can be, biting the words off like poisoned threads: *Don't you* dare *tell me those quacks at the Clarke Institute have it right, Doctor – that my daughter's an... early-onset child schizophrenic, a psychopath, for Christ's own sake. That she's mentally goddamn ill.*

But: *Isla's* angry, *Mrs Decouteau*, Dr Lavin replies, maddeningly calm as always. *Abandoned by one parent, pathologized by the other... You've got your own stresses to deal with, I'm sure, but those aren't my problem, except in terms of how they manifest through Isla's various behaviors. What she needs most right now is to let herself forget the ways in which her fits of rage cause her to let you down – forgive herself for them, eventually, if she can. But that will never happen until you learn to stop pressuring her. She'll only come to terms with what she does when she's pushed beyond her limits. When she's ready. Not at my convenience, or yours.*

(Or hers.)

The next night you have another dream entirely, lying silent next to Amaya, who's curled away from you with her pillow tucked over her face. This time there is no beach, no shell, no voice. Just Nan's house the way it used to be back when you lived here, however briefly. She's already gone out and left a list of things for you to do behind: one of those weird scrawled, barely legible ones she used to tape to the basement apartment door before you came up in the morning. But this time the house is full of animals you've apparently agreed to look after, a random bunch of pets Nan – animal-hater that she was – would never have owned in the first place: cats, dogs, birds, rats. Plus some sort of *thing* you can't even begin to recognize, something truly awful, unnatural... long and hairless, with a ferret's slithery body but the head of a leech or lamprey, all teeth, no face. And it's going around swallowing the smaller animals down whole with its jaw unhinged like a snake, as you watch, horrified. And you want to interfere but you don't want to touch it long enough to, for fear it'll turn that fierce appetite *your* way before you can – too afraid your disgust will take over and make you beat it to death with a skillet, then having to explain that to Nan afterwards, too revolted by the idea of having to take responsibility for its actions, or your own lack thereof. Because Jesus, it's not *your* pet, after all...

Which is exactly when you notice it's shitting as it swallows, of course, but also giving birth at the same time, as messily as possible – all these tinier versions of the same animal sliding out onto Nan's spotless vinyl-tiled kitchen floor slimed head to toe with crap, stinking and spilling, humping and squirming. The *sound* of this horrible unknown creature panting, grunting in painful effort, its very pain repulsive. The fucking *smell*.

It makes you want to scream, to set the house on fire. Makes you wake up crying so hard you think you're going to go blind, choking and shuddering as Amaya bolts upright, cringing away when she tries to hug you. And teetering throughout on the brink of some memory too painful to access at all during your waking hours. Of something, something, *something so bad—*

"I need to tell you about what else happened, after Nan threw me out," you begin, later that morning, as Amaya glances up from her smartphone's screen.

"Your mom blame you for that, too?"

"No, actually. No, she was... occupied... with something else, back then. Someone else." You swallow, throat dry.

"The boyfriend she *didn't* marry."

"Mmm. Which kind of worked out for me, as it happened, but anyway. Not the point." Your hands work against each other, massaging the knuckles as if you can already feel the arthritis both Mom and Nan have probably passed on in your genes. "You see, I didn't just go straight home."

Amaya tilts her head, silently, patient as always. You make yourself go on. "Nan locked me out of the basement; I kicked a hole in the door, but I couldn't get it open. Still, I wasn't going to leave everything I cared about behind – so instead of leaving, I went into her room and hid under her bed, to wait for her to come back. Just lie there 'til she was asleep then sneak out and get the new keys off her ring, that's all I was thinking... all I *think* I was thinking. But—"

The darkness and silence of Nan's bedroom, stinking with overflowing cigarette trays, thick dusty air, talcum powder – then at long last an opened door, stumbling steps, clothes dropped to the floor, a body settling back onto the mattress, so frail the box spring barely creaks. Wait 'til the light goes out plus an hour more, counted by heartbeats, breathing slowly through your nose, before finally slithering out, straightening up. Tiptoeing to the dresser and the purse left there, open far enough for you to rummage through it, your own silent anger outlining every shadow like it's boiling out through your pores, a radiation-sickness halo—

From the bed, there's a sudden sickly gasp as Nan jolts upright, eyes bulging, too disoriented to recognize the threatening black shape in the corner as her granddaughter: that rigid-backed thing already turning on her, its mouth gone square and teeth bared, eyes hateful enough to scald. You'd probably scare you too, you remember thinking, if you could see yourself: good, good. *You* should *be scared, you horrible old—*

But here the gasp is cut off by a squeal, then a thick, disgustingly hoarse rattle; the sound alone's enough to cut your horribly happy pleasure at her fright right off at the root as Nan's gaze glazes over, one eye skewing and mouth going slack on the same side, face half-melted. As she slumps over, settling into a permanent lean, with you all the while thinking, equally terrified: *Oh God, what happened, what did I* do?

(That voice, coolly: You *know*, Isla.)

"A stroke," Amaya says, out loud. "You frightened her into a stroke."

"That's right."

"Okay, well, um… that's really, really bad, obviously. But it was… that was an *accident*, babe."

You snort. "Fucking her brain forever, just because I wanted my *stuff* back? Yeah, I can see how you'd like to think so, and me too. But no."

"Oh, c'mon, Isla! I mean, how could it not be? There's no way on earth you could've known that would happen, and – well, she survived, right? I remember you saying. Your nan didn't die until—"

"Five years later, right. And how do you think she was all that time, Maya? I know I told you *that*, too."

You see her stop and take a breath, thinking. Hearing your voice in her head, maybe, recounting Nan's subsequent downward plunge into dementia, paranoia, sheer outright insanity. How she went from simple bitch to raging harridan in what seemed like zero to sixty, only to let her house degenerate into a human rat's nest so bad it had to be almost entirely gutted and rebuilt from the studs after she died.

"*I* did that," you tell Amaya, perversely glad to hear the words out loud. "Me. I knew something would happen when I moved in with her, just not what—"

"Yeah, but you thought it would be a blow-up or a fight, something you were actually *responsible* for. As opposed to her just chucking you out for nothing, because she was a bitter, verge-of-nuts bitch – your mom squared, basically. Because she's where your mom gets it from."

You shake your head. "I was a guest. She let me into her home, and—"

"Hey, you need to stop. That is *not* your fault."

"Oh baby, it *is* my fault, and more than you know. More than even I remembered, up 'til now."

Back in the bedroom, you watch Nan's expression distort like a fist-crushed clay mask. Obscenities explode on a cloud of spit, too fast and slurred to make any sense – yet you know you've heard them all before already, more snidely, more subtly. And here's the primal raw hatred version, flayed and bleeding: how you're worthless, unlovable, a monster who'll make nothing but more monsters, a waste of time and breath and life. How everything you've ever dreaded is true, and worse.

You should feel sorry, and you do. Guilty. You do.

It also makes you hate her, more than ever.

You pick up Nan's keys from the floor and leave the bedroom; her ranting doesn't change or stop, not even when you close the door on her. You unlock the basement door and go down to collect your belongings, as much as you can take in a single trip, and—

(This is the part you don't tell Amaya, because...)

(...well, it sounds *crazy*, even to you.)

—you see the *Jaundice Bitters* bottle by your bedside, its silver patina glimmering in the dark; stare at it a moment, before making the decision. Then pick it up, work the cork out carefully. In a series of whispers, tell the empty air inside the bottle what you did, feeling the story slip from your shoulders as you say it aloud – slip out and down, inside, settle at the bottle's bottom. Shove the cork back in with your last word, hard, to keep even the faintest shred of it from leaking back out. Go over to the closet, move as much of the stuff inside as you can, make a hole; lifting the bottle up to the top shelf seems to take disproportionate effort, let alone shoving it in, far as you can.

The minute you let go, though, it's like you've already forgotten it. Like it was never there.

(And here we go back to reality, the agreed-upon version.)

You shut the door, hump your things back upstairs, toss Nan's keys onto the living room floor and leave without looking back, front door cracked open to the cold, cold night. Don't even bother calling 911 'til you're at the bus station.

Amaya's taken your hand at some point during your story, studying you closely; she waits for a pause long enough to suggest you've finished, then swallows. Begins: "That's—God, Isla, I'm *so* sorry that happened to you. I can't even imagine how that feels."

You gawk. "I don't... Were you *listening?* I don't think you really heard what I—"

"Of course I did, and it sounds traumatizing, to say the fucking least. But I still think you're blaming yourself too much for what happened, especially after all these..."

"The paramedics could have got there faster, maybe could've... done something, I don't know. But I didn't let them, because – well, I *hated* her, okay? Always. So that's on me."

"She sounds legitimately hateable, babe. And you were young – younger. You're not that person anymore."

(*Oh no?*)

"Maya, you really don't get it, do you? I'm responsible for weaponizing her craziness, then walking away, knowing Mom would have to deal with the result.

And now I know it again, I'm *glad*. I knew how bad her health was, what a sudden shock could do to her—"

"Goddamnit, *no!*" Amaya so seldom interrupts you at all, let alone this forcefully, that surprise is enough to stop you. "Strokes don't *work* like that, Isla; it could've happened at any time. It's even odds you had nothing to do with it at all – and even if you did, A) being angry isn't the same as legal malicious intent, and B) it sounds like she damn well deserved it!" She stands, eyes blazing. "So if you want forgiveness, then fine, *I'll* give it to you! Good enough?"

"That easy, huh? You 'forgive' me, and I'm just supposed to feel better?"

Amaya's fists tighten. "What I'm *saying* is, there's nothing to forgive. The only person in this house who thinks you did something wrong that night is you."

(*And yet.*)

You almost turn your head this time; the impression of a *voice* is so strong. But Amaya clearly hears nothing.

And yet, what? you wonder. *Is this only that secret, constant worm of doubt, the one that fears Amaya's only ever been humoring you? Or is it something—*

(some *one*)

—*else?*

"I'll *always* be 'that person'," is all you snap back, however – quoting her savagely, throwing her own words back in her face – before you can think not to. Watching her flinch and feeling like flinching yourself, but walking away again instead: down, this time.

Back to the basement, half-lit with daylight seeping in through the shades, with the bottle's furtive gleam. To which that murmur behind your eyes replies, just as simply: *Yes.*

(*You will.*)

Amaya's voice reaches you through the basement bathroom door, now, barely audible over not just the shower's roar but also that hiss, that thrum, that oceanic back and forth building inside your inner ear, your skull, your entire pounding body. The one that meets every fervent pledge of love and support she makes with its own litany of self-fulfilling prophecy, advice you don't even want to hear, let alone follow...

Just listen, keep on listening.

You promised to help me, Isla.

Don't be afraid, you'll like it.

You'll want to.

You'll feel so *much better once you do.*

Remember: Amaya thinks she knows, but she doesn't – she never will. She can't. She can't, can't ever be allowed to know.

(*how bad you are, have always been, how awful*)

(*she'd stop loving you if she knew, and that would just be...*)

I'd rather die, you think. And hear something sigh in pleasure, somewhere deep inside: *Yes, exactly.*

Exactly.

"Baby, come on," you think you hear Amaya plead, from so much farther away than through three inches of door. "Come out of there, Isla, please. Everything's going to be okay, I promise you."

You clear your dry throat, raise your voice just a bit. "You should go, Maya. I don't want to…"

"Don't want to what?"

"Doesn't matter. Just… go home, all right?"

"I don't—"

"Christ, can you just trust me, for once? Go *home*, Amaya! Why won't you just go home?"

A pause, during which you can almost see her draw her breath: so determined, so loving. So innocent.

"You couldn't *make* me go home, Isla," she says, at last. "Remember? I'm here for *you*."

Staring down at the razor in your hand, one leg half-done, you wonder exactly how best to pop the blade inside out without letting Amaya know what you're doing, so you'll never have to shave the other one. So you won't have to worry about hurting her, or hurting yourself. And hearing it still, all through these breathless seconds – another voice in yet another room, then in this one, then inside *you*: go here, do that. Telling you how nothing you've done in the years since you bottled up your crime and left it behind has meant anything, if it can all be wiped away so easily; telling you how no one ever really changes, how even that stroke you gave Nan simply broke the mask she wore and let what was always inside spill out. Telling you – oh so plausibly, rationally, soothingly – how if she really knew you at all, that *friend* of yours, she'd surely want to kill you, too. So…

…kill *her* first, *then* kill yourself. Leave the house empty as your sin-catching bottle.

(*It only makes sense; you know it does.*)

But: *Goddamnit, no. NO.*

I won't, you think. *Not that, not ever – not to her. And you can't make me.*

(*Oh…*

…can't I?)

By the time you finally come out, hair still wet, she's already asleep. So you creep back upstairs, lock yourself in Nan's former room, crawl under the bed and lie there with eyes wide open in the dark, looking up. Like you're trying to count the bedsprings.

All at once, you find yourself aware of something scurrying in the darkness, a lithe, wet scuttle. Is it that thing from your other dream, shitting its slimy-blind progeny out everywhere it goes? So you roll out once more, up on all fours, teeth bared. Follow the sound more than any movement, its nailed feet clicking fast towards the bedroom door, and scrabble just as quick at the handle – twisting it to and fro, hard enough to strain your wrist – before finally throwing it open, stumbling out into, not the hall, but that long, black beach under a silver-glazed sky. Mica and volcanic grains beneath, gray-blue above, pale smears of cloud like the peeling patina under raised letters, J-A-U-N-D…

There's a plop to your right, a watery swish as that *thing* immerses itself in the surf, speeding away. Something buried bruises your heel as you step back. Another shell?

No. A half-circle, then a stem, then the rest. You scrape away sand from every side, freeing it, and raise up the result.

The bottle.

On impulse, you raise it to your lips. Breathe across the rim like you're testing a flute, light but long, evoking a low, pale note – then inhale once more without thinking, only to taste that same note in your mouth like a lover's tongue or a drug's first hit, narcotic, numbing. Feel your lungs start to ache with that rush, and whisper: *Who are you?*

You, the voice replies, or seems to.

(You're almost certain.)

Who?

You.

(*I am* you.)

That voice in the dream, in the dark. That voice.

It's yours, you realize. *Oh God.*

It always was.

Anger is a ghost. Guilt is a ghost. This confession is a ghost.

You are a ghost.

You are your own ghost.

* * *

And here you recoil, throw the bottle into the sea, the incoming waves. But all at once you can see the sky is tightening, shrinking, and you start to see *through* it to a bent, warped reflection of your room – as if you're somehow trapped inside an infinitely larger version of the bottle you've just discarded. You yell, pound on the bottle's sides as it moves inwards, crushing you down into a mere flickering light. And as you shrink, the world outside the bottle gets clearer – you begin to perceive what you're looking at, that smeary room (the basement), that smeary figure (yourself). Standing over the bed, occupied by Amaya. Holding a knife.

On the bedside table, the bottle starts to move, to slide, to fall, to crash. Inside the falling bottle, you feel yourself start to wink out.

This is when you'll wake up, you can already tell, looking down on the self-made pattern of your own ruin. The room will be dark, dark enough it takes your eyes a moment to adjust. Staring up at you is Amaya, the one you love so much your heart hurts, with her red mouth open and teeth beginning to pull apart, her soft black pansy eyes gone wide and hard with terror.

Because: *Did you really think love would save her, or you? A girl like you, everything you've done, allowed yourself to* forget *you've done... What sort of love do you think you deserve, hmmm?*

(*That's right: none.*)

* * *

Oh, you should not rest
  Between the elements of air and earth,
  But you should pity me.

THE MARVELLOUS TALKING MACHINE
Alison Littlewood

It is across a distance of many years that I remember the events of 1846, and yet it might have been yesterday that I first heard the voice that haunts my dreams. It is not the words that have troubled me so, ever since I was a boy; it is the way they were spoken – and the fact of their emerging from no human throat.

I was twelve when I first heard of the inventor Professor Joseph Faber. Now my hair is grey, and yet inwardly I feel much the same. I still remember my father's theatre, the magnificence of its halls; the sense of never knowing what wonders would pass before my eyes; the idea that perhaps, truly, they were not entirely of this world.

My father set me to work early, not because we were in need of funds, but because I begged him to release me from the tyranny of slate and desk. For what were schoolrooms to me, when life itself – and such life – passed daily before my eyes at the Egyptian Hall?

The edifice itself was a curiosity to behold. Part of the row of mansions lining Piccadilly, it was yet a thing apart; for its gargantuan figures, winged globes and lotus motifs would be better suited to an ancient tomb of Egypt than the heart of London. The mysteries continued within: vast pillars suggested the great avenue at Karnak, while indecipherable hieroglyphics adorned every surface. Its ever-changing displays were equally entrancing, having included extraordinary statuary, dioramic views, historical artefacts – including Napoleon's coach – and indeed human entertainments; we had hosted a family of Laplanders offering sleigh rides, the Anatomic Vivante or Living Skeleton, and a mermaid – this last, alas, sadly pretend.

Indeed, it might be said that I was accustomed to wonders, and yet, when faced with something more remarkable still, I longed only to turn my face away. But I was not alone in that, for Joseph Faber's was one of our most poorly received attractions.

My first sight of the man was not promising. A hunched fellow he was, wearing a frock-coat with too few buttons, and those dulled with time. His beard was untrimmed, his shoes smeared with street-dirt and his features were unprepossessing; his eyes, which were dull likewise, looked askance when he was addressed, even by me, a mere child.

He gave his name softly and with a slight German accent. It was only when he directed the placement of his boxes and crates that his expression became sharp, even mercurial in his assiduousness. I showed him to the chamber wherein his display would appear and he glared about before closing its door in my face, presumably to prepare himself. Later, my father sent me to offer any assistance he may require. I knocked and a voice responded with some phrase that I had no doubt meant, "Go away".

I did not go away, however, for I was young and curious; or perhaps it was stupidity that made me press my ear to the door and listen.

He was constructing something; that was certain. I decided I must ask my father what it was, for I had been much distracted by the imminent arrival of General Tom Thumb, a fellow celebrated for his diminutive stature and comic scenes, and had paid little attention when he had told me of it. I knew only that it was some kind of machine, and so it seemed, for I detected the sound of wood being slotted into place and the clearer sound of metal striking metal. But it was Faber's mutterings that interested me the most.

It did not sound as if he were talking to himself. He would murmur in a low voice and then pause so that I could sense him listening before giving some reply. It sounded as if he were engaged in conversation with someone I could not quite hear.

Suddenly my ear stung as my father cuffed it. He told me to step sharp and see about the scenery flats in the main theatre, in tones so loud that Faber, shut up in his room, must surely have heard. And so I left him in there, alone yet not alone, speaking to whoever would listen; and to prepare for his performance that evening, whatever that may be.

* * *

I stared down at the handbill. THE MARVELLOUS TALKING MACHINE, it proclaimed. I had wasted no time, after dressing the stage for the hilarious capers of Tom Thumb, in obtaining a copy from the ticket-seller.

So perhaps here was the answer to the sounds I'd heard coming from Professor Faber's room. The bill informed me that not only could his machine speak, but that a full explanation would be given of the means by which the words and sentences were uttered. It said that visitors may examine every part of his Euphonia – that was what he named it – not only demonstrating a wonder of science, but providing a fund of amusement to young and old alike.

All at once, I understood. Examination notwithstanding, it was clear to me that Faber was a cheat; for of course he must have some accomplice who would be concealed somehow within this "wondrous" machine and speak on its behalf. It had been done before. Almost a hundred years ago, Kempelen's chess-playing Turk was heralded as the most magnificent automaton of its age, until it was discovered that its contests were won by a mere human hiding within its base. Thus it was made plain: it was a feat of wonder for a machine to mimic a man, but a matter of imposture and derision for a man to mimic a machine.

I could not confront Faber or reveal him as a fraud, however, for were we not his hosts, and party to all that passed? Yet I was determined to see for myself how the trick was done, and I confess I longed to lay eyes on whatever little creature may be concealed so cunningly. For, of course, it occurred to me that he or she may prove even tinier than Tom Thumb himself.

My disappointment may only be imagined when my father asked me to sort through a heap of mouldering costumes, to put some aside for repair, others for disassembling and yet others for the ragman. I knew I would never finish in time to take my seat for the start of Faber's demonstration, and it being held in a somewhat small chamber, I could not then disturb those who had paid their shilling by making my entrance.

Still, as the time came for it to end, I could not resist waiting in the passage to glimpse what I may when the doors opened. This time, I could more distinctly make out the sounds from within. People called out in turn, the audience I supposed, and something answered, though in tones the like of which I had never encountered. The voice was flat and dead and empty, and it made me shudder, and then the first notes of music sounded, and the awful voice began to sing. It was the National Anthem, but emotionless and dry, as if the life was missing, or perhaps the soul, as if the voice progressed from the very heart of a tomb. But of course this must be Faber's Talking Machine, his Euphonia, and I grasped the reason at once. For he could not wish it to sound human; if it did, all would guess at its true nature and his imposture would be discovered. It must perforce sound like something long dead – indeed, like something that had never lived. And yet I could not quite shake the chill as I pressed my eye to the keyhole.

But the door suddenly shook and swung open. I started back; a gentleman stood there, with commodious whiskers and a gloriously shining top hat. He gave me a disdainful look before leading the exodus from the room, and I made a hasty bow, gesturing towards the exit as if I'd come especially to point the way.

All the ladies and gentlemen filed past me, and as they went, I realised something odd about them. Usually, our patrons left smiling and laughing, exclaiming over what they had seen. But these did not smile; they did not laugh. They were entirely silent as they moved towards the cabs and carriages that awaited. There was no light in their faces; the only emotion that emanated from them was dismay.

I looked away from them and saw Faber, his skin pallid, his eyes as lightless as the rest – and fixed upon mine.

I mouthed an apology, catching a glimpse of the contraption behind him: a wooden frame, through which I could see the back of the stage; an arrangement of keys and levers and bellows; and, affixed to its front, a human face. It was in the form of a woman – or rather, a girl – with reddened lips and gleaming ringlets, but with a cold and empty expression. It unnerved me to look upon it, and I knew in that instant that there was nowhere for anyone to hide, even had they been half the size of Tom Thumb.

Faber stepped towards me and I turned and closed the door between us. I did not leave, however, but leaned heavily against the wall. Thankfully, he did not follow; after a time I heard shuffling sounds and the scraping of wood against the floor.

Then I heard a soft call of "Good night".

I froze, thinking he called out to me, then the light that crept from under the door was extinguished and I was left in near darkness. Faber was to sleep in the chamber, then, with his machine. Whatever his trick, it seemed I would not discover it that evening.

The next day, I asked my father what he knew of the strange inventor who remained ensconced within our chamber. In response, he pulled a face.

"His takings are underwhelming," he said.

I opened my mouth to enquire further and found myself unsure what it was I sought. However, he went on regardless.

"He's a scientist, not a performer, and a mad one at that. This isn't his first talking machine, did you know? He burned the first one."

"Why did he do that, Papa? Didn't it work?"

He looked as if he'd like to spit. "Who knows? Drove himself maniacal with it, I reckon. It's clever – more than clever, some would say – but people don't like it all the same. There's some asked for their money back."

"It really speaks, then, his machine?"

My father affirmed that it did, and I remained silent, musing on that. It seemed intolerably sad to waste such an effort, if the professor really had somehow made the thing work. But perhaps his first attempt had failed?

I did not realise that I had voiced my feelings until my father replied. "Sad, you say? There's worse things, boy. Sleeps in the same room with it, he does. Insists he can't leave it by itself. It's not good for a man to become so obsessed – mark that. And—"

"Yes, Papa?"

He hesitated before he spoke and when he did it was with reluctance, as if it were something better left unsaid. "It's just – I did hear tell he gave that machine his dead sister's face."

I recoiled, thinking for an instant he meant it was made from flesh and blood; but of course it could not be so. I remembered the Euphonia's visage, her bow lips, her pretty ringlets – her lifeless eyes. And it came to me of a sudden that "euphonious" meant pleasant, honeyed, bell-like; agreeable. How could Faber give his deathly sounding machine such a name – and such a face, one that was dear to him? But perhaps he hadn't meant it to sound as it did. Perhaps that was why he had been driven mad, why he burned his first machine – perhaps he had realised the gulf between what he hoped to achieve and reality. And yet, if his machine could truly speak, he was responsible for a miracle – was he not?

* * *

That evening, I witnessed the miracle for myself.

I did not know if Faber saw me as I scuttled inside and took a seat at the back of the room. I did not see him, only his machine, its pale face and shining hair standing out from the shadows. The edges of the room were dimly lit, though the stage was bright with gaslights, hissing and sputtering and highlighting each strut and lever and key – making it abundantly clear to all that no one could be concealed within. Those lights would not be lowered, not for this performance. Everyone could see as much as they wished.

Faber stepped forward. In a halting voice, he begged the liberty of introducing us, one and all, to his Marvellous Talking Machine – his Euphonia. His voice softened when he said this last, and he looked upon the immobile face with something like affection. I saw that he had suspended a white dress beneath it for this performance – a dress that hung limp and empty almost to the floor, swinging slightly in some unseen draught. The hem, I noticed, was a little frayed, and I wondered where he had come by it. Had this, too, been his sister's?

Faber took his seat at the instrument as at a pianoforte, stretching his hands from his sleeves like a great proficient before placing them above a set of ivory keys.

A noise like a great intake of breath filled the room. It was the only sound; no one moved or spoke. Then the Euphonia opened her mouth. Slowly – so slowly – she said, with a slight German accent, "Please excuse my slow pronunciation. Good evening, ladies and gentlemen… It is a lovely day… It is a rainy day."

I realised I was leaning forwards in my seat. I wondered what expression must be written on my features. Despite the ordinariness of the words, I was repulsed – fascinated. Her lips moved like human lips. Her tongue lolled within her mouth like a human's. She breathed like a human, and yet none could mistake her voice for a human voice.

I think my feelings were shared, for it was only when she ceased speaking that those around me began to move again as people do, shifting in their seats, rubbing their lips. No one applauded, however. No one cheered.

I looked at Faber, whose mouth was compressed into an unhappy line, his brows drawn down.

He invited the audience to provide words for his machine to copy. One soul, braver than the rest, bid her say, "*Buona sera.*"

No doubt he intended it for some trick, but say the words she did, though slowly, sounding each syllable as if she were learning his language. Another called out a line from *The Taming of the Shrew*. She could pass no comment upon it, only copy his words. Another demanded something about the fineness of the summer and this she spoke too, all with the same languor, although sunshine and warmth seemed a long way from this accursed chamber.

Then Faber demonstrated how, with the turn of a screw, the Euphonia could whisper. This was even worse. In this way, she gave out the words of a hymn, though such a horror of a hymn I'd never heard. Still, I could not take my eyes from her empty gaze until I became sensible that someone else was watching, someone standing at the back of the stage.

It was a girl, almost concealed by the curtain. Her hair was shining, her dress white, her face pale. I did not look at her directly but even from the corner of my eye, I could see that her lips were moving. Was this Faber's accomplice after all? I turned my head to better focus on her, and I saw that no one was there. It was only a fold in the curtain, nothing more, and I shook my head. I told myself I was unsettled by the dreadful voice and the dismal man operating it. Little wonder he had burned his first effort – would that he had burned the second!

Then everyone around me rose from their seats, and I realised it was time to inspect the machine. I did not wish to go closer, yet I followed, not wishing to remain alone either, and in the jostling of the crowd I found myself standing directly before the Euphonia's face.

Close to, it appeared more lifeless than ever, more like a doll, and I wondered that I could have imagined it to be made of flesh. And Faber explained its workings: the replicated throat and vocal organs made of reeds, whistles, resonators, shutters and baffles, and then he showed how the bellows drove air through it all, and the Euphonia opened her lips and let out a long exhalation. I started away. It felt like breath on my cheek, but cold – cold as the grave.

I turned and, hidden amidst the bustle, I slipped from the room. I had heard the Euphonia speak. I had no wish, now, to hear her sing.

I could not keep away, however, for after the crowds had dispersed, I returned to that little room. I did not know what drew me there, only that I had been unable to cast it from my thoughts. Perhaps it was pity, for poor mad Professor Faber. I expected to find him lost in despair at the horror induced by the thing he loved, but no; even from the passage I could hear voices and the clanking of keys.

Quietly, I opened the door and slipped inside. He was seated once more at his infernal machine. He had not seen me enter, for his head was lowered as he played upon it. The Euphonia's mouth gaped and twisted. She was singing after all, but not "God Save the Queen" or any such thing. I had not heard its like before, but I guessed this must be some German nursery song, perhaps even a lullaby.

My gaze went to the place by the curtain where I had imagined seeing a young girl. With those sepulchral tones resounding all about me, I could almost believe I had truly glimpsed the spirit of his dead sister.

Faber suddenly let out a cry of despair and slumped across his machine, folding his arms before his face.

And yet – I can see it still – his machine sang on. Her lips continued to move; her eyes still gazed blankly at me, holding me there until her song was done.

Slowly, Faber began to unwind his arms and lift his head. I did not wait to see his sorrow, or whatever message his expression might hold, however – I grasped for the door again, pulled it open and I fled.

That was many years ago. Faber left us soon afterwards, saying he had an opportunity with Barnum in America, and yet success was never his. I heard sometime later that he had destroyed his beloved Euphonia once more; and he too had then perished, by his own hand. It seemed plain to me, upon receiving the news, that they must always have risen or fallen together.

And could I believe that his was only a machine – that the glimpsed figure was an illusion conjured by my overwrought imagination? Sometimes, perhaps. But more often it seemed to me that he created not a Talking Machine, but a vessel; and that something immeasurably distant yet always close to him had come to reside within it.

I have thought upon it more than ever after my wife, Mary, died. Like Faber, we had no children; my father died long before. I was the last of my line. I was grown old and was alone, and lonely. Mary went before me into the dark, and I wondered – what would I not do to bring her back, to have my dear wife speak to me again?

The question would have signified nothing, of course, if it were not for the parcel addressed to me that arrived at the Egyptian Hall, years after Faber's death, but not long after my wife's.

The writing within was in a tongue strange to me, yet I saw its purpose at once. For there were plans and diagrams within: plans with levers and keys and shutters and baffles, and an empty space where a face should be.

Some unknown beneficiary of the professor must have sorted through his sad possessions at last – yet it seemed almost meant to be so. It appeared that Faber had not been able to entirely destroy his life's work, but had decided to pass it on; to let some other man make the choice whether it should live or die. The only name he had bethought himself to write on the stained, torn envelope containing all his wisdom was mine.

And I began to dream of it, that awful, dry, dead voice whispering as I slept. Would it be worth the cost, I wondered, to have my wife speak, but in such a voice – dead – soulless? But perhaps, I told myself, it needn't be so. I pored over the plans with increasing avidity. Could not the arrangement of baffles be improved upon a little? And the whistles and resonators could surely be of finer make than had been available to Faber. If I followed the plans carefully, exactly, and yet made my own little improvements here and there, surely the vessel would be perfect. I would hear her the way she was in life, her honeyed tones, her bell-like laughter…

I could only pray it would be so. It took many more months of hearing that voice, of wondering, but eventually I could resist its call no longer. I had the papers translated piecemeal, so that none but I would learn their whole secret. And I started to build, creating lungs, glottis, vocal cords, tongue, lips. I laboured long in closed rooms, my beard becoming unkempt, my clothes as stained as Faber's had been. It consumed me, this thing, and yet still, I hoped.

Now it is nearing completion. With his footsteps carved into the earth before me, I have achieved what cost Faber many years of torment. Soon it will be time to take my place at the machine and see what emerges from its waiting lips.

The time has come to try my creation. I sit at its keys, regretting the arrangement that has Mary's face turned outward, so that I cannot see it. I wonder what expression might be revealed upon it? But it is of no matter. If my wife returns to me, I will know; I will feel her presence.

I place my hands so that they are just resting on the ivories, and I fill her artificial lungs with air. She takes a breath. We are ready.

I touch my fingers to the keys, and in answer she begins to speak. I press and press and her vowels turn into words that become sentences, and still I cannot stop, though I want to; with my whole heart, I want to. But my fingers betray me. They keep pressing, performing their dance, and I do not know what drives them; perhaps it is horror. Perhaps it is only that I wish, so very badly, that it is not true...

The voice speaks with a German accent. It is unmistakable, even in its hoarse whisper. And there is so little life in it that I can almost convince myself I am wrong, but as it speaks to me, I know: the voice is not a woman's, but a man's. It is Faber's voice I hear.

I sense a presence, though not hers; not the one I longed for so badly. I can picture the dishevelled, hunched figure standing at my back, watching me with narrowed eyes. I feel his sorrow, his yearning, his unfathomable despair, and still, I play. I make my machine whisper. I make it sing, but even then, the truth does not change.

I press my hands to the keys more firmly than ever. I am driven onward by something – madness, perhaps; yes, it is likely that. And yet there is fascination too, with the terrible miracle that is before me. Most of all, though, I realise it is fear. For what would happen if I ceased giving it these words – my words? The thing might not stop speaking. It might keep opening its lips – and what might I hear then?

I keep feeding it, and as I do, I feel my own humanity slipping from me. I do not mourn it as it goes. I think of Faber shutting himself in a room, setting fire to his machine, to himself. I can almost sense the flames that await me, that are waiting to consume us both.

* * *

Historical note:

Joseph Faber's sister is fictional, but the inventor himself was very real, as was his display of the Euphonia at the Egyptian Hall in 1846 (though Tom Thumb actually appeared there two years earlier). Sadly, the audience's reaction to his machine is also a matter of record. One theatre manager of the day, John Hollingshead, said: "Never probably, before or since, has the National Anthem been so sung. Sadder and wiser I, and the few visitors, crept slowly from the place, leaving the Professor with his one and only treasure – his child of infinite labour and unmeasurable sorrow."

ACKNOWLEDGEMENTS

I owe some very special thank yous; first to the authors who kindly contributed to this anthology – and also to Cath Trechman, Miranda Jewess, Ella Chappell, Davi Lancett and the team at Titan Books, Jamie Cowen and, as always, Paul Kane for all their help and support in bringing *Phantoms* into being.

ABOUT THE AUTHORS

Angela Slatter is the author of eight short story collections including *The Girl with No Hands and Other Tales*, *Sourdough and Other Stories*, *The Bitterwood Bible and Other Recountings*, *Black-Winged Angels*, *Winter Children and Other Chilling Tales* and *A Feast of Sorrows: Stories*. Her novels *Vigil* and *Corpselight* were released in 2016 and 2017, with *Restoration* published in 2018.

Angela has won a World Fantasy Award, a British Fantasy Award, one Ditmar Award and six Aurealis Awards. She has an MA and a PhD in Creative Writing, is a graduate of Clarion South and the Tin House Summer Writers Workshop. She was an inaugural Queensland Writers Fellow in 2013/14, and the Established Writer-in-Residence at the Katharine Susannah Prichard Writers Centre in Perth in 2016. Her work has been translated into Japanese, Russian, Spanish, French, Chinese and Bulgarian, and the film option to her novelette "Finnegan's Field" has been purchased by Victoria Madden of Sweet Potato Films (*The Kettering Incident*).

Robert Shearman has written five short story collections, and between them they have won the World Fantasy Award, the Shirley Jackson Award, the Edge Hill Readers Prize and three British Fantasy Awards. He began his career in the theatre, and was resident dramatist at the Northcott Theatre in Exeter, and regular writer for Alan Ayckbourn at the Stephen Joseph Theatre in Scarborough; his plays have won the Sunday Times Playwriting Award, the World Drama Trust Award, and the Guinness Award for Ingenuity in association with the Royal National Theatre. A regular writer for BBC Radio, his own interactive drama series *The Chain Gang* has won two Sony Awards. But he is probably best known for his work on *Doctor Who*, bringing back the Daleks for the BAFTA-winning first series in an episode nominated for a Hugo Award. His latest book, *We All Hear Stories in the Dark*, is to be released by PS Publishing in 2019.

Joe Hill is the #1 *New York Times* bestselling author of *The Fireman*, *NOS4A2* and *Strange Weather*. He lives in New Hampshire.

Tim Lebbon is a *New York Times* bestselling author of over forty novels. Recent books include *Blood of the Four* (with Christopher Golden), *The Folded Land*, *Relics*, *The Silence* and the *Rage War* trilogy of Alien/Predator novels. He has won four British Fantasy Awards, a Bram Stoker Award and a Scribe Award. The movie of his story *Pay the Ghost*, starring Nicolas Cage, was released

Halloween 2015. *The Silence*, starring Stanley Tucci and Kiernan Shipka, is due for release in 2018. Several other movie projects are in development in the US and UK.

Find out more about Tim at his website www.timlebbon.net

Laura Purcell is a former bookseller and lives in Colchester, England with her husband and guinea pigs. Her historical novels were followed in 2017 by chilling ghost story *The Silent Companions*, which *The Guardian* described as "intriguing, nuanced and genuinely eerie". Laura's latest novel, *The Corset*, was published by Bloomsbury in September 2018.

Catriona Ward was born in Washington, DC and grew up in the United States, Kenya, Madagascar, Yemen and Morocco. She read English at St Edmund Hall, Oxford and is a graduate of the Creative Writing Masters at the University of East Anglia. Her debut novel, *Rawblood* (Weidenfeld & Nicolson, 2015), won Best Horror Novel at the 2016 British Fantasy Awards, was shortlisted for the Author's Club Best First Novel Award, and was selected as a Winter 2016 Fresh Talent title by W H Smith. *Rawblood* is published in the US and Canada as *The Girl from Rawblood* (Sourcebooks, 2017). She lives in Devon.

Catriona's second novel, *Little Eve*, was published by Weidenfeld & Nicolson in July 2018.

Muriel Gray graduated from Glasgow School of Art, and worked as an illustrator and museum exhibition designer. After presenting the iconic music programme *The Tube*, a long career in broadcasting followed, including founding a television production company. An award-winning opinion writer in many publications, she is the author of three horror novels, *The Trickster*, *Furnace* and *The Ancient*, and many short stories. She was the first female rector of Edinburgh University, is chair of the board of governors of Glasgow School of Art, and a trustee on the board of the British Museum. She lives in Glasgow.

John Connolly was born in Dublin in 1968. He is the author of almost thirty books, including the Charlie Parker mystery series, *The Book of Lost Things* and *he*. He divides his time between Dublin and Maine, and is mostly kind to animals, old people and small children.

M. R. Carey read English at Oxford University and taught Media and Communication at secondary and FE levels before resigning in 1999 to pursue writing full time. He writes across many different media but is best known as a novelist and comic book writer. His graphic novel series *Lucifer* has been developed as a major TV series. His novel *The Girl With All the Gifts* has sold over a million copies in English-language editions and became a critically acclaimed motion picture based on his own screenplay, for which he received the British Screenwriters'

Award for Outstanding Newcomer. He has also written eleven other novels, including two collaborations with his wife Linda and their daughter Louise.

Josh Malerman is the author of *Bird Box*, *Black Mad Wheel*, *Goblin* and *Unbury Carol*. He's also one of two singer/songwriters for the rock band The High Strung, whose song "The Luck You Got" can be heard as the theme song for the hit Showtime show *Shameless*.

Helen Grant writes thrillers with a Gothic flavour, and ghost stories. Her first novel, *The Vanishing of Katharina Linden*, was shortlisted for the CILIP Carnegie Medal and won an ALA Alex Award in the US. Since then she has produced six other novels, the latest of which is *Ghost* (Fledgling Press, 2018), and a collection of short supernatural fiction, *The Sea Change & Other Stories*. Helen has lived in Spain, Germany and Flanders, and now lives in Scotland. Her novels and stories are largely inspired by these places and other intriguing locations she has visited.

Formerly a punk-cabaret singer and composer, **A. K. Benedict** is now "one of the new stars of crime with a supernatural twist" (*Sunday Express*). Her debut novel, *The Beauty of Murder*, was shortlisted for the eDunnit award and is in development for an eight-part TV series. Her poetry and short stories have appeared in *Best British Short Stories*, *Magma*, *Great British*

Horror, *New Fears* and *Best British Horror Stories*; her audio drama includes episodes of *Doctor Who* and *Torchwood*. Her second novel, *The Evidence of Ghosts*, published by Orion, explores her obsession with haunted London. She lives in Rochester with writer Guy Adams and their dog, Dame Margaret Rutherford.

Kelley Armstrong is the author of the Cainsville modern gothic series and the Rockton crime thrillers. Past works include the Otherworld urban fantasy series, the Darkest Powers & Darkness Rising teen paranormal trilogies, the Age of Legends fantasy YA series and the Nadia Stafford crime trilogy. Armstrong lives in Ontario, Canada with her family.

George Mann is a *Sunday Times* bestselling novelist and scriptwriter. He is the author of the Newbury & Hobbes Victorian mystery series, as well as four novels about a 1920s vigilante known as The Ghost. He has also written bestselling *Doctor Who* novels, new adventures for Sherlock Holmes and the supernatural crime series, *Wychwood*.

His comic writing includes extensive work on *Doctor Who*, *Dark Souls* and *Warhammer 40,000*, as well as *Teenage Mutant Ninja Turtles* for younger readers. He has written audio scripts for *Doctor Who*, *Blake's 7*, *Sherlock Holmes*, *Warhammer 40,000* and more, and for a handful of high-profile iOS games. As editor, he has assembled four anthologies of original Sherlock Holmes fiction, as well as multiple volumes of *The Solaris Book of New Science Fiction* and *The Solaris Book of New Fantasy*.

His website is at www.george-mann.com.

Mark A. Latham is a writer, editor, history nerd, proud dogfather, frustrated grunge singer and amateur baker from Staffordshire, UK. An immigrant to rural Nottinghamshire, he lives with his wife, Alison, in a very old house (sadly not haunted), and is still regarded in the village as a foreigner.

Formerly the editor of Games Workshop's *White Dwarf* magazine, Mark dabbled in tabletop games design before becoming a full-time author of strange, fantastical and macabre tales. His Apollonian Casefiles series, and his Sherlock Holmes novels, *A Betrayal in Blood* and *The Red Tower*, are available now.

Visit Mark's blog at http://thelostvictorian.blogspot.co.uk or follow him on Twitter @aLostVictorian.

Paul Tremblay is the award-winning author of seven novels including *The Cabin at the End of the World*, *A Head Full of Ghosts*, *Disappearance at Devil's Rock* and *The Little Sleep*. He is currently a member of the board of directors of the Shirley Jackson Awards, and his essays and short fiction have appeared in the *Los Angeles Times*, *Entertainment Weekly.com* and numerous "year's best" anthologies. He has a master's degree in mathematics and lives outside Boston with his wife and two children.

Formerly a film critic, journalist, screenwriter and teacher, **Gemma Files** has been an award-winning horror author since 1999. She has published two collections of short work (*Kissing Carrion* and *The Worm in Every Heart*), two chap-books of speculative poetry, a Weird Western trilogy (the Hexslinger series – *A Book of Tongues, A Rope of Thorns* and *A Tree of Bones*), a story-cycle (*We Will All Go Down Together: Stories of the Five-Family Coven*) and a standalone novel (*Experimental Film*, which won the 2016 Shirley Jackson Award for Best Novel and the 2016 Sunburst award for Best Adult Novel). All her works are available through ChiZine Productions. Her novella *Coffle* has just been published by Dim Shores, with art by Stephen Wilson. She has two upcoming story collections from Trepidatio Publishing (*Spectral Evidence* and *Drawn Up From Deep Places*), and one from Cemetery Dance (*Dark Is Better*).

Alison Littlewood's latest novel is *The Crow Garden*, a tale of obsession set amidst Victorian asylums and séance rooms. It follows *The Hidden People*, a Victorian tale about the murder of a young girl suspected of being a fairy changeling. Alison's other novels include *A Cold Silence, Path of Needles, The Unquiet House* and *Zombie Apocalypse! Acapulcalypse Now*. Her first book, *A Cold Season*, was selected for the Richard and Judy Book Club and described as "perfect reading for a dark winter's night".

Alison's short stories have been picked for several year's best anthologies and have been published in her collections *Quieter Paths* and *Five Feathered Tales*. She has won the Shirley Jackson Award for Short Fiction.

Alison lives with her partner Fergus in Yorkshire, England, in a house of creaking doors and crooked walls. You can visit her at www.alisonlittlewood.co.uk.